Moment of Truth

Michelle D Rayford

Barrington Drive Publishing

Columbia, SC

Barrington Drive Publishing
10120 Two Notch Road, #307
Columbia, SC 29223
www.michelledrayford.com

Publisher's Note: This is a work of fiction. Names, characters, places, and incidents are a product of the author's imagination. Locales and public names are sometimes used for atmospheric purposes. Any resemblance to actual people, living or dead, or to businesses, companies, events, institutions, or locales is completely coincidental.

Book Layout © 2017 BookDesignTemplates.com
Cover Design: CoversinColor.com

Moment of Truth/ Michelle D Rayford -- 1st ed.
ISBN 978-0-9997303-0-0
Moment of Truth/Michelle D. Rayford – 2nd ed.
ISBN 978-0-9997303-8-6

To Stanley, Ashley and Megan – My three heartbeats

Tell the truth, or someone will tell it for you.

—STEPHANIE KLEIN

CONTENTS

Section I	Moment of Discontent
Section II	Moment of Clarity
Section III	Moment of Truth

CHAPTER ONE

Moment of Discontent

ADRIENNE

I wish I could go back in time. Back to a time when I'm not sitting in an examination room waiting on the doctor to return and tell me what I already know to be true.

Closing my eyes to the harsh glare of fluorescent light, I shift on the exam table as the paper crinkles beneath me and blow out a stream of air. I tell myself I have this all wrong. A missed period can be caused by any number of things. I have put off this visit for weeks, content to live in denial. Now, I cross my arms and wince. My tender breast ache and my stomach is queasy.

Three months into my marriage and I've already messed up. I will have to tell my husband. And Logan will not be pleased

My stomach churns. I hop off the table and make it to the small restroom in two strides, kneeling in front of the toilet. While on my knees, I send up a prayer that my husband will accept this gift and forget about my reluctant agreement. Logan's demand to not have children almost doomed our marriage before it began, but I relented to his terms after weighing the option of being left alone again. Marrying a lawyer put me at a disadvantage in arguing a point.

I hear the *tap, tap* of someone knocking at the door. Dr. Taylor has returned with the results.

"Be right out," I yell as I flush the toilet. At the sink, I stare in the mirror before washing my hands. I don't recognize the woman staring back. All my confidence is gone. I want to run, but my legs go weak and I grab the sink for support. *Get it together,* I tell myself. Being pregnant is not a death sentence. My marriage may end, but I've been through worst. I will my limbs to move and open the door.

When I walk back into the exam room, Dr. Taylor and his nurse are beaming. He presents the positive test to me. The plus sign marked in blue makes me ecstatic and terrified at the same time.

I think back to that Saturday a month before we were married. I had convinced Logan to accompany me to one of my student's soccer game. As a kindergarten teacher, I enjoy interacting with my students outside of the classroom. It helps me connect with the children and their parents. One of my favorite students, Keenan, told me about his soccer tournament and I had promised to be there.

Five minutes into the game, Logan leaned over. "Why did I agree to come to this again?"

"You didn't want to miss the "Tiny Titans" advance in the playoffs," I teased.

"No, I think you got me in a moment of weakness."

"What weakness? You were conscious."

"Maybe, but I believe you were naked at the time." His eyes warmed and I knew he was reliving the memory of the night before and the shower that morning.

I elbowed him in the side. "Would you focus? I thought you might enjoy this. Didn't you used to play soccer?"

"A long time ago." Logan tucked the blanket around my legs. I liked the way he used any excuse to touch me.

"But you were good, right? Your mother said you had a soccer scholarship to college."

Logan sighed. "That's right and then I buckled down and got serious. I left that childish game behind and concentrated on my studies. I had to get ready for law school."

Logan once told me his father never approved of the game. He was expected to follow in the family business and take over the law firm. I suspect there is more to that story, and I started to ask him about it when I spotted my student.

"There he is," I pointed. "There's Keenan. Number 5."

We watched as a skinny sandy haired boy streaked down the field with the ball rolling in front of his nimble feet. The kid was pretty good considering most of his teammates were running in place, looking at someone on the sidelines or utterly clueless.

"Yes!" I jumped to my feet and clapped. "He scored. Way to go, Keenan!"

Keenan pumped his fist and did a dance. When he heard my voice, he looked toward the stands and blew a kiss.

I laughed and sat down. "I told you he's a mess."

"I thought teachers weren't supposed to have favorites," Logan said.

"We don't. Unless we do," I nudged him in the side.

Logan pulled me close. "What's up with you and this kid? Is he trying to take my girl?"

"Are you jealous, Mr. Rutherford?"

"No way. Besides, he is not old enough to do this." He turned my face to his and kissed me.

I remembered getting lost in the promise of that kiss. I was a lucky woman to have a man like Logan love me so completely. And then, my illusion of the perfect man disappeared in a single breath.

After the game, we exited the bleachers and went to meet Keenan and his parents. I kneeled for a hug from my student and stood to make introductions. We made small talk for a few minutes before the conversation turned to our upcoming wedding.

"I bet you guys can't wait to have children of your own," Keenan's mother said.

Before I could respond in the affirmative, Logan piped in. "That's not something we plan to do."

A pit formed in my stomach, but I held my questions until we were in the car. "What did you mean back there? Why would you say we aren't having children?"

Logan stared straight ahead and shrugged. "I meant what I said. I don't need to have any children."

We argued on the way home. I loved kids. That's why I became a teacher. I wanted the dream marriage and two rug rats of my own. I pleaded with Logan, but he wouldn't budge. He lost all patience and said, "This is a non-negotiable item for me. I don't want any children. We aren't having any children."

When he saw the hurt on my face, his voice softened but not his stance. "All I want is you. I'll give you everything, Adrienne. I love you and I want you to be my wife. We don't need children to be happy."

We discussed the issue for days followed by bouts of strained silence with neither of us willing to concede. Then Logan threw down the final gauntlet. "The woman I marry needs to understand that there will be no children."

I realized I had to choose. But this positive test changes everything.

"When was the date of your last period?" Dr. Taylor repeats the question.

I struggle to remember. The wedding and honeymoon were a blur. Logan and I dated for five months before he proposed. We planned a wedding in a month. And now, we are about to be parents.

Based on the best guess of my last period, Dr. Taylor notates that I am exactly twelve weeks along. He conducts an exam followed by an ultrasound to confirm the time frame. In six months, I will have a baby.

I leave the doctor's office with a prescription for folic acid, several pamphlets and the book, *What to Expect When You're Expecting*. Too bad there wasn't a manual to explain telling your stubborn husband we are expecting. I sit in the car, cell phone in hand and stomach in knots.

I debate calling Logan at the office, instead my fingers punch in another familiar number.

"I'm on my way over."

"Well, hello to you too, Sister. Why aren't you at work?"

"I took the day off. Be there in a few." I pull out of the downtown parking garage and head for the interstate. The balmy fall day does nothing to bolster my sullen mood.

The best thing about living in Columbia, South Carolina, besides the mild winters, sweltering summers and Carolina college football games, is that you can get to almost any part of town in less than thirty minutes. Today, I make it to Kim's in fifteen.

Pulling into the driveway of my first major purchase after college always makes me smile, but not today. I want to celebrate my good news, but the thought of Logan's reaction tempers my attitude.

I have a key, but I ring the doorbell. Kim opens the door and I blurt out, "I'm pregnant."

"Oh. My. God," Kim screams, opening her arms to me. "I'm so happy for you."

I exhale and hug my sister. Everything will be okay now. Kim will help me make sense of things. I have always looked up to my little sister, literally. The woman is six feet tall without heels with a model-thin body. She has our father's height. I am six inches shorter with the curvaceous build of our mother.

I follow Kim through the house into her office, taking in the most recent decorations. I marvel that I once lived here. My sister's eclectic tastes are noticeable throughout the bungalow and reflect our differences in taste, especially her home office. The walls are painted a faux stone texture and compliment the wicker fan back chair that I am offered.

Kim slides behind her wrought iron glass-topped desk and clicks the mouse. "I'm on deadline for this website design." Her hair falls in ringlets around her shoulders as she works.

"Was Logan excited when you told him?" Focused on the computer screen, she doesn't see my pained expression.

"I haven't told him yet."

Kim stops typing and looks up. "Things haven't changed?"

I shake my head. "His decision is final on the subject. I couldn't change his mind."

"Men say that all the time, but they don't do anything to prevent it."

"That's true." Once we got married, Logan threw out his box of condoms in a symbolic nod to his commitment to our marriage.

"Then he should know that nothing is one hundred percent effective. No birth control is."

"Yeah, but he doesn't know I stopped taking the pill before we got married."

Kim leans back and frowns. "You know that's not cool."

"I know, I know. But I'm already thirty. I thought I would have been married a long time ago with at least two kids by now."

"Is that why you got married so quick? Because of Christopher?"

The mention of his name makes my heartbeat fast. The love I lost. "This isn't about Christopher."

"This is me you're talking to. It's always been about Christopher. I was there, remember? You dated the man for two years and then it was over. The way he ended it. Don't try to pretend he didn't hurt you."

"Okay, yeah. He hurt me." I concede the point. "But that's history. I think I'm over it now."

Kim shoots me a look and walks over to the printer. She exams her design and smiles, "If you say so. Anyway, Logan will get over himself and be fine. Or not. Either way, I'm going to be the coolest auntie."

I hang my head and groan. "What am I doing?"

"Don't beat yourself up. You know you'll be an excellent mother. You raised me and look how good I turned out," Kim says with a wink.

I smile. "I guess. You are kind of great."

"Thanks to you. I know what you gave up."

I wave my hand. We are not having that conversation again. "No one else would take care of a bratty thirteen-year-old. I was stuck with you."

Sometimes I wondered how either one of us turned out sane after dealing with so much grief. Mom died after a long illness and we had adjusted to having lost her when Dad passed less than a year later. We lived with dad's brother, his wife and our cousin until I turned eighteen. They were our relatives, but they made us feel like visitors. Visitors that had overstayed their welcome. I got us out of there as soon as possible. It's been Kim and me ever since.

"I wish they were here too," Kim says, picking up on my mood without me having to say a word.

"I miss them at times like this. They would be so excited to be grandparents."

I nod my head. "Yes, they would."

"Which Al Green song do you think Dad would play?"

Dad had Al Green's collection and would play the album every night. Our lullaby was a soulful soundtrack about life and love. Kim leans over her laptop and clicks the mouse a few times. The strains of *Look What You Done for Me* sing from the computer speakers. "This is a celebration," she says. "Brother-in-law will come around."

We listen for a few minutes, chatting about due dates and possible baby names. Then the first notes of *How Can You Mend a Broken Heart?* start to play. Kim turns off the music but the vibe in the room changes.

"Every time I hear this song, I think of Dad playing it over and over after Mom died." Kim's voice breaks.

She reminds me of the scared little girl she used to be. I lean over the desk and squeeze her hand. She squeezes back, and I walk around the desk to pull her into a hug. We take a moment to honor our shared history.

"You know what I think?" Kim sniffs.

"What?" I step away to grab a tissue.

"I think we should be celebrating. You are going to be a mommy."
Kim does a dancing jig and boogies out of the room.

I follow her into the kitchen, wishing I could match her enthusiasm.
I shiver and place a hand over my stomach. I hope Logan is ready for
this because there is no turning back now.

I am keeping my baby.

CHAPTER TWO

ADRIENNE

I stand in the doorway to the living room watching Logan fix his spirit of choice, rum and coke. I decided to wait until after dinner to tell him. Logan smiles and pats the space beside him. I take a deep breath and join him on the couch, trying to calm my beating heart. I'm struggling to find the right words when the phone rings.

"Hello, Mother," Logan taps his fingers on my leg as he listens to his mother. "We'll come by for dinner tomorrow, okay?" I can tell he is half listening to his mother's mundane requests. He keeps trying to nuzzle my neck and one hand is inching up my thigh. "Yes, mother, I remember the dinner at church. We'll be there. It's next Sunday, right?"

I swat his hand away playfully. He takes my hand and then straightens up.

"Yes, Mother. I understand the firm has a reputation. I'm doing my best." Logan updates his mother on the status of clients and cases at the firm. Client/attorney privilege doesn't matter between those two. I use the momentary distraction to observe the man I married.

Logan is not like the men I am usually attracted to. He has a natural slim physique that comes from hours spent on the golf course and playing racquetball at the club. According to his mother, his light pecan sandy complexion is the product of proper breeding. Add to that his clean-shaven face and close-cropped hair and you have the perfect image of a corporate attorney. Kim calls Logan my bougie rebound.

We met in a graveyard. Not a romantic place to meet your future spouse but for two lost souls like us, it was perfect. I was putting fresh flowers on my parents' graves, something I still do once a month, when movement to my right caught my attention. A man kneeled on a newly dug grave about fifty yards away. I couldn't make out what he was saying, but he kept pounding the dirt and shaking his head.

I don't know what made me walk over. The closer I got I heard him repeating one word. "Why? Why? Why?"

Logan hangs up the phone and reaches for the remote control. "Mom says hi."

I know she didn't, but I play along. "How is Marilyn doing?"

"You know, Mother." Logan clicks through the channels. "How was your day?"

"Interesting." I don't know if I should blurt it out or show him the ultrasound picture and play a guessing game. What is the script for telling a husband that doesn't want children you are pregnant?

"Oh yeah. Did some kid refuse to take a nap?" Logan laughs at his own lame joke.

I elbow him in the side. "Very funny. I'm serious."

"I am too." He stops channel surfing on CNN and kisses me. "Have you thought anymore about what I suggested?"

Here we go again, I think. The man is relentless when it comes to something he wants. I used to think that was an admirable quality. Now it gets on my nerves.

I reach for a throw pillow and bring it to my chest, playing with the fringes. "I know I don't have to work. I want to work," I repeat the same line I've been saying since we got married.

I tamp down my aggravation and snuggle closer to him. "You may get your wish." I use his "my wife doesn't have to work" spiel he's been giving me since we returned from our honeymoon as an opening to share my news.

Logan sets his drink down and wraps his arms around me. "I know a wish you can make come true right now." He kisses my neck and nibbles my ear. "You smell good. Let me taste you."

I grab the hand wandering up my thigh.

"I'm pregnant."

His entire body becomes rigid. "How did that happen?"

I look at my husband. Total confusion about human reproduction plays across his features.

"Well, when a man and woman love each other…" I launch into the dissertation every middle school student has heard in health class, thinking it would make him laugh.

Instead, he slides away and holds his hand up to stop me. "No, I mean how can you be pregnant?"

The accusation knocks me off balance and I shift in the seat. I avoid his gaze by focusing on the picture sitting on the end table. The picture of us on our wedding day. We were happy then. Will we be happy after this?

"No birth control is one hundred percent effective."

"I know. But you are on the pill. You are on the pill, right?"

I shake my head. "With the stress of moving and the wedding, I may have missed a pill or two." A lie sounds better than the truth. I dare not confess I accidentally missed those pills on purpose.

Logan grabs his drink, swallows it in one gulp and stands to fix another one. He slumps into a chair beside the sofa and drops his head. "How could you? We agreed we wouldn't have kids?"

I get up and kneel in front of him, taking his free hand. "You know how much I wanted a baby. This child, our baby, will make our family complete."

I massage his hand, trying to get him to understand. He pulls his hand away and shakes his head. I try once more to bridge the distance, but when I stroke his arm, he stiffens.

"How long?" he croaks. His voice is a mixture of confusion and disbelief.

"What?"

Logan looks at me. His eyes reflect more pain than anger.

"How far along are you?"

I put one hand over my belly. I pray he doesn't suggest an abortion. I couldn't forgive that. "Twelve weeks."

Logan looks at me like he is seeing me for the first time. I watch his eyes narrow as he does the calculation in his head. He snatches his arm away and the drink spills. The pungent smell fills the air and I feel nauseous.

"How could you?" The words echo around the room as my heart races. *What if he leaves? What if every man I love leaves?*

"This is not a bad thing. I know this is sudden. We just got married and all. But, we have enough love to share. Imagine if it's a little boy that looks like his father. We can name him Logan Charles Rutherford the third. Carry on your father's name." I talk fast. He has to understand.

Logan jumps up and I lose my balance falling into the puddle of alcohol.

"How could you do this? You think I would give your baby my father's name?" He spat the words like bullets, each one finding its intended target. My heart.

"How could you?" he repeats and walks out the door.

CHAPTER THREE

ADRIENNE

Four years later

Logan's warm fingers caress my back and wake me from a sound sleep. "Babe, you up."

Without opening my eyes, I know it is 5:30 in the morning. The man is a sadistic alarm clock. I feign a deep coma like sleep, which is hard to pull off with Logan grinding into my back.

"Adrienne," Logan whines. "Come on, baby. You can go back to sleep later."

No sane woman can resist such a romantic declaration, but I still don't respond. Logan works my nightshirt up until it bunches around my neck. When he starts to fondle my breast, I squirm away.

Logan takes any slight movement as permission to plow ahead. Four years of marriage and I know how this will play out. With a sigh, I give in. If I don't get with the action, Logan will pound away and I will be left unfulfilled. He enters me and starts pumping. I turn my head to avoid the full blast of bad breath. I don't open my eyes so I can pretend that I am somewhere else. I pretend I am with someone else. It works most of the time.

I start to feel the faintest stirrings of pleasure when Logan grunts and collapses on top of me, his body pressing down on me like dead weight. He doesn't move fast enough so I push him. Hard.

"Sorry, babe," he mumbles and jumps up. I watch him stretch and then stroll into the bathroom. The toilet flushes and the shower comes on.

I lie there staring at the ceiling and wonder, not for the first time, how did we get into this rut. I always suspected marriage had an ebb and flow; a natural rhythm most relationships go through. Strained is an accurate description of our union. Logan doesn't even kiss me during sex anymore. He might as well have been masturbating.

The air conditioner clicks on and chills my skin. I grab the shirt wedged under my arm and yank it down. My hand brushes the raised ridges on my stomach. My badge of honor. Four years ago, I received the caesarean scars from the birth of my baby, our son, Nicholas. I have everything I thought I wanted - a husband, a beautiful baby, a house in the suburbs. We have enough money to allow me to be a stay-at-home mom. I should be happy. But I can't seem to shake the feeling that something is missing.

The water shuts off in the bathroom and I look at the clock. I have about an hour before Nicholas gets up. Enough time to relax in a bubble bath.

The bathroom is my favorite place in the entire house. Our home is decorated in the traditional sense with heavy wood furniture and muted colors, but I took control of designing the bathroom. The architect implemented all of my requests and created an oasis of comfort. The walls are painted soft yellow, which makes the large room seem huge. The marble countertop houses his and her ceramic vessel sinks separated by a vanity for my perfumes, hair and makeup items. The chair level commode is housed in its own room for privacy. The dual shower heads with slate-colored tiles are a bear to clean but perfect for the times when we want to shower together. And then there is the tub. A porcelain thing of beauty with enough room to lay back and relax with whirlpool jets for stressful days.

Logan is standing at his sink shaving when I walk in. I feel his eyes on me as I turn on the water to fill the tub. I sprinkle jasmine scented bath beads in the water and adjust the temperature. He is still staring as I undress and slip into the water. I relax against the pillow and ignore him. "Adrienne…" He calls my name, but I don't open my eyes.

"Adrienne, what do you have planned for the day?"

I take a deep breath and let the aroma of flowers take me away. Logan knows I do the same thing every day. Why can't he let me enjoy my soak and stop trying to make conversation?

"Adrienne," his voice echoes off the tile.

I slowly open my eyes and stare at him. He puts down the razor and turns around.

"You okay?"

"Sure, why wouldn't I be?" I sink further into the watery cocoon.

He doesn't respond to my question. He knows what the issue is. We keep having the same argument because he refuses to listen to reason. He stands there for a minute looking at me then glances at the clock. Shaking his head, he turns around.

Logan takes the towel from around his waist and tosses it toward the hamper. He misses. Again. Not that he notices. I look at the wet crumpled heap and know it will stay there until I pick it up. He walks naked into the bedroom.

I tuck a stray a hair behind my ear. "Tell me again why I can't go back to work?"

Logan re-enters the bathroom in black cotton briefs and black dress socks. He walks past me into the closet.

I raise my voice. "I asked you a question."

He clears his throat. "What, Adrienne? We discussed this last night."

Logan emerges from the closet with his pants unzipped and his white dress shirt hanging open.

"Look, I don't think now is a good time for you to go back to work." He holds up two ties. "Which one? I have an important meeting with a potential client today."

He is wearing his lucky black suit. I am not going to be distracted by asking about this client like he hopes I will. I could care less which tie he wears. I point to the burgundy one and he goes back into the closet.

I sit up and water sloshes over the side. "I have to let them know something soon. The new school has three openings for kindergarten teachers."

"What new school?"

I sigh. Does the man listen to anything I tell him? "The school I mentioned last night. This district is opening a new elementary school and one of my former coworkers told me about the positions. This is a good opportunity for me to get back in the classroom."

I hear him clear his throat again. I know what that means. He is preparing his arguments.

"I don't understand why you can't support me on this." I fight to control my tone. "When we decided I would stay at home with Nicholas, it wasn't going to be forever. It was necessary. I needed to stay with Nicholas when he was a baby. But we have to treat him like any other child and let him be around other kids."

"He's two years old. What do you plan to do with him while you teach other people's children?"

"Nicholas is three. His birthday is today. Remember? He is old enough to start preschool and I found a good program at a church not far from here. I checked them out. They have a good reputation. I told them about Nicholas's health issues and they're willing to work with us. You should have seen Nicholas's face when we stopped by. He wanted to stay and play with the other children."

Logan walks out of the closet dressed, complete with the gray tie and a smirk on his face. I've seen that look before. He thinks he has an edge in this discussion. I replay our conversation in my head to figure out what he will try to use against me.

"What's the rush? Are these people equipped to handle a child with sickle cell anemia? Do they know what to do if he has an episode? Could you handle it if Nicholas got sick at school and you weren't there? I think it would be better if you wait until he's older and can articulate his needs to a teacher. You're his mother. We need you at home right now. We can revisit your returning to teach in a few years."

"In a few years? Do you have any idea what I do every day? I need something more challenging than cleaning the house. I've drilled the alphabet and numbers into Nicholas. He knows all the colors and can spell and write his name. We have gone to visit every museum and park in the city. We no longer need a map to navigate the zoo and the librarians know us on a first name basis. The rest of my time is spent browsing the internet for imaginative ways to make chicken for dinner. Dinners that you are too busy working late to eat. If I have to watch one more episode of "The Wiggles," I might lose it."

"I like having my wife at home," Logan deadpans and turns to open a drawer. "Where are the nail clippers?"

His dismissal gives me courage to force the issue. "Look, Logan. I'm not asking your permission. But I would like your support."

"What else is new? You are good at deciding things for yourself," he mumbles.

And there it is. I thought I had braced for it. I knew Logan would use my unplanned pregnancy as his weapon. It remains a sensitive subject. The emotions surrounding Nicholas's conception and birth hover over every tense conversation. My determination to have a baby and Logan's acceptance, albeit reluctant, is the delicate string that holds our marriage together. Guilt is the shaky foundation.

Funny thing about guilt, it makes you compromise on things you would normally fight. I lean back against the tub. "I don't think that's fair."

"I don't think it's fair that you are still taking these." Logan holds up my birth control compact. I know I am in the tub, but I feel exposed. I should have hidden them better.

"Logan—"

"I thought you stopped a month ago. Didn't we agree to try to have another baby?"

I twist the washcloth in my hand and avoid making eye contact. "I didn't agree to anything."

Logan's voice echoes off the tile as he paces back and forth. "We did agree. I want another child. Why do you get the final say on whether we can add to our family? You decided to get pregnant damn near on the honeymoon, now all of a sudden you don't want another baby."

"That's not it," my voice cracks.

"Then what is it, Adrienne? You don't want to have my baby?" Logan pauses to catch his breath. "Another one of my babies."

I see the hurt and rejection on his face, although Logan will never admit it. I fight to hold back the words, but they escape around the mass in my throat. "I don't want to have another sick child."

The thought is unspoken but ever present. We already brought an illness on our baby. The mutated trait we both share gave Nicholas the disease that he must live with for the rest of his life. Now that I know, I can't take the chance of passing it on to another child.

Logan stares at me so long I want to reach for a towel. He drops the pack on the counter and searches for a dry spot to sit on the side of the tub. He kneels instead and wipes away a tear I didn't know had fallen. "It's okay. You know I didn't mean to upset you."

I don't trust myself to speak. I know he meant every word. Logan always wins.

"It's just…sometimes you make it hard. I want to take care of you and Nicholas. My dad worked hard to do that for my mom and me. He taught me that a man provides for his family. That's all I'm trying to do."

Logan lifts my chin to meet his gaze. "Babe, please don't fight me on this. I hate to see you look so sad. You know I love you, right?"

"I know."

Logan grins and kisses my forehead. "And think, with Nicholas in school, the baby will keep you busy."

My neck snaps back and I raise my eyebrows. I didn't see that one coming. He would make an offer of acceptance as long as I follow his plan. I start to question his manipulation, but he stands to leave.

"We need to talk," I call after him.

He turns and I see the face of the man I believed I could spend the rest of my life with. The man that chose me. The one man that didn't leave.

"Sure. We can talk later. And maybe work on adding that new member to the family." Logan winks and then he is gone.

I slide further down in the tub and stare as the bubbles, like my hope, disappears.

CHAPTER FOUR

LOGAN

I guide my car into my designated parking space outside of a building that bears my name. The Rutherford Law Firm is housed in a small two-story brick structure that was designed by the state's first black architect. Senior was proud of that fact.

I shut off the engine and settle against the buttery leather seats to gather my thoughts, get the foolishness with Adrienne out my head and focus on what's important. If I sign this client, it will be the biggest one in the firm's history. Senior never landed a CEO with this much prestige. The meeting today has to be perfect.

I take a deep breath and inhale the new car scent. It's the drug I need for further clarity about what is at stake. Signing this client will ensure I can continue to make the lease payments. I am already calculating the hefty fees I can bill. The firm will be in the black this quarter.

A brand-new Acura TLX parks beside my vehicle and I watch as my paralegal, Sheila, steps out teetering on a pair of black high heels. She has on the black power suit with the red camisole I requested. Sheila has been with the firm since I started interning here. Senior introduced me to the buxom brunette and explained she was a diversity hire. We bonded instantly. Two newbies trying to prove to Senior we were good enough.

"Are you ready?" Sheila asks. She leans against the door so I can get a view of her cleavage. I won't be distracted this time.

"Today's the day. Is the presentation finished?"

Sheila sighs and stands up straight. "Made copies last night."

I step out of the vehicle and reach into the back for my jacket and laptop case. Her perfume tickles my nose. She has upped her game today. "I can always count on you."

"For whatever you need," She teases.

I gesture for her to lead the way and follow her into the building, holding the door for her. Playing the role of a gentleman rewards me a view of her ass as she switches. The sexual tension between us is a welcome distraction from the stresses of the day. We have an unspoken understanding. Flirting but no touching. The new rules since my marriage.

I walk through the front doors and that familiar sensation envelops me. My stomach clenches and I take a deep breath. I belong here, I tell myself. I have to repeat it three times before I can move forward.

Beatrice is already at her perch. She was one of the first employees Senior hired. Mother was the original secretary but when she got pregnant with me, Beatrice took her place at the receptionist desk.

"Good morning, baby," she says and gets up to pour a cup of coffee. She ignores Sheila who walks to her office without a word. "You ready for our big day?"

"Yes, ma'am." I sip from the cup she hands me. "Can you make sure the conference room is all set?"

"Already handled. But you may want to speak with Gregory."

"Why?" I hope my voice sounds neutral. Gregory Atkins has been a tolerated nuisance since Senior hired him. "You need competition," my father told me.

Beatrice takes my laptop and jacket. "I'll put these in your office. Go see."

I leave the cup of coffee and march upstairs to Gregory's office. When Senior was alive, Gregory pounced on every opportunity to kiss up to him. He loved to point out any mistake I made too.

All of that stops today. He can either get on track with our new direction or suffer. I open the door to his office unannounced; preparing to remind him that it's my name on the letterhead. The words get stuck between clenched teeth when I see the stack of boxes.

Gregory is taking a frame off the wall and doesn't turn around. "I knew Beatrice would send you up here first thing. The old girl is loyal."

My heartbeat quickens. "What are you doing?"

"Exactly what it looks like." He turns to look at me. "Making the move I should have made as soon as the old man died. I knew you couldn't handle this place."

"Handle the place? This is my family's firm. My father knew he could entrust it to me. You should be grateful I let you stay on."

Gregory laughs. I could punch him in the face right now. Or maybe I should aim for that gut he has growing. The man loves doughnuts as much as he loves questioning every decision I make.

He walks around his desk and puts the frame in a box. "Like you had a choice. The other two lawyers bailed a month after the old man died taking their paralegals with them. One month. I was all you had. Well, besides Beatrice who is still loyal to your father and Sheila because you're screwing her."

"I am not sleeping with Sheila." I glance down the hall to see if anyone heard my outburst. I step into the office and shut the door.

"Cut the crap, Gregory. We both know what this is about. You wish you were me. Maybe then Sheila would take you up on your offer of a 'drink' after work. You wish Senior was your father instead of the deadbeat that ran out on you and your mother."

Gregory's eyes narrow. I knew I could shake his cool demeanor. Instead of hurling an insult back, he pulls out his chair and takes his time settling in. "Now, why would I want to be you? You don't have anything I want. I'm the one keeping this firm going. I figure I can go start my own. When was the last time you brought in a client? The few remaining ones you have are connected to your father."

"The new client coming in this morning isn't connected to Senior. It's a major opportunity to have Christopher Michaels consider the firm."

Gregory leans back in his chair. "And why do you think that is?"

Any decent attorney knows not to ask a question unless you already know the answer. Gregory is an excellent attorney. I feel the setup coming but can't stop myself.

"It's obvious the man heard about the stellar reputation of my firm. The Rutherford name carries weight in this city. Any businessman moving here would want the best." I pace back and forth.

"You're right about the 'stellar' part," Gregory says. "That's why Michaels asked for me specifically. Bet Beatrice left that part out of the message."

I freeze. I can't afford to let this client walk out the door. If Gregory thinks I'm going to let him steal the Michaels account, he is mistaken.

I am in front of Gregory's desk in three strides. I grip the edge and lean over. "You can leave. But if you try to take any of my clients, I will sue your ass for breach of contract."

Gregory pushes away from the desk and stands. I cross my arms and stare him down, daring him to make a move. He blinks first.

"Calm down, Junior. I already spoke with Michaels to inform him of my exit. He isn't an official client so no breach there. For some reason, he wants to honor the appointment. This is my last gift to you. Don't mess it up." He turns and starts to remove books from the shelf.

I relax my stance and smirk. "Make sure you are out of here before ten." I want no traces of the traitor when the man arrives.

I hurry down the hall to rework the presentation before doubt can hinder my progress. Gregory just did me a favor. Time to step up my game. I'll make Senior proud today.

CHAPTER FIVE

ADRIENNE

"**N**icholas is full of energy today," Vanessa says, passing her baby to me. "That's a wonderful birthday present."

"It is," I pull little Morgan in close and inhale her baby scent of milk and bananas. I'm rewarded with a toothless grin when I tickle her plump belly.

Maybe I could have another baby. I look at Vanessa for inspiration. We've known each other since freshmen orientation where we shared a dorm room and a major. Even back then, Vanessa's goal was to marry well and be a mother. My friend is the definition of a super mom. She has three kids and makes it look easy. I watch as she gathers the boys together. With the precision of a drill sergeant, she makes them clean up their sandwich wrappers, wipes Matthew, her oldest son's face with a napkin, ties Miles's shoe and helps Nicholas adjust his birthday hat. She releases the kids and they race back to the jungle gym. It was her idea to have a birthday lunch for Nicholas before his party this weekend. The weather was too nice to keep the kids inside, so we moved it to the backyard.

"Spill it, girlfriend." Vanessa rummages in the baby bag and pulls out a diaper and some wipes.

I stand Morgan on my lap and she marches in place. "Spill what?"

"It's Nicholas's birthday. It's a beautiful spring day and you are hanging out with your best friend."

"Yeah. And?"

"And you've been quiet. You have that look you get when you're in deep thought about something. So, spill it."

Morgan blows bubbles and I bounce her up and down. "You ever miss it?"

"Miss what?"

"Miss working. Teaching. Having a job?"

Vanessa leans back against the picnic table. "I have a full-time job taking care of these kids. I don't think I'm missing anything."

I look at Nicholas climbing the ramp. His squeals of laughter follow him down the slide. I smile at his happiness. I love being his Mom, but I need more than that.

"I've been thinking about going back to work," I confess. "Logan's against it."

"That figures. You know, my Moses is all for me staying home with the kids. Men love to be able to say their wives don't have to work."

Vanessa's husband is an assistant football coach at the university. She stopped working as soon as she got pregnant with Matthew.

"Maybe. But what if I want to work. It's not about my husband's ego."

Vanessa shoots me a look. "Are you crazy? Do you know how many women would kill to be able to stay at home? The most important job you can have is being a mother."

I nod. "It is an important job. But it doesn't have to be the only one." Morgan stops bouncing and scrunches her face. Her brow furrows. The stench informs me she wasn't in deep thought. Vanessa reaches for her.

"This girl is a regular stink pot. Yes, she is," Vanessa croons. Morgan smiles and kicks her legs.

"Maybe something is wrong with me," I muse.

"Something is wrong with you." Vanessa cleans the baby and snaps her onesie close. "There is no greater job than motherhood. And you have a special needs child. Even more reason for you to stay home."

"He has an illness. He's not special needs."

"You know what I mean," Vanessa says. "He's different."

I cut her off. "He's no different from your Miles." I point to the two boys chasing Matthew with a football. "He can do anything a three-year-old can do. I refuse to treat him, or let anyone else treat him, like he's fragile."

"Alright, girl. Calm down, Momma Bear. I was trying to say that no one will take care of your baby better than you. Why would you want to leave him and go to work?"

I open my mouth to respond but no words escape. I cross my arms and stare at Vanessa. She turns her head to avoid eye contact. "You know, I'm right. You should be grateful for the gift you have. If a woman has children, she should be the one to take care of them. It's the way we are designed."

"Do you know what year it is? You can't possibly believe that mess?"

"Yeah, I believe it and I live it every day. You need to stop being selfish and think about Nicholas. He needs his mother at home."

I roll my eyes so hard I give myself a headache. "You know what, 'Nessa. You can take that 1950 mess somewhere else."

I stand and call for the boys.

Vanessa tucks Morgan in the stroller and looks at her watch. "It's time for us to head home anyway. I need to start dinner and get them down for a nap."

Nicholas bounds over and hugs my leg.

"Not ready, Mommy." His sweaty face smiles up at me.

I wipe his face and pull a water bottle off the table. It doesn't help his condition if he gets overheated.

"You can play later. Miles has to go home now." I take his hand and lead the way around the house. "Let's walk our guests to the car."

Nicholas skips along beside me, and I hear Vanessa pushing the squeaky stroller over the grass. The boys jostle behind her whining about something.

I stand on the porch while Vanessa buckles her crew into their car seats. She turns on the car and then comes to the bottom of the stairs.

"I'm sorry if you're upset, but I'm telling you what I think is best. You know that, right?" She shields her eyes from the sun.

"Whatever, 'Nesa. You do know there is not one way to be a mother. Plenty of women work and their kids are fine."

"I know that. But they have to work. You don't. Don't block the blessing. That's all I'm saying."

I look down at my friend and shake my head. I know she means well, but it still pisses me off. I'm not trying to take away anything from Nicholas. I'm trying to find something for myself.

"I get it," I say.

Vanessa stands there swatting a fly away. "Are we okay? I can't leave unless I know we are good."

"We're fine. You can go. Your kids are getting riled up." I point to her vehicle. The boys are throwing something around and Morgan looks like she is about to scream.

Vanessa looks at the van, runs up the three stairs to give me a hug and hurries to the vehicle. Super Mom is back in effect as she calms the situation in the van. She rolls down the window before she backs out. "See you Saturday at the party."

****

I thought my day couldn't get worst, but I was wrong. The doorbell chimes, and I look through the peephole. Marilyn, in her usual outfit of below the knee skirt, white blouse and pearls accompanied by a designer handbag and sensible shoes. I think about pretending I'm not at home. Instead, I take a deep breath and open the door. "Marilyn."

"Adrienne," she air kisses the space near my cheek and pushes past leaving a trail of Yardley Lavender perfume. I follow her into the family room where she perches on the edge of the couch with her back ramrod straight.

Marilyn is popping in for a visit. Again. Logan's mother feels as if she has the right to stop by unannounced whenever she likes. Logan gave her a key so she could let herself in, but I put a stop to that foolishness by developing a tendency to walk around the house naked. I remember the look on my mother-in-law's face when she walked in one day to find me at six months pregnant lying across the couch wearing nothing but a bowl of praline & butter pecan ice cream. Now Marilyn rings the doorbell. Small victory.

"I just put Nicholas down for his nap." I pick up a toy car that crashed into the coffee table earlier and parked.

"Oh no. I was hoping to see him today. I brought him a gift. Each birthday is a miracle, you know." She hands me a box wrapped in blue birthday paper topped with a white bow. Marilyn always refers to Nicholas as a "miracle." She is convinced it was her prayer group that got him through his first crisis when he was five months old. I would never let Marilyn know I think it was a miracle too. Having to watch my child struggle to breathe was a helplessness I never want to feel again. But I know the real reason Marilyn won't call Nicholas by name. She can't accept that we didn't name him Logan the third.

I sit the gift on top of the teacher recertification application I was working on when the bell rung.

"I really want to see my grandson on his birthday," Marilyn says. "I have a busy schedule today, but maybe I can swing back by before dinner."

Marilyn launches into some description about a charity event she is helping to organize as her eyes inspect the cleanliness of the family room. I follow her gaze. There are books scattered across the rug, a gang of action figures huddled in front of the fireplace and Elmo is situated in a compromising position with a stuffed Spiderman. I think a house should look lived in. I'm certain Marilyn is adding the unkempt room to the list of the ways I come up short as a Rutherford wife.

"I did want to speak with you, Adrienne."

My eyebrows shoot up. *What is it now?*

Marilyn picks at imaginary lint and places her hands in her lap. I brace for the blow to my self-esteem.

"I was speaking with Logan this morning and he mentioned your desire to return to work. While teaching is a very honorable profession, I need to remind you that your first obligation is to your husband and child. I feel Nicholas needs the stability of being at home with his mother. He does require special care. As you know, I stayed at home with my child, and I think it benefited him immeasurably."

Marilyn pauses, anticipating a response from me, but my mouth and brain are no longer coordinating.

She continues. "Logan needs you to be available to support him as well. He's done an admirable job running the firm after his father's passing, but he is under a lot of stress. I'm sure you don't want to be a burden. We both need to make sure that his home is a place of peace."

This is a new twist. I've heard the dutiful Rutherford wife speech before, but she is working a new angle.

"Logan told you all this today?" I manage to squeeze the words out between clenched teeth. I shake my head trying to process the betrayal.

"Of course, dear. Logan and I talk every day. There is nothing we don't discuss. He tells me everything." Marilyn sits on the couch with her head held high. A proud queen bee. If she wore glasses, she would be peering over them at me. She reminds me of the ladies on a daytime soap opera; dressed up with nowhere to go.

"I'm not sure what Logan has told you, but whether or not I return to work is a decision we will make as a couple. And while I am sure you mean well, I don't think it's your place to tell me what is best for my family."

Marilyn's face draws up like something smells funny. Probably my attitude.

"I am trying to give you the motherly advice that I'm sure your own mother would." She waits a beat. "God rest her soul."

I sink back into the chair from the low blow. Marilyn loves to criticize under the pretense of fulfilling a motherly duty. My stomach clenches and I struggle for a snappy comeback. Then I remembered something my mother used to say. 'Don't argue with fools.'

This one will make Mom proud. I stand.

"I appreciate you bringing Nicholas a gift. I'm sure he will love it. Now, if you'll excuse me, I really need to get back to my household duties." I even manage a smile.

Marilyn looks confused for a second. Before she can compose herself, I see the truth hidden under all that makeup. She is just a lonely old woman. My fight is with my husband.

Marilyn takes her time rising to her feet. "Well, I'll let you get back to your chores."

I follow her to the door. "We are planning Nicholas's party this weekend. I hope you can join us."

Marilyn studies my face. She recognizes the gift I'm offering but turns away from my look of pity. "Before I forget, Logan mentioned that he is bringing a client home for dinner. You may want to clean up and prepare a decent meal."

The smug smile on her face is the last thing I see before I close the door.

CHAPTER SIX

ADRIENNE

I wait for Logan to come home. After his mother left, I got Logan on the phone and start in about him discussing our business with Marilyn. He cuts me off.

"I need you on this one, babe," he said. "Your glazed chicken will help me close this deal."

I gave in like always and perform the role I am expected to play and support my husband. The house is clean, the food is warming, and Nicholas is in bed.

I greet Logan in the foyer with a smile.

"Hey, babe," Logan says and kisses me. "Something smells good."

I open my mouth and the usual "Must be me" retort lodges in my throat.

"Are you okay?"

I nod, realizing Logan never mentioned the name of his client. Christopher Michaels stands in my foyer smiling like he knows a secret.

The man I have been trying to forget since my wedding day. The man that still invades my dreams and slips into my thoughts when I least expect it. That man stands here with my husband. I focus on breathing and look from Christopher to Logan. What is going on here? Is this some sort of twisted joke?

Logan slides to my side and pulls me close. "I'm sorry, babe. Let me introduce you to someone I hope will be our newest client. Christopher Michaels, meet my wife, Adrienne."

"Nice to meet you," Christopher extends his hand.

I hesitate and Logan nudges me. I swallow and send up a quick prayer. My prayer isn't answered when our skin touches and I feel the familiar sizzle of attraction. I drop his hand, the heat too much to bear. "N-n-nice to meet you, too."

"Come on in and have a seat," Logan says. He leads Christopher into the living room. "What's your pleasure? Rum, scotch?"

I know the answer will be sweet tea before Christopher echoes the choice of beverage. Logan looks at me and I almost trip over my feet to get out of the room.

I pace the length of the kitchen trying to make sense of things. Why is Christopher here? What do I tell Logan? How do I sit through dinner? I need to call Kim.

"What is the hold up in here?" Logan's voice snatches me out of my thoughts.

"Just checking on dinner." I open the oven and let the heat camouflage my flushed face. I remove the pan of Balsamic Glazed Chicken and drizzle the pan drippings over the red potatoes. If I stay busy, I won't have to go back into the room. I take the glass from Logan and remove the pitcher from the refrigerator.

"Do you know who that guy is?" Logan asks.

Time stops. My hand shakes and tea spills on the granite countertop. I force myself to take a deep breath when Logan continues talking.

"That man is worth over ten million dollars and he came to the Rutherford Law firm. I have to sign this guy and I can sense he's close. He left for other meetings, but I got him to agree to meet for dinner. I played on being hospitable to the new guy in town. Made him think I do this for all my clients. Once he gets a home cooked meal, I can get that signature. The firm will be back in the black."

"Is the firm in trouble?" I use a paper towel to wipe up the puddle.

"Not anymore." He winks at me. "Now come on. Can't keep the man waiting."

I lean against the counter and take a deep breath. I can get through this. It's obvious that Christopher hasn't said anything about our past. Maybe it doesn't matter to him. Perhaps this is a mere business meeting for the CEO of Michaels, Inc. Two can play that game. This is a simple business dinner like all of the ones I've hosted before.

I transfer food into serving dishes and put everything on the dolly, check my reflection in the hall mirror and get ready to perform my part as the executive wife.

Logan has given Christopher the seat at the head of the table. That works to my advantage. I place the dishes on the table and move my place setting to sit beside Logan away from Christopher.

"Everything looks delicious," Christopher says.

Logan takes my hand. "I knew you would appreciate a home cooked meal. My Adrienne has perfected this dish."

"I can tell this is going to be good." Christopher spoons two pieces of chicken, a heap of potatoes and some string beans on his plate. Logan does the same. I have lost my appetite but put some food on my plate. When we are all served, Logan stops to bless the food.

I take the moment to appraise the man invading my territory. He still looks good. His hair is shaved close and his full beard and mustache are trimmed neat. His grayish green eyes dance with amusement when he catches me sneaking a peek. I tear my eyes away. It has been four years, and he still makes my stomach flip.

I listen to the guys talk while I pick at my food. I've sat through a few of these dinners, and I know my role is to be the silent supportive wife. I have no qualms remaining in the background. I don't trust myself to speak.

"Like I stated earlier in the office, we are a small firm but you can be assured of our total dedication to your business and interests," Logan says.

Christopher doesn't look up from his plate. He cuts a piece of chicken and nods as he chews. I wonder if he remembers how I used to cook for him.

"We take total care of our clients," Logan continues. "We can draft bylaws for the board, file the articles and make sure you have all the proper licensing required in South Carolina."

"Since I sold the stock brokerage, I've been acquiring real estate holdings. I just purchased a franchise with some partners. Can you review the paperwork?"

"No problem," Logan says. "I just need your signature on the agreement and I'll get started."

Christopher spears the remaining beans off his plate and savors the last bite. He wipes his mouth with the linen napkin and places it on his plate. "Now that meal brought back some pleasant memories. It's been a long time since I've had food this good."

I pretend I don't hear the compliment meant to evoke memories of times spent in   Christopher's kitchen. I look at my watch. I shouldn't have to endure this charade much longer.

"At the Rutherford firm, we treat our clients like family," Logan puts a hand on my knee underneath the table.

"Speaking of family, where's the baby?" Christopher asks.

I look up. "Baby?"

"I saw the family portrait in the other room. A baby boy, right?"

Logan laughs. "That's an old picture. Nicholas turned three today. He's asleep. Adrienne has him on a schedule so we can have quality time in the evenings."

Logan is looking at me so he misses the wince on Christopher's face. I wonder what it means. Then I wonder why I'm wondering what it means.

"Mommy," a tiny voice calls from the doorway. Nicholas stands in the doorway with his blanket in one hand, rubbing his eyes with the other. "I look for you, Mommy."

"I'm right here, baby." I push back my chair to get up, but Logan springs into action.

"Hey, buddy." He scoops Nicholas up and rocks him. "You're supposed to be asleep."

"I wake up. Potty break," Nicholas says.

I walk over and rub Nicholas's back. "I'll take him back up."

"I've got him," Logan whispers. "Entertain the client for me."

Knowing that's not a good idea, I try to reach for Nicholas but Logan turns to Christopher. "Let me put my son down and then we can finalize things."

"No problem, man. Family first. I respect that," Christopher says.

Logan winks at me and leaves me standing there. He is putting on a good show. I can't remember a time he has ever put Nicholas to bed without prodding from me.

"You're looking mighty fine, Ms. Adrienne."

I turn to glare at Christopher. He smiles like he knows a secret.

That pisses me off and I cross the room to stand over him. "What are you doing here?"

He leans back. "Like Logan said. I'm a potential new client."

Before I can process what that means for me, Christopher stands to look me in the eyes. He moves a strand of hair behind my ear. "You grew your hair out."

"My husband likes it long." I try with little success to distance myself from the feelings his touch ignites.

"But what do you like? I bet I can remember." He strokes my neck and I flashback to our last night together. The kissing. The touching.

I put a hand on his chest and push him away. "Don't touch me." I glance at the door and start stacking dirty dishes. Anything to keep my hands busy.

"Sorry if I'm being forward. I'm getting ahead of myself. It's just seeing you again has me…"

I don't look up. "Are you going to tell me why you are here? It's been a long time."

"Four years, seven months. Give or take a few days." Christopher sits back down.

I continue as if he didn't speak. "You show up with my husband and you didn't tell him anything. What's your angle?"

He doesn't say anything until I stop scraping dishes and look at him.

"I missed you."

The glass shatters when I drop it. My mind races. I need to get out of here. If I leave now, I can make it to the garage before Logan comes back. My keys are right beside the door.

"Careful." Christopher is on his feet. "You don't want to step in glass."

I bend over to pick up the larger pieces. "I've got it."

He kneels beside me. "Does this mean you missed me too?"

Our hands touch when we both reach for a chunk of glass. I stand up so fast I'm lightheaded. I grab the back of a chair to steady myself.

Christopher stands and reaches for me. "Are you okay?"

No, I'm not. Nothing about this is okay. I step back. "I'm fine. I need to get a broom… to get up the glass."

I hurry from the room and run into Logan.

"Whoa," Logan catches me before I can walk past. "What's the rush? Nicholas is all tucked in."

I take a breath and explain about the glass.

"Take your time," he says. "I'll take Michaels into the study and close this deal. We can celebrate later." He pats my behind.

I lean against the washing machine and try to calm down. I am thrilled and terrified seeing him again. In my fantasies, I would flaunt how fabulous my life is without him. I would flash my ring finger to show him that someone chose me when he left. I wanted to be sexy and cool and reject him as he groveled at my feet. In the real-life version,

I'm hiding out in the utility room using a dirty towel to wipe perspiration from my face.

Time to snap out of it. Logan will finish his business meeting and Christopher will be gone soon. I won't have to see him again and I'll have a funny story to tell Kim. I grab the broom to go clean up the mess in the dining room.

I manage to tidy up the dining room and stack the dishes in the dishwasher without further incident. I can hear the guys talking in the study but I have no intentions of stopping as I pass by on the way to the stairs.

"Adrienne can help you with that. She used to be a teacher, so she probably knows these places," Logan says.

"I don't want to impose. She may have other plans tomorrow."

"It's no problem," Logan says.

"What's not a problem?" I walk into the study.

Logan puts down the glass of rum he is holding and crosses the room. "I was going to tell you later, but I need you to escort Michaels here to a few schools. He needs to find one for his daughter."

His daughter. The reason he left me.

I look at Christopher, but he keeps his head down. The file folder in his hand must hold the secret to getting time alone with an ex.

"Figured you can get Mother to watch Nicholas for a few hours. I would do it, but I have to be in court in the morning." Logan moves so close I can smell the alcohol on his breath. His eyes plead with me to agree as he squeezes my arm. Hard.

I know I should tell him. If he knew the truth about my history with Christopher, he would freak out. If he knew about our past, I doubt he would want me around the man. If he knew my secret, it would destroy us.

"Sure," I say and move his hand from my arm. I hold his hand instead. "Anything to help."

Logan kisses me. A bittersweet reward for my secrecy. Then he kisses me again. Longer for show.

"Thanks, babe," he says and goes to retrieve his drink. He pours a glass for Christopher and offers toast. I back out of the room to go check on Nicholas.

Later that night, I make love to my husband with purpose needing to remove any doubt in my mind. I am over Christopher so there is nothing to tell. I am over the man and I'll prove it to myself by taking him around.

Long after Logan falls asleep, I lay awake. My thoughts are racing and can't seem to settle down. I snuggle closer to my husband, and he wraps me in his arms. This is the man I love, I tell myself. The past doesn't matter. I repeat that mantra until I drift off. Knowing the whole time, it's a lie.

CHAPTER SEVEN

ADRIENNE

"Guess who came to dinner?" I march past Kim and stand in the middle of her living room.

Kim closes the door. "Where's Nicholas?"

"Marilyn. Guess who came to dinner?"

"Wow. You look nice." Kim looks me up and down. "What's up with you?"

"That's what I'm trying to tell you. You won't believe who came to my house last night."

Kim circles me and points. "I can't remember the last time I saw you in dress clothes. I mean, the yoga pants are functional but hardly fashionable."

"You need to focus." I put my hands on my hips. "You'll never guess who was at my house…Last night."

"Who?"

"Christopher." Saying his name makes my heart race. I collapse on the couch.

Kim sits in the oversized chair across from me. "Wait. What?"

"You heard me. Christopher was at my house. Last night. For dinner."

Kim's eyes widen. "Your Christopher?"

I nod.

"Let's go into the kitchen. This sounds like I'm going to need a drink."

The leather sofa crackles when I stand to follow her. The kitchen is painted sunshine yellow. Everything in the room screams "Get Happy" right down to the yellow smiling face cookie jar. The white appliances gleam and I take pride in the cleanliness. I taught her well. I sit at the old wooden table that belonged to our mother and immediately feel better. I am home.

Kim reaches into the cabinet and takes out two wine glasses. "It's too early to get Goose Induced but wine should be fine. This sounds major."

I laugh. "Goose Induced?"

"This guy I was dating used to drink Grey Goose vodka. Mixed it with cranberry juice and a splash of pineapple juice. It's pretty good. Unfortunately, this dude got induced almost every day."

I momentarily forget about my craziness and escape into Kim's life. "You dumped him, right?"

"Of course. A girl doesn't have time to go to AA meetings."

"You are crazy. When are you going to stop the serial dating?"

Kim shrugs her shoulders. "Why stop? I'm having fun. Enough about me. Let's get into this."

Kim retrieves a bottle of wine from the fridge, pours two glasses and sits beside me. She watches me gulp down half a glass. "Start at the beginning. And don't leave anything out."

I give her the dirty details.

Kim takes a drink and leans back in the chair. "Let me get this straight. Your husband invited your ex-boyfriend to dinner. Not knowing he's your ex, of course. And wants to sign him as a client?"

"Logan wants me to escort Christopher around. He picked out this outfit. He dropped Nicholas off at his mother's." My husband has never been so helpful.

"So, take the man around and that's the end of it. What's the big deal?"

I sigh. "The big deal is I don't know what Christopher is doing here. Why did he go to Logan?"

"Only one way to find out. Ask him."

I stand up and take my glass to the sink. I turn and lean against the counter. "But don't you think it's odd? Shouldn't I tell Logan about the past?"

A slow smile spreads across Kim's face. "You still love him, don't you?"

"What? Are you crazy? The man left me, remember?" I try to conjure up the familiar feelings of anger. Instead, all I recall his scent. I must be going crazy. My life was fine until Christopher showed up at my house. I don't know what he expects but I am a married woman…with a child.

"I know. Doesn't mean you stopped loving him. Or that he stopped loving you."

I shake my head. "That doesn't matter now. He made his choice and I made mine. Too late to go back now."

"But if you could, would you?"

That's the loaded question. If I didn't marry Logan, I wouldn't have Nicholas. I would never undo that. Choices. No matter how much you think a decision only affects your life, you are wrong. Some decisions can change everything.

Kim is still talking. "We had some good times, right? Remember when Christopher called himself cooking out for the fourth?"

I remember. It was our first holiday as an official couple and Christopher wanted to show off his grilling skills.

"Yeah, and the man couldn't get the charcoal started. Maybe the coals were old or something, but they wouldn't burn."

"I didn't think pouring a whole bottle of lighter fluid on them was a good idea."

I look out the window and see the remains of the burn marks on the patio. "One minute, we're arguing about who was going to the store and the next minute that fire ball shot out of the grill."

"Man, I took off running." Kim laughs.

"Me too. Christopher didn't move fast enough." The picture I took of Christopher's singed eyebrows is probably still somewhere in this house.

I return to the table. "There are a lot of memories of Christopher in this place." I can still feel his presence in the redecorated space.

"Chris was my favorite out of all your boyfriends."

"Including my husband."

Kim picks up on my teasing. "Don't get me wrong. Brother-in-law is cool. But he is sort of intense."

As if on cue, my cell phone rings.

"I bet that's Mr. Uptight now," Kim says.

I go get my purse off the couch and take out the phone. The man doesn't even say hello.

"Have you gotten to Michaels yet?"

No, I haven't."

Logan explodes. "Why not? I thought we agreed you would help me on this. It's not like you're busy."

"You need to calm down. I said I would do this and I will."

"When Adrienne? Because I told Michaels this would happen. Are you trying to make me look bad?"

Logan continues to rant. I pull the phone away from my ear and can still hear him. The man is stressing out. I hear water running in the kitchen sink and the clink of glasses. I know Kim can hear this man yelling so I walk down the hall.

"Logan," I snap. "I'm going like I said I would."

There is silence on the other end. We listen to each other breathe.

"Okay," he says and clears his throat. "I know you'll do it. I don't understand the delay. But this is very important. Like we discussed last night, you agreed to help. Everything must be perfect for this guy. I need Michaels as a client."

Logan's half ass apology doesn't make me feel any better. "I understand." I retort, ending the call.

"Brother-in-law sounds higher strung than usual," Kim searches my face to gauge my mood when I walk back in the kitchen.

"Yeah."

"Is everything okay?"

"Sure. Everything's fine." I know Kim isn't convinced. "It's important, you know. Logan needs Christopher as a client. I can't let my past get in the way of the future." I almost convince myself.

Kim isn't easily swayed and raises an eyebrow. "I hope you know what you are doing."

That makes two of us, I think. I take a deep breath and dial Christopher's number.

CHAPTER EIGHT

CHRISTOPHER

I wake up this morning to thoughts of Adrienne. No different than any other day. That woman is the first person I think of in the morning and the last person I pray for at night. My mother was right. I regret leaving Adrienne every day.

I unplug the vacuum cleaner and return it to the closet. I have already dusted and cleaned the kitchen. I saved the bathroom for last. Extra effort goes into scrubbing the tub. I remember how much Adrienne loved to take baths. The memories of walking in on her and being pulled into the water make me smile. *Don't blow it*, I tell myself. I am going to be alone with her. I need to regain the trust I threw away years ago.

I am a cheater. Correction, I am a reformed cheater. I gave in to temptation one time and it cost me everything. The thing that gnaws at me is I was never a dog like most of my friends. I preferred to be with one woman. There was no sport in it for me to run game on several women and take chances on breaking hearts.

If I could turn back time, I would never have slept with Lisa. I think back to the time when I was the hot, young stockbroker and Lisa was the other Black person in the office. Circumstances and meddling coworkers threw us together at every opportunity. One moment that changed my life forever.

I wring out the sponge and store the supplies under the sink. I'm getting dressed when my cell phone sings. Lisa's mobile number flashes on the caller id.

"Morning, Daddy."

I smile and sit on the bed. "Mya Papaya. How's my favorite girl doing?"

Mya giggles at her pet name. "I'm good, Daddy."

"Then why are you whispering?"

"Mommy is making me wear the blue pants to school. But I want to wear my pink dress. Can I wear the dress? Please, Daddy."

I pick up the picture of Mya I keep by the bed. I miss my baby. Lisa has started to be a little less accommodating with visitation. I suspect it has everything to do with her new fiancée, Troy. "You need to listen to your mother. Wear the pink dress for me this weekend, okay?"

"Oh. Okay, then."

I marvel at how well Mya adjusted after the divorce. I made sure that Mya memorized my phone number and I see her every chance I get.

Mya starts going on about her friends at school and then I hear Lisa in the background. "Girl, didn't I tell you about taking my phone."

I hear the phone drop. "Sorry, Mommy."

"Who are you talking to anyway?" Lisa picks up the phone. "Who is this?"

"It's me."

I swear I can hear Lisa roll her eyes. "I should have known. Your daughter has a bad habit of sneaking my phone. Half the time I can't find it."

"I'll get her a phone then."

"A five-year-old does not need a phone."

"She needs to be able to get in touch with me whenever she wants."

"Maybe you should pay my cell phone bill instead."

I take a deep breath. It always comes down to money with this woman. The generous divorce settlement and child support payments aren't enough for her because it's never enough.

"I'll be there on Friday around six to pick up Mya."

Lisa instructs Mya to go to her bedroom and change clothes. "About that, I was going to call you. You'll have to get her on Saturday. We have something planned on Friday."

I fight exploding. "What are you talking about? I couldn't get her last weekend because of some gymnastics tournament."

"You got to see her, didn't you?"

"Cheering from the sidelines is not quality time with her. We agreed I could get her on weekends when I didn't contest you moving to another state. Why are you making things difficult?"

"It's one day, Christopher. I don't know why you are making a big deal out of it."

I pace around the room. This is the reason I married the woman in the first place. Trying to parent from a distance is fucking hard. I loved it when I shared my home with my daughter. Too bad her mom was there too. I don't regret having Mya. I regret having her with the wrong woman.

"How long are you going to punish me?" I ask. She acts like she doesn't know what I am talking about. "Come on now. We both knew our marriage was a sham, but we tried to make it work."

"At least one of us tried. You spent more time at the office than you did at home."

I don't want to have this argument again. "How many times do I have to apologize for being a lousy husband?"

"I don't know. Why don't you start by admitting I could never compete with your ex? I know I deserved better. I could have had any man I wanted. I chose you."

"You chose me because you saw dollar signs."

"I chose you because I saw potential. I wanted the Huxtable dream. You couldn't let go of the past."

I resist the urge to tell Lisa *The Cosby Show* wasn't real. Our problems couldn't be resolved in thirty minutes.

"You know what? You're right. I messed up. I couldn't be the man you needed." How did I deal with this spoiled woman for five years?

"Doesn't matter. I'll have a *real* husband soon." I don't miss the emphasis on the word real.

"How is Troy?" She thinks it bothers me that she found a replacement. I'm happy Lisa found someone else to put her claws in. She needs someone else's money to spend besides mine and he has some. *I'm not saying she's a gold digger.* Kayne West was singing my life with that tune.

"He is fixing his family breakfast," Lisa brags.

"About this weekend, all I'm asking for is time with Mya. She needs her daddy."

"She has a daddy," Lisa spits. "Troy is here with her every day."

I freeze. "What the hell did you just say?" If Lisa was standing in front of me right now, I would have to plead temporary insanity for my actions. She might as well have kicked me in the balls.

"You heard me. Mya has a daddy right here. She doesn't need you." Lisa's smug tone makes me lose control.

My words shoot out like a bullet. "You bitch. Are you sure you want to play this game? You think you've won because I didn't contest you following that man and taking my daughter with you?"

"Listen—" Lisa tries to interrupt.

"No, you listen. I expect Mya to be ready on Saturday morning."

"Whatever."

I hear the dial tone and throw the phone on the bed in disgust. Time to handle this woman. I'm not rich because I'm stupid. I'm rich because I know how to execute a plan. I grab the phone and call my attorney. I leave a message with his secretary. Lisa's not going to drive a wedge between me and my daughter. I'm not going to be like my father. Time to change our custody arrangements.

The thought of Mya brings the weight of emotions back and I collapse on the bed. I look at the picture of my baby again. A part of me understands how some men can give up on having a relationship with their children. It is hard. Damn hard when the mother tries to sabotage your efforts. My own Dad couldn't find the courage. I vowed to never repeat that behavior. But I never thought I would have the crazy baby mama drama either. I guess this is my retribution.

The phone rings and it takes a moment for the sound to register. Lisa again.

"What?" I bark.

"Daddy, I forgot," Mya whispers.

Damn. I take the temper out of my voice. "Forgot what, baby girl?"

"Forgot to tell you I love you."

Just like that the world is right again. At least it feels that way. "Love you too, Mya Papaya. See you this weekend."

CHAPTER NINE

ADRIENNE

I turn into the parking lot of Christopher's building and glance at the clock. I am late, but I stall further by taking a few minutes to survey the surroundings. Christopher lives in a condo in the Sandhills Development. It is a mixed-use retail center made up of specialty stores, boutiques, restaurants and department stores. It also has a movie theater, a grocery store and several bank branches. An ideal resident would be one that owns a store and lives in the condo above it. Or single professionals like Christopher. The complex is about three years old and I am curious to see the housing floor plans. I tell myself the excitement of seeing the condos is making my stomach flip and not the person that will be my tour guide.

I enter the lobby, get buzzed in and take the elevator to the fourth floor. When I turn the corner, Christopher stands in the doorway of his suite. The walk down the hall gives me the opportunity to stare without being obvious. He is wearing a pair of jeans, a causal button-down shirt, no shoes and a cocky smile. My pulse quickens. He envelops me in an embrace that feels like home.

"Ms. Adrienne," his greeting is as warm as his hug. "I'm glad you could come." I allow a moment to breathe in his scent and step back. This is business.

"Are you ready?"

I think I see disappointment in his eyes. His hand lingers on my arm for a moment longer than necessary. "I'll be ready in a minute. Come on in. I need to throw on some shoes." He steps aside and ushers me in. "Look around. I apologize for the boxes. I'm still unpacking."

I move into a small foyer with hardwood floors that leads into a kitchen and living room. The granite countertops gleam and accent the modern stainless-steel appliances. The living room is littered with unpacked boxes, a leather sofa and a flat screen television mounted on the wall. The wooden blinds are open to display a view of the water fountain, which marks the center of the shopping complex and is the staging area for various musical acts in the summer and fall.

I keep my back to Christopher. What am I doing here? I'm not supposed to be here.

"I like the view too." I turn. Christopher's eyes broadcast his intent. He is not talking about the landscape.

"What the hell are you doing?" I spit. A cascade of emotions overtakes me. Anger being the clear winner.

Christopher throws up his hands. "I'm not doing anything. Trying to give a beautiful woman a compliment is all."

"Don't do that. Don't act like you aren't trying something. Why am I here, Christopher? Why are you trying to manipulate my husband to spend time with me?"

"First of all, I didn't have to trick Logan into doing anything. I mentioned I needed to find a school for my daughter. He gladly offered up his wife, the former teacher, to be my guide. I took advantage of the opportunity to see you again."

"But you knew Logan was my husband before you made the appointment with him."

"No. That was fate. One of my friends gave me the name of an attorney. Gregory Atkins. When I realized it was your husband's firm, I couldn't believe my luck. I'll admit I wanted to meet the man you married. And I wanted to see you again. I didn't know how I would accomplish that part, but Logan made it easy."

I cross my arms. "Because he doesn't know our history."

"Because he's a fool. What kind of man offers up his wife to a man he just met?"

"I don't know. What kind of man cheats on a woman he says he loves?"

He steps closer to me. Closes the distance with his heat. His eyes locked with mine. "The kind of man with regrets."

"Regrets, huh?" I bark a laugh. "Which regret? Sleeping with a coworker, getting her pregnant or telling me in the airport that we were through?"

He steps back and lowers his head. "All of them. I should have given us a chance. If you could have forgiven me, I should have fought for you."

The anger evaporates with his admission. That's the real reason I agreed to Logan's insane request. I needed to hear this man admit he was wrong. "Why didn't you tell me this the last time we saw each other?"

"The last time we saw each other there wasn't much talking going on." The cocky smile returns.

I turn away embarrassed by the memory. "That was about me getting closure. It was so easy for you to leave me and I needed to show you I was over you."

"Is that you what you thought? That it was easy. It was fucking hard to do that. Hell, it's taking all my willpower right now not to touch you."

I tuck a strand of hair behind my ear and turn to face him. Our eyes lock and the history of our time together plays like a symphony. The highs and lows. Christopher licks his lips and I have to look away.

"Well, let me put some shoes on," he says. He sits in a chair and pulls a pair from beside the couch, sliding his long feet into a pair of sexy Salvatore Ferragamo shoes. I think about the implications of those big feet of his. *Shit, I'm in trouble.*

I shake my head. "I don't want to do this anymore. Let's not talk about our history."

"Let's," he says. "I know I messed up with Lisa. I know sleeping with a coworker was stupid, but Adrienne?"

I interrupt him. "Your daughter is what, five years old? Do you have any idea what kind of school you want?"

"You and I both married the wrong people for the wrong reasons."

I frown. "You don't know anything about my marriage or my husband."

"I know he's struggling to keep his business afloat. He's desperate, Adrienne. He needs me in a way that he shouldn't at this stage in his career."

Logan was stressed. I thought about how he'd tried to coach me this morning on how to behave and what to say. And Chris was right; he was completely unconcerned about me spending time with another man.

"What's the second reason?" I ask rolling my neck.

Christopher raises an eyebrow. "Second reason for what?"

"You always do that. Start a conversation with 'first of all' then never have another point."

He smiles. "You remember."

I don't smile back. "I remember a lot of things. Like getting dumped in the airport."

"Wait. I already apologized for that. I regret how I handled things that day." He starts toward me, but I hold up a hand to stop him.

"Forget it. Tell me the second reason why you're here."

Christopher pauses for a second. "It's easier to show you." He reaches for my hand. I don't trust myself to touch him so I ignore it.

"What are you talking about?"

Christopher points. "Follow me."

We walk down the short hallway and Christopher stops at an open door. "This is the bathroom and here is the first bedroom which is my office."

The office is the only room that is unpacked. He has a traditional wooden desk, silver laptop, printer and fax machine. There is a matching file cabinet in one corner with a bookcase in the other. We go across the hall to another room.

"This is the reason I'm here. This bedroom will be my daughter's. I had them paint it pink and yellow. Her favorite colors. The furniture should be here tomorrow." His eyes betray sadness. I touch his shoulder.

"Must be rough not seeing her."

He touches my hand to acknowledge the gesture. "I'll get her soon. She's the smartest and prettiest five-year-old ever and I'm not just saying that because she's my daughter."

Christopher becomes animated when he talks about his daughter. I can feel the love he has for her, and I begin to relax. This is the Christopher I remember. Once someone or something becomes a part of his world, he is passionate in expressing his feelings.

I have a revelation that I dismiss as soon as the thought forms. I've never seen that look on Logan's face when he talks about our son. I'm glad when Christopher distracts me by continuing the tour.

Christopher leans against the door to the master bathroom and watches me inspect the place. "You like?"

"Yes. This is nice. How long have you been here?" I run my hands over the countertops and peer up at the recessed lighting fixtures. The art deco claw foot bathtub is calling for a soak. I reluctantly turn away.

"About three months."

I make note of the timeframe. "How did you even know about this place?"

"I met the developer through some business associates. He talked about his concept of retail and mixed-use properties. When I decided to relocate, I figured this would be ideal for me. Everything I need is within walking distance. And I'm thinking about opening a franchise here on the property."

I'm not sure I hear him correctly. "So, you plan to be here for a while? In town, I mean."

"I have some unfinished business here."

He locks eyes with me so the meaning is explicit. I am that unfinished business.

I tuck my hair behind my ear and shift my purse to the opposite shoulder. It is starting to get warm in here. "Maybe we should get going. Logan said you were interested in private schools and I made some appointments." I hope the mention of my husband will diffuse the vibe in the room. It doesn't. But Christopher stands up straight and goes to the closet to pulls out a blazer.

"I'm ready whenever you are, Ms. Adrienne."

The statement has a double meeting. I don't doubt it for a second.

CHAPTER TEN

CHRISTOPHER

I didn't know it could be so hot in an air-conditioned vehicle. Being this close to Adrienne has me sweating. Christ, I was an idiot to let this woman go.

"Did I ask the wrong question?"

I blink. "I…uh…what did you ask?"

"How do you feel about Lisa remarrying?"

I shrug. "I don't care what Lisa does. My only interest is Mya. Besides, I had the guy checked out and he seems to be decent."

Adrienne stops at an intersection and gives me the side-eye. "Checked out? As in investigated?"

"Right down to his social security number. If that man is going to be around my baby, I need to know everything about him."

"Well, all right now," she murmurs. "What's your plan?"

"I'm going back to court. Lisa plays fast and loose with accommodations. She tries to punish me for not…" I stop talking. I want to regain Adrienne's trust by putting all my baggage out there, but I don't want to push it.

"Go on," Adrienne says. "Punish you for what? Did you cheat on her too?"

I wince. "No. Lisa was the one that did that. That's the real reason for her move. Her fiancé got a job in Greenville at BMW. I followed to make things easier. I'm not trying to keep Mya from her mother, but she needs me too."

Adrienne nods and proceeds through the intersection. I can tell she is processing this new information. I hope she knows I'm being totally honest about everything. We ride in silence for a few miles with music from the radio filling the car.

We turn into the parking lot of the first school and Adrienne shuts off the engine. "Did you have the Rutherford Law firm investigated?"

I turn to face her. "Of course."

I notice her grip on the steering wheel tightens. She hesitates and then asks, "And, what did you find out? Tell me the truth."

I nod. "It's a small firm with an excellent reputation, mostly because of Rutherford Senior. After he died, the senior associate managed the firm with Logan being groomed to take over. When the partner retired, Gregory was the main guy. Now that Logan is flying solo, let's just say the jury is still out on that one."

I spare her the detail about Logan having a reputation for avoiding court at all costs and losing all his employees. She probably knows about his staffing issues.

Adrienne takes a breath. "Are you going to hire Logan?"

"I signed the papers this morning. I'll fax them when we get back."

"If you've already decided, what is this about? Why am I here playing chauffeur like he still needs to win over a client?"

I unbuckle my seat belt and take her hand. "To be honest, it was never about hiring a law firm. I needed a reason to see you."

She slides her hand away and tucks a strand of hair behind her ear. I missed seeing her do that. "So, you are using Logan to get to his wife. Isn't that shady?"

"Using Logan? Isn't he using you to recruit a client?" The man is nuts to send his wife out with me alone.

Adrienne grips the steering wheel hard. Maybe that is a sore point.

"Listen," I lean across the seat and turn her my face to mine. "Let's not make this bigger than it is. I needed a local firm to represent my interest with a local buyer. Most of the deal has been put in place by my attorneys. If I can give your husband some business and get to see you at the same time, what's the harm?"

I can see the conflict play out in her eyes. She is loyal to her husband, but I can feel the familiar chemistry. I want to kiss her so bad it hurts. But I don't want to give her an excuse to dismiss me. I'm happy being near her again. I lean back in my seat.

Adrienne unbuckles her seat belt. "We're going to be late."

"It's never too late," I say. Husband or not I'm hoping like hell it's true.

The first school we visit, I dismiss as elitist. "If that man used the phrase 'high caliber of student' one more time, I was going to tell him to kiss my high caliber ass."

Adrienne laughs. "I agree."

The second school lacks diversity. "Did you see a child of color anywhere in that school?" I ask when we walk out the door.

"Maybe two," she says. "And they looked miserable."

By the time we arrive at our last stop, we are laughing like the friends we used to be. I can feel Adrienne's guard come down. I keep her entertained with stories of bad business deals and famous people I've met.

"You wouldn't believe how short most of them are," I say.

"Everyone is short to you. What are you? 6'3"?"

"6'2 and ½ but I'm glad you remembered to round up."

"That ½ makes a difference, right," Adrienne teases.

She remembered one of our running jokes. I'm making progress. I hold the door for her as we walk into the last school on the list.

Patricia Hamm, head mistress of the Harrison Hall greets us with a warm smile, graying hair and a killer Jones of New York blue suit. I recognize the brand. My ex-wife has a closet full of them.

"Thank you for coming in today," she says and shows us to the couch in her office. A love seat. Adrienne and I are close enough for our legs touch. The close presence of this woman makes my mind wander to places I've been trying to avoid since I watched her walk down the hall to my condo. I focus on snatches of the conversation. The academic standards of Harrison Hall, the 100% graduation rate, the varied racial composition of the school, extracurricular activities and scholarship to insure a diverse student population with a mixed social economic status as well.

"Our students not only excel academically, we ensure they are well rounded individuals that can help change society," Mrs. Hamm concludes.

"Well, I'm impressed," I say and turn to Adrienne. "What do you think?"

"What is the student/teacher ratio?" Adrienne asks. "How do your students perform on state required tests? Are programs in place to assist students who learn differently?"

Mrs. Hamm winks at me. "Nice being married to a teacher."

I take the opportunity to take Adrienne's hand. "Yes, it is. How did you know she was a teacher?"

"Educators know other educators. It's who we are." Mrs. Hamm goes to her desk and returns with a folder. "You'll find the answer to all of your questions in here. Where do you teach?"

I put my arm around Adrienne and answer for her. "Nowhere at the moment. She took some time off to stay at home with our son. But she is looking to get back into the classroom."

"As a matter of fact, we have an opening. I can get you an application."

When Mrs. Hamm leaves the room Adrienne whispers. "What are you doing?"

"Just go with it," I say. "We're about to hook you up with a job."

"Who says I want a job?"

"Your eyes. Every time we've entered a school today, I see the joy. You belong in the classroom, Ms. Adrienne."

"I have been thinking about it. But Logan thinks—"

I interrupt her. "What do you want? That should be the only consideration."

Mrs. Hamm returns with the application and explains the process. The semester begins in four months, and they would like to have all their instructors in place.

We settle back in the car when I tell Adrienne that today was a success. "We found my baby girl a school and a job for you."

Adrienne starts the car and pulls out of the parking lot. "What makes you think I'm going to take the position?"

"First of all, you have got to be kidding, right? I know you can already see yourself walking down those hallways. We both know you want to get back into teaching."

I watch the struggle for an excuse play across her face. Something, or rather someone, is holding her back from returning to the classroom. My gut tells me it her husband. All is not well at home. I make a mental note of that.

"I can't see myself teaching in a private school. Not that there is anything wrong with it, but I've always been an advocate of public education."

I hold up my hands in mock surrender. "I know, I know. I think I've heard your 'public education is the foundation of society' speech a time or fifty."

Adrienne laughs, and it is the sweetest melody. "You still remember that?"

"I remember everything about you."

The mood changes, and I stare at her until she glances my way. She stops at an intersection and starts to tuck a strand of hair behind her ear. I do it for her and lean close.

"I remember your touch and the way you taste when I kiss you. I remember the way you would curl up beside me in bed and hold my hand until you fall asleep. I remember how passionate you are about teaching and your belief that everyone can learn. I remember the first time we made love." I pause. "And the last time."

Adrienne stares back at me and I wish I could read her mind. My heart is pounding. I hope I didn't make her uncomfortable, but I couldn't hold that in any longer. She starts to say something but a car horn blares behind us. The traffic light is green, interrupting the moment.

"Are you hungry?" Adrienne asks after a beat. "We could stop for lunch."

I rub my hands down my pants legs and sigh. "Sure. Let's go somewhere nice. It'll be my treat for helping me today."

She doesn't want our time together to end, I think. I may still have a chance.

The Blue Marlin Restaurant is located downtown in a strip of restaurants that were converted from an old train station. The old platform remains, now littered with metal art sculptures from local artists. The inside of the restaurant has been renovated with heavy cherry wood accents from the wooden beams in the ceiling to the bar and hardwood floors. The smell of fresh baked bread perfume the air, mingling with the aroma of grilled seafood. We arrive after the lunch rush, so we are immediately shown to a booth. I see it as a good sign that she brought us here. We used to come here together when we were dating.

During lunch, I try to get Adrienne to open up about her marriage. All I can ascertain is that she and Logan didn't date long before marriage and had their son nine months later.

"Things happened fast," I say. "I bet that was a surprise. Married one day and a baby the next."

She remains evasive so I switch subjects. "Tell me how baby sister is doing?"

The waiter sits our plates in front of us. I offer up a quick prayer.

"Kim is great. She graduated college and works for herself as a graphic artist."

"I always admired the way you took care of her after your father passed."

Adrienne waves off the compliment. "I did what I had to do."

I remember the struggles she had losing both parents. Her strength drew me to her.

Adrienne must be thinking of her parents too because her eyes start to water. "This Cajun grilled salmon is spicy," she says.

I spear a shrimp and pop it in my mouth. "You know, my mom still asks about you."

"After all this time?"

"Yeah. She mentioned you yesterday as a matter of fact. You know my Mom will always call me out on my mess. Like you used to."

Adrienne puts her fork down. "Oh yeah. And what did she tell you?"

"That I was a fool to marry Lisa."

"What are you doing?" Adrienne's eyes tighten.

I feign surprise. "What do you mean?"

"I don't want you to get any ideas. I'm here because Logan asked me to take you out. And I'll admit I was curious about the life you left me for. But we are not going to keep trying to rewrite the story of us."

"Fair enough. But, I do hope we can be friends." I back off. For now. I look around the restaurant and note that we are the only patrons left.

Adrienne takes the napkin to wipe her mouth. I can tell she is considering my words. She studies my face. "And?"

"And I know you're married. But I have to make sure you're okay."

"Friends?" She considers it.

"I think I'll make a great friend." I give her a full smile and raise one eyebrow.

Her laugh is all I need. I motion the waiter over for the check. Adrienne reaches for her purse, but I stop her.

"My momma told me to always pay for a woman's meal. That way she'll have to put out." I hope she will remember the familiar routine we shared on our dates. I would tease that once I paid for a meal she had to give me some. Of course, that was never a problem between us. Anytime we were alone I could get some loving.

Adrienne's face flushes. "You know good and well your mom didn't tell you that. And since we are strictly friends, you get none of this."

I sign the check and stand to put my blazer on. "A brother can try, can't he?"

I offer Adrienne my hand so she can stand. When she takes it and turns to me, I envelop her in a hug. At first, she stiffens but her body remembers how to fit against mine. I breathe in her familiar scent and get dizzy. Then her cell rings.

Adrienne breaks free and grabs the phone from the table. She mouths that it's Logan and walks away to take the call. I make a quick stop to the restroom and meet her at the car.

The drive back to my place is quiet with the radio providing background noise. I feel comfortable with the silence. The woman doesn't say a word, but I feel the heat between us. Maybe there is a still a chance for us one day. One major barrier to that happening is her phone that keeps vibrating on the console between us. Logan is calling again.

Adrienne parks the car back at my building but doesn't shut off the engine.

"Aren't you coming up?" I ask.

"My job here is done."

"Is that all this day was for you? A job?"

Adrienne hesitates before answering. "Yes."

I lean over and whisper in her ear. "Liar."

She swallows hard. She starts to say something, but that damn phone is buzzing again. "He wants to know if you are planning to sign the retainer agreement."

"Of course. I signed it this morning. I'll fax it when I go upstairs," I wait until she looks at me. "How else am I going to be able to see you?"

She smiles. "I'm glad. I mean, I'm glad you have decided to come to Rutherford Law Firm."

The tension hangs in the small space between us. I wonder if I should try to kiss her. I wonder if she would let me. I stare at her and she licks her lips. My breathing slows and I run my hands down my pants leg to keep from grabbing her. Something has to give here.

"I need to go," Adrienne says.

I nod and reach for the doorknob. "There is one more thing."

Adrienne picks up her cell phone and frowns. She takes a deep breath and starts fiddling with the phone. Perhaps her mind is on her persistent husband. I repeat the question and she freezes.

"Is there a chance that Nicholas is my son?"

CHAPTER ELEVEN

ADRIENNE

My mind is racing as fast as I can navigate the car toward home. Christopher's question brings up an issue I have buried for the last three years. Could he be Nicholas's father? I told him some nonsense to get him out of the vehicle, but I could tell he didn't believe me. In fact, he looked more disappointed than skeptical. I wanted him to drop it and never bring it up again.

The truth is that day in the airport when Christopher dropped the bomb on our relationship wasn't the last time I saw him. But no one needs to know about that.

The vibrating phone saves me from thinking about the possibilities.

"Why haven't you been answering your phone? Where the hell are you?" Logan yells.

I remove the phone from my ear and take a deep breath. Logan is still screaming my name when I get back on the line. "Logan, calm down. My phone was on vibrate in my purse. I didn't hear it."

He lowers his voice. "I need an update. Are you still with Michaels?"

"No. I'm on the way to pick up Nicholas from your mother."

"Did Michaels find a school for his kid?"

"I guess so. He found one that he likes. And they have an opening for a teaching position."

Logan ignores my comment and continues to talk about the firm. "Good, good. He has to agree to let us represent him now. I bet Greg will come begging for his job back. I would love to tell him to go to hell. No one thought I could do it, but I'm going to move this company further than my father ever could."

"Did you hear what I said? One of the schools offered me a job." I remember how encouraging Christopher was and I want my husband to do the same. Sure, he has never supported this effort before but I hope for a positive response.

Logan laughs. Laughs.

"I hope you told them you don't have to work because your husband is the man."

My stomach sinks and I blow out a frustrated breath. I try not to, but I begin to wonder how different things would be if Christopher was on the other end of the line. I shake my head to clear away those thoughts. Logan doesn't notice I have gone mute. He continues to offer praises unto himself. "Hey, babe. Got to go. Michaels is on the other line."

I put the phone down along with any hope of getting back into a classroom.

****

"Hey, Mommy," Nicholas calls to me when I walk into Marilyn's living room. He is lying across the sofa and his voice is weak. "I want you, Mommy."

"Are you okay?" I ask. Nicholas reaches for me and I scoop him up. He feels warm.

"Did you already give him something for the fever?" I ask Marilyn.

She stands there looking hesitant. "No, he said he was tired so I had him lay down and rest."

I fumble through my purse until I find Nicholas's ibuprofen. I always carry it and Nicholas has some in his backpack. Fever can be the first sign of an upcoming episode. It is best to head these off before it becomes a full-blown crisis.

I stroke Nicholas's head and administer the proper dose. I hate this. You can have months of good days and when you are lulled into a false sense that everything will be okay, the disease returns to attack my baby.

"Are the Spidey senses tingling?"

Nicholas holds me tighter. I feel his heart racing. "Spidey senses" is our code so I'll know if he is in pain.

"It's okay, baby. Tell Mommy. Are the Spidey senses tingling?"

Nicholas nods his head. I don't realize that I have been holding my breath until I have to gulp for air.

"Where, baby?" Nicholas points to his left leg. I take his skinny limb and touch it. He winces. It is tender. A bone crisis usually affects an arm or leg. Watching my baby cringe, I can feel the pain. For the billionth time, I wish it were me with the disease. It's my fault he's sick. My head knows I can't control genetics, but my heart tells me it should be me in his place. I pull Nicholas close.

"Is he okay?" Marilyn asks. I forgot she was even in the room.

"No, he's not," I snap. "What did you do today?"

Marilyn sits in the recliner. "My friend Pearl came over with her granddaughter. We let the children play outside since it is such a nice day. Pearl and I discussed the upcoming church anniversary. I am Chairperson of the Committee and we needed to get a lot of things organized. We—"

I cut her off. "How long was Nicholas outside?"

She shifts in her chair. "Not long. About thirty minutes."

I figure that means at least an hour or longer. I've witnessed Marilyn and her so called society church friends. They gossip for a couple of hours and call it volunteer work.

"Did you make sure he stopped to rest?" Most of the time Nicholas will stop playing when he gets tired, but not if another child is involved. Playing to exhaustion can trigger a sickle cell crisis. Before Marilyn can respond, I fire another question. "Did you make sure he took water breaks? It's important that he maintains fluids."

I continue to lecture her on the proper care for Nicholas. I've explained this a million times. Dehydration can also cause a crisis. Nicholas travels with a water bottle. He likes flavored waters and Gatorade. I don't care if he drinks Kool-Aid as long as he drinks something, especially if he is playing outdoors. "Why didn't you call me?"

"You were busy, dear." Marilyn flicks imaginary lint off her skirt. "Helping Logan with the law firm is very important. I can take care of Nicholas."

"Oh, that's obvious. You've done such a wonderful job today." I gently hoist Nicholas on my shoulder and grab his bag. I turn to Marilyn. She has her hand on her cheek as if she's been slapped. The thought does cross my mind.

"And for the record, do not assume the Rutherford Law firm comes before my child. I don't care if I was second chair to help Logan try a case before the Supreme Court. Nicholas comes first. If I can't trust you to make that decision, then you can't be trusted to babysit anymore."

Marilyn looks wounded, but I don't care. It's all her fault.

I take Nicholas home and call his doctor. We've been through this before, so the routine is as familiar as a pair of well-worn jeans. Dr. Patrice Payne is a pediatric hematologist or blood specialist. She has been Nicholas's doctor since he was diagnosed at birth. We both like her. She has an easy-going personality and the patience to answer all my questions. Fortunately, when I call, she is in between patients and calls me right back.

"What's going on with our little web slinger?" Dr. Payne asks. She knows of Nicholas's affinity for Spiderman. I explain the pain episode.

"Let's see," she says. I hear her flipping pages. "According to Nicholas's chart, this is his second episode in four months. With the first one the pain wasn't severe, and you were able to treat at home. How is it this time? Where is the pain located?"

"It's his leg. I gave him an over-the-counter pain reliever a few minutes ago and he seems to be resting okay." I sit on the edge of Nicholas's bed and adjust the sheets around him. He tries to smile. My baby is so brave.

"Do you still have the prescription for anti-inflammatory drugs we used before?"

I reply in the affirmative.

"Okay, give him the prescribed dosage of that and let's see how he responds. If it gets worse overnight, take him to the ER and call me at home. If things stabilize, let's make an appointment to check on things in the morning. Hold on and I'll transfer you back to the nurse." Dr. Payne then adds for my benefit. "Things will be okay. How are you doing? Did you follow my advice about getting help as a caregiver? You need to make sure you get a break too."

"I know," I reply, thanking the doctor for her time. *I took a break today and see what happened. Anytime I relax, the disease attacks my baby.*

Nicholas takes his medicine and I curl in the bed beside him. We lay there and watch cartoons until he drifts off to sleep.

Logan hasn't returned the call I made earlier so I try his office again.

"Oh," I say when Sheila answers Logan's direct line. "How are you?"

"Just fine, Mrs. Rutherford."

"It's good to hear Logan was able to persuade you to return. I'm sure he appreciates your help."

"Return?" Sheila asks. "I mean, yes, he does, Mrs. Rutherford."

Why does Sheila keep repeating my name? We have never been this formal before. Any other time I can't get the woman to stop talking and today she sounds as if we have never met. I don't have time to try to figure her out. "Let me speak with Logan."

"I'm sorry. He is with a client." Sheila has to repeat it twice.

"It's urgent that I speak to my husband."

Sheila doesn't fall for my power play. "He asked that he not be disturbed. I can give him a message if you like."

I am seething. Why is Logan screening his calls when I called his direct line that rings on his desk and bypasses Beatrice? One minute he says Sheila quit and now he has her answering his phone.

"When Logan can tear himself from work, tell him to call home immediately. It's about Nicholas."

Sheila loses some of the attitude. "Is he okay?"

"No, he isn't. Can Logan be disturbed now?"

She is so quiet I can hear a printer in the background. I also hear a door open and the muffled sound of Logan's voice. Has he been there the whole time?

"I'm sorry, Mrs. Rutherford. Logan says to call him if Nicholas must be admitted. Otherwise, he'll give you a call later."

The dial tone shrieks in my ear and snaps me out of my shock.

CHAPTER TWELVE

LOGAN

My cell phone buzzes and I hit the Ignore button. Adrienne's call will have to wait. I can't talk now. I can't form coherent words. All I can do is feel. Pleasure ripples through me and I look down at Sheila. She is in my favorite position, on her knees with her head in my lap.

I have been able to resist rekindling my relationship with Sheila until this moment. Rules of professionalism were established once I got married. I may have dipped a time or three, but Sheila understands the deal. I must maintain a standard as an honest hardworking family man. A Rutherford man cannot succumb to temptation. I make sure I get my fix every morning from my wife, but I was thrown off today. I had to keep Adrienne focused on charming Michaels.

A lesser man might worry about his woman being alone with another man. Not me. I know Adrienne would never betray my trust again. When she told me she was pregnant, I learned my wife's kryptonite. Over time I learned how deep Adrienne's abandonment issues go.

Women are easy to read. My mother needs to know she raised an upstanding Rutherford man. My wife needs to know her husband can provide for her. And Sheila. Well, Sheila needs to think she has a chance.

When Sheila came into my office with the signed agreement from Michaels, I breathed a sigh of relief. When she walked back in with the certified check for retainer fees, I knew I was the man. This check would put the firm back in the black for the first time in months. It was time to celebrate. When Sheila closed the door and reached for my pants, I didn't stop her.

The thought of money makes me harder. I grab Sheila's hair and lean back in the chair.

"Damn, baby," I moan.

Sheila can't respond. Her mouth is full.

I deserve this. I've been stressed for months. My phone vibrates across the desk. The wife is calling again. I have a momentary speck of guilt, but it is replaced with the thrill of getting my dick sucked at the office. A blowjob isn't sex. I can stand up in court and say I did not have sexual relations with this woman.

Sheila does that thing with her tongue, and I lose control. I close my eyes and buck my hips. The release is powerful and Sheila keeps up the suction. She takes in every drop and licks her lips when she is done.

She smiles up at me. "How was that for a celebration?"

"Perfect," I mumble. The last remnants of ecstasy have me totally relaxed.

"You know what would be perfect," she says. Sheila grabs some tissue off the desk and wipes her mouth.

"An encore," I laugh.

"Us back together."

Afterglow is all gone now. I stand and fix my pants. "What are you talking about? This doesn't change things. You know the deal."

"I know I'm getting the bad end of this deal." Sheila crosses her arms and stares at me.

"Nevertheless, you agreed. Now you want to renegotiate because of a blowjob. I've kept up my end of things. Don't I pay your bills in addition to your salary?"

"The car payment was late this month."

I continue talking. "You know I had to get married to inherit this place. Senior saw to that."

"You could have married me."

My mother would never allow that to happen. But I don't tell Sheila. I stick to the lie that she accepted years ago. I clear my throat.

"I told you my parents had it arranged. I had to marry Adrienne. She's the niece of Senior's first partner and best friend. The merging of two families and all that."

Sheila shakes her head. "Even if I believed some old-fashioned mess like that it doesn't answer my question. You don't have to stay married. You have the firm. What's keeping you there?"

"It takes time to get a divorce. I have assets to protect. Right now, I can't afford alimony and child support. My wife doesn't work, you know?"

"And why can't she get a job? Ungrateful bitch."

"She wants to stay at home with the kid. It's always about the kid." I wonder if Adrienne keeps calling about Nicholas. She is always worried about every sniffle with him. I don't have time to placate her anxiety.

Sheila drops her arms and leans against the desk. She starts to say something and then drops her head. When she looks up again her eyes are moist. "I need to know where I fit in, Logan. I can't keep doing this. Pretending to just be colleagues when I want more. I love you, but I can't wait on you forever."

A part of me wishes Sheila would find someone else. Let him deal with her drama and get her out my pocket. I know I can get her to come back to me for the occasional blowjob. But there is no way I'm leaving my wife. I love Adrienne. Still, I play my part.

"Come here, baby."

Sheila hesitates but steps into my embrace. She tries to resist but melts against me.

"I need a little more time," I say. "I know you are the one that has been there from the beginning. You know how I feel about you, right?"

Sheila nods and I kiss the top of her head. She lingers for a moment then steps back. "Do you want me to deposit Michaels' check in the trust account?"

I breathe a sigh of relief that Sheila is back to business. "No, I'll do it myself. How about you go get cleaned up? I'll get Beatrice and the Rutherford firm can go celebrate. Dinner and drinks are on me."

Sheila leaves and I pump my fist like I used to do after I scored a goal. Things are going my way. Senior would have been impressed with the way I closed the deal with Michaels. This is a new chapter for the firm. Now I can use Michaels' connections. Get in front of the right people and get a more consistent cash flow of fees. I can expand the firm. Hire some new lawyers that are loyal to me. My mind darts between different scenarios for making the Rutherford firm the best in the state.

Adrienne calls again, but I still don't answer. My dutiful wife had a part to play in this and I'll thank her properly later tonight. Right now, I'm going to take this check to the bank.

CHAPTER THIRTEEN

ADRIENNE

I try to call Logan again and it goes straight to voicemail. That's it. I'm not trying again.

I walk out of my bedroom and go across the hall to check on Nicholas. We seem to have avoided a full-blown crisis. He fell asleep when we got home but woke up long enough to eat and have a bath. I watch the rise and fall of his chest as he sleeps. I worry about my baby every minute. Why hasn't his father called to check on him?

I leave the door to Nicholas's room ajar and go downstairs. Now that the crisis has passed, I have nothing to do but think. To avoid doing that, I pick up the phone to call Vanessa.

"Hey, girl," she says on the other end. "What's up?"

I tell her about Nicholas's crisis. "I may need to postpone the party. I don't want him running around and have another flare up."

"Totally understand. We can get the kids together and go to a movie instead. I think that new Disney flick started today."

"That sounds like a plan." I hesitate to share my dilemma with Vanessa but I need another married woman's opinion. "Let me ask you something."

"Sure."

Before I can get it out, I hear a child shriek in the background followed by a crash.

"You are going to be in so much trouble when your father gets home." Vanessa yells. "Girl, let me call you back."

She hangs up before I finish saying goodbye. I go into the family room and turn on my Al Green Greatest Hits CD. My Dad's salve. I find myself falling into the same routine whenever I have something heavy on my mind, cleaning and singing along with Al. Thoughts race through my mind in tune with the soundtrack of my misery. I work to avoid it, but Christopher invades my thoughts. Traces of our old connection remain. He was a good boyfriend. Right up until the time he was the worst.

And how is the man I married any better? Logan wasn't like this in the beginning. He was kind and considerate showing a vulnerable side of himself that he keeps hidden from everyone. Behind his perfectly crafted façade of the uber-professional, hard-core attorney is a man terrified of failure. A man that said he loved me because I didn't expect him to be anything but himself. All of that changed and the memory of that night cause me to shut off the vacuum and sit down. It was the moment I told Logan I was pregnant.

The CD changes and the refrains of my favorite *How Do You Mend a Broken Heart?* sail from the speakers and bring tears to my eyes. Thoughts of Christopher interplay between the choruses. He was the one. Hell, he is still the one and there is nothing I can do about it.

The ringing phone interrupts my thoughts. The caller id dashes my last hope. It is Kim. "How is our little man doing?"

"Fortunately, the pain has subsided. He's asleep now."

"Sounds like you need a break," she says. "I'll come over tomorrow and do the Chuck E, Cheese thing. You can go relax somewhere."

The gesture is appreciated. "Thanks, but I'll watch Nicholas tomorrow. Make sure he has recovered. Vanessa and I will probably take the kids to a movie."

There is a pause and then Kim asks, "What's wrong?"

"Nothing," I automatically reply.

"No, there is something. I hear Al Green."

I smile. No one knows me better than my sister. "I'm fine. Really."
I try to convince both of us this is true. "Just tired."

Kim isn't buying the act. "Where is Logan?"

Good question. It is after 10 o'clock.

"Working late," I say like it is okay that I do not know where my husband is in the middle of the night.

"Um hmm," Kim says. She knows the routine. I have called her many nights complaining about the late hours Logan puts in at the office.

"He's working hard." I tell her.

"Why do you always defend him? The man acts as if he doesn't have a family at home. Has he even called to check on Nicholas?"

"Don't do that," I say. "Don't talk about my husband like that."

"Like what? It's the truth."

"Don't insinuate that he doesn't care about Nicholas. That's his son. Of course, he cares. He is extremely busy making sure we are provided for. He's been short staffed at the firm and has to take on more responsibility."

I continue to justify Logan's actions. I don't mention the conversation with his paralegal, Sheila. I am still trying to process what that means if anything. Instead, I look around the room at everything my husband has provided for his family. The spacious family room has a fireplace with the 50-inch flat screen mounted over the mantel. The supple leather sofa and love seat are a deep burgundy that highlights the rich wood grain of the end tables and built-in bookcases. The hardwood floors are accented with a Persian rug and the walls are painted the color of oatmeal. The material things are lovely. Logan has given me everything I never asked for.

"He has to work hard," I continue. "The firm needs new clients since one of the senior associates left."

"Okay, I get the picture," Kim says. "Logan is a good provider."

She thinks I deserve more. I am grateful she doesn't say it. I need to believe my marriage is strong.

"Can we change the subject?" I ask. I finish straightening up the room and turn off the stereo.

"Sure," she says. "Let's talk about Logan's new client. How was your date with Christopher?"

"It wasn't a date," I clarify. "It was a business meeting."

"Whatever. How was it? And tell the truth. You enjoyed it, right?"

I climb the stairs and sit on the edge of my bed. "I'll admit I had a nice time. Christopher was always fun."

Kim is silent for a second. "You know that should have been my brother-in-law."

"He left, remember?" I stand and pace the room.

"I remember." Kim's voice is so soft I have to strain to hear.

"He made his choice. And I made mine."

"It's not too late. It can be like that scene in 'Pretty Woman' when Richard Gere goes in that white limo and rescues Julie Roberts."

"Well, that must have been a hell of a traffic jam because Christopher is late. I'm married with a child. I don't need rescuing."

"Maybe you do, and you don't know it yet."

I'm tired and collapse on the bed again. Kim has started a train of thought I don't have the strength to endure. I change the subject again and Kim goes along. We talk for about twenty minutes and call it a night. She promises to visit Nicholas tomorrow. I get ready for bed and settle in to wait for my husband.

When Logan stumbles into the room I look up from the book I am pretending to read.

"Where have you been?" I glance at the clock on my nightstand. It is after midnight.

Logan glares at me and starts shedding clothes. He leaves his suit jacket and pants on the floor and walks into the bathroom. The smell of rum and coke are left behind. He returns damp from the shower with a towel wrapped around his waist.

"Did you get my messages?" I ask.

Logan continues to ignore me. I speak louder. Maybe the alcohol has affected his hearing.

"Why didn't you return my calls? Didn't Sheila tell you it was important?"

At the mention of Sheila, Logan gives an exasperated sigh.

"Am I bothering you? You have some nerve. I've been trying to reach you all day, and you act like I'm the one that stayed out all night."

Logan turns and faces me. "What is it, Adrienne? What was so important?"

My eyes widen. He must be drunk. "If you had bothered to return my calls you would have known that Nicholas was sick."

"Was being the operative word. I just looked in on him and he seems fine. You need to stop overreacting to every twinge the boy has."

"Overreacting? Have you forgotten that our son has a disease?"

Logan shakes his head. "How can I? You won't let anyone forget."

"And what is that supposed to mean?"

Logan walks over to his side of the bed without answering. He sets his alarm clock and sits on the edge of the bed. The book I was reading falls to the side. I kick it further and twist to face Logan's back. "Answer me. What do you mean I won't let anyone forget?"

"What did you say to Mother today?" Logan's back is rigid and he doesn't turn around.

"What?" My minds races and rewinds to Marilyn's house. I remember being scared that Nicholas was having a crisis. I don't remember what I said.

Logan stands and narrows his eyes. "Nothing to say now? You had a lot to say to my mother. I'm only going to say this once. Don't you ever threaten my mother again."

"Threaten her? When I picked up Nicholas he was in pain and your mother didn't call me. I told her…"

Logan points a finger at me. "Mother called me hysterical and told me what you said. I was in the middle of signing our first major client and I had to stop and calm her down."

"But you took her call, right? You didn't have Sheila tell her you were in a meeting and couldn't be disturbed."

Logan clears his throat. "That is my mother. Of course, I took her call."

I jump out of bed and stomp around to stand in front of Logan. My chest is heaving and I talk through clenched teeth. "And I am your wife and Nicholas is your son. We matter too."

Logan takes a deep breath. "You matter too. Look, Sheila didn't mention anything about the kid. She told me you called. Mother told me Nicholas was tired and you went psycho on her."

"That still doesn't excuse you from not calling me back or staying out all night. It's inconsiderate and selfish," I continue to rant.

Logan stares at me and licks his lips. "You're beautiful."

I lean back. "What?"

He reaches for my hand and pulls me close. His voice deepens. "You're beautiful, Adrienne."

I wipe the water off my face. He didn't dry off from his shower. "What are you talking about?"

"I don't want to fight. Today was a good day for the firm and we should be celebrating."

"Celebrating?" My mind is slow making the transition between anger and lust. Logan's isn't. His hands circle my waist and gropes lower.

"Michaels agreed to let us represent his company. You had a small part in making that happen. I saw the way he looked at you the day I brought him here. He wants what he can never have."

Logan tries to kiss me, but I turn my face. "What are you doing? We have some issues that we need to resolve now."

"I have an issue right here," he says and drops the towel. "I want to thank you properly."

"I'm not in the mood for this."

Logan eyes darken. "You better get in the mood." He pushes me on the bed. Before I can sit up he is on top of me.

"What are you doing?" I struggle to get up and Logan pins my arms over my head.

"You spend time with another man and now you don't want me. You are my wife." Logan keeps my arms trapped with one hand and rips my underwear. I struggle to push him off but he gets more excited. He pries my legs apart with his knees. He growls when he enters me, and I suppress a scream. I don't want to wake Nicholas and have him witness this.

Whatever this is.

I stop squirming and let Logan pound away. He is too far gone to stop. He tells me that this is the beginning. He'll give me the world. He tells me that he'll never leave me. He tells me he loves me. His eyes are closed so he doesn't see the tears running down my face.

With one final thrust, Logan groans loudly and collapses. "You're still the best," he whispers. His breath suffocates me.

I wait until his body relaxes and he releases my hands. I slap him hard enough for the sound to echo around the room. Logan touches his face and falls away. I scramble across the bed and stand on the other side. My hands are fists.

Logan blinks several times and shakes his head. He stands and takes in the scene and grabs the towel. His mouth opens in apology. Instead, he shakes his head. "She's right. You are an ungrateful bitch."

CHAPTER FOURTEEN

MOMENT OF CLARITY

ADRIENNE

The next day I am a zombie. I couldn't stand to be in the same room with Logan so I spent a sleepless night locked in the guest room. I manage to doze off and when I hear Nicholas calling this morning, Logan is already gone.

I go through the day on auto-pilot. I tell myself over and over that last night wasn't rape. Logan was drunk and got a little carried away. A husband can't force his wife. I almost convince myself that last night was merely a misunderstanding until I remember his last words. Who is the "she" that called me an ungrateful bitch? Would his mother say such a thing? I decide right then that I am done feeling guilty about Nicholas. I am done feeling guilty about everything. I figure last night means we are even.

I get my mind off the sorry state of my marriage and focus on Nicholas. My baby is back to normal with no lingering effects from the mini crisis. We spend the morning at the movies with Vanessa and her crew. We do lunch at Chick fil-A and the kids play on the jungle gym. Back at home, we mix up a batch of Nicholas's favorite chocolate chip cookies.

Kim arrives when we take the last batch out of the oven. "How's my favorite nephew?" She follows me back to the kitchen where Nicholas is at the table drinking milk.

When Nicholas sees Kim, he laughs and runs to wrap himself around Kim's legs. "Hey, Auntie. Want some cookies?"

"Did you make them?"

Nicholas nods. He takes her hand and leads her to the table. Kim takes a cookie and Nicholas pushes his cup in front of her. He climbs back in the chair and swings his feet.

Kim turns to me. "He seems like his usual self."

"He has been practically bouncing off the walls today."

"You look stressed. How about I take Nicholas and put him down for a nap?"

I smile my gratitude.

"I not sleepy, Auntie," Nicholas whines. "I not tired."

"I know. How about you read Auntie a story?"

Nicholas runs to find a book and Kim follows. I clear the table of Nicholas's dishes and my knees get weak. I slump in a chair at the table and rest my head in my hands. Kim finds me there when she returns.

"Who sent the huge bouquet of flowers?" Kim is looking back into the great room where the delivery man placed the obscene floral apology so she misses the look of fear on my face. By the time she turns, my mask is back in place.

"Logan." I return to the sink to wash dishes.

"What did brother-in-law do now?"

"What makes you think he did something? Maybe it's a "just because" bouquet."

"Because most men send flowers for three reasons. Valentine's Day, birthdays or I'm Sorry Today. I know it's not the first two. And he did come home late last night."

I rinse the mixing bowl and place it in the dish rack, thinking about what Kim said. Damn if it isn't true.

"Well, what is it?" Kim sits on a stool at the counter and crosses her arms.

"You do not want to know." I put the last spoon in the rack and empty the water from the sink.

"Girl, tell me what is going on."

I shake my head. I'm not sure if I can verbalize what happened. "Nicholas asleep?"

"That boy was out almost as soon as he lay down. And don't try to change the subject."

I hang the dishtowel over the edge of the sink and go into the great room. Kim follows. The flowers coat the room with a sickening sweet scent. I struggle to breathe. "How long do you think you can be punished for one mistake?"

"What?"

"How long are you punished?" I repeat.

Kim looks from me to the flowers. "You are starting to scare your sister."

I can't stand the sight of the flowers anymore. I pick up the vase, its weight like a bowling ball, and march out the patio door. I find the trashcan and toss the flowers inside.

Kim stands in the doorway. "What was that about?"

I don't answer. Instead, I sit on the edge of a chair and gaze across the backyard.

"Tell me what's wrong? I haven't seen you this weirded out since Christopher…" Kim catches herself and comes to kneel in front of me. She takes my hand.

"Did Logan leave?"

I shake my head. When Christopher left me, I mourned his loss like a death. Kim was there to help me recover. What Logan has done is much worst. How do I recover from that? I look at my sister and take a deep breath.

"Logan and I had an argument last night."

Kim nods. "You guys argue all the time. I figure that's the way y'all communicate."

"This was different."

"How?" Kim leans back. "Did he hurt you?"

The tears spring to the surface, but I refuse to let them fall. I swallow and blurt it out, giving Kim all the details of last night. When I finish, Kim stands. "That punk bastard."

"It's okay," I say automatically. The words ring hollow to my own ears.

"Okay? Are you serious, Adrienne? You tell me that Logan forced himself on you. That he raped you and it's okay?"

When she says it like that, it does sound bad. "I'm not excusing what he did. He was drunk and got a little rough. I wouldn't call it rape."

Kim throws her hands in the air. "What would you call it then?"

"I don't know. He's my husband, Kim. There have been times when he wanted sex and I didn't. But I rolled over anyway. It's what a wife does. That doesn't make it rape."

"You know this is something different or you wouldn't be upset. Why do you keep making excuses for him?"

"I don't."

"Yes, you do. All this time I've been trying to figure out why. What has he done to deserve it? I know you love him, but let's face it. He isn't the nicest guy." Kim looks to the heavens for answers. The answer she finds rocks me in the pit of my stomach.

"Maybe it's this house. Must be the Lexus you drive and the fact that you don't have to work. Have you gotten so comfortable with his material things that you'll accept his abuse? Mom and Dad would turn over in their graves. You were raised better than that."

Disappointment flows between us like the breeze. Is that the type of woman I have become? It hurts to the bone to hear my sister accuse me of being weak.

My voice is a whisper. "Is that what you think of me?"

Kim turns toward me, but I bury my head in my hands. I'm afraid she'll see the truth in my eyes. I'm not a gold digger. I'm a cheat. Married to one man and still in love with another. Kim doesn't know about my indiscretion the night before my wedding. I have to keep it that way. I don't want to lose what little respect she has left for me.

"No, I don't think that about you." She hugs me tight. "I love you and I know you deserve better than this."

I manage a nod.

"What do you want to do?" Kim squeezes in the chair beside me. She takes my hands and looks at me with wide eyes. I see the little sister that looked to me for all the answers and pat her hand.

"I'll handle Logan."

"You know if you and Nicholas need a place to stay, our house is still there."

"I know."

"Of course, you'll have to take the smaller room now."

I nudge her with my elbow. "Big sister gets the bigger room."

"Hey, when you move, you lose. It's mine now."

We joke back and forth for a minute and then sit there. I have always been able to sit with Kim. Reminds me of the days after our parent's death when it was the two of us. I thought it was rough then, but we made it through. Mom made me promise to look after Kim, and I've been doing that. I made it through that, and I'll make it through this thing with Logan.

I slide back in the chair and enjoy the warmth from the sun. I feel the tension ease out of my muscles. Kim's next question causes them to clench.

"Talk to Christopher today?"

Another man that I've been avoiding today. He left a message on my cell phone last night and called again this morning. I tell Kim this.

"Why haven't you called him back?"

The real answer is I'm afraid the conversation will lead to questions about Nicholas's paternity. But I tell Kim I've been dealing with other things. Nicholas was sick. Logan. I recap the last twenty-four hours in case she forgot.

"I know, I know. But maybe you should give him a call."

"Why?"

Kim starts to fiddle with her ear. "No reason. I mean, you can use a friend. And you and Christopher used to be friends."

I raise my eyebrows. "What are you up too?"

"Nothing," The word is out of her mouth before I finish the question.

"I raised you, girl. Whenever you start playing with your ears, I know there is more to the story. Have you been talking to Christopher?"

Kim starts laughing. Busted. "Well, yeah."

I shake my head. "Not cool. I am a married woman."

"Maybe you shouldn't be."

And there it is. Kim has voiced the nagging truth that has been in the back of my mind all day. I wait until Kim turns to me before I respond.

"Don't do that," I say. "Don't dismiss my marriage like it's nothing."

"Why not?"

"I'm not the type of person to walk out on a relationship because of a bad patch. Logan and I may be having some problems, but we'll work it out. I told you those things to vent. Not for you to use it as an excuse to hook me up with another man."

Kim starts to protest, but I cut her off.

"And the second reason is Nicholas."

"I know, okay," Kim accepts defeat and stands. "I'll let it go."

I stand too. Time to get back in the house before Nicholas wakes up. I have some more housework to get done. I walk Kim to the door and she gives me a hug.

"Take care of yourself."

"I will."

"If you need me for anything…"

"I know," I say.

Kim turns to go out the door and pauses. "I want you to be happy. I remember when you were with Christopher, you were happy. Can you honestly say that now?"

I have no response.

"Think about it," Kim hugs me again. "I'll call you later."

CHAPTER FIFTEEN

LOGAN

I gulp the last of my drink and the waiter appears like magic.

"Would you like another, Mr. Rutherford?" he says. I think his name is Todd.

I look up at him. No judgment on his face. That's what I like about coming to the club. All your needs are anticipated and met with the professionalism benefitting an upstanding member of the business community.

But I decline another drink. I won't find the answer I need by getting drunk at one o'clock in the afternoon. "Bring me a sweet tea."

"Very good, Mr. Rutherford. And are you still waiting on your guest?"

I nod and Todd leaves the table. I take a folder out of my briefcase and check that all the documents are in order. I invited Michaels to meet me here for lunch. I have the business documents ready for his signature, and I want to impress him with the club.

The Capital City Club is a "members only" establishment for business and community leaders. I look around the dining room at the panoramic view of the State Capital and downtown skyline. The décor screams old money with traditional rich colors and wood accents. The clatter of silverware hits the fine china on each table. The cuisine is some of the best in the city. I can smell the prime rib on the lunch buffet.

It's my favorite and I take a large serving of it back to my table. I'm glad I was able to catch up on the monthly dues this month.

Business is picking up for the Rutherford Law firm. Signing Michaels was the first win. Then I settled two cases in favor of my clients. Hefty fees for me. Everything at the office is under control.

Home is a different matter. This past week has been tense around the house. I'm baffled by this thing with Adrienne. Ever since that night, my wife sleeps in the guest room. She walks around the house like I'm the bad guy. Like I raped her or something. A man can't rape his wife. She belongs to me. When I want sex, she has never denied me before.

I think back to that night. Yeah, I was a little drunk but nothing I couldn't handle. I remember being angry with her because of Mother. Then when she was standing in front of me going off about something, all I could think was how beautiful she looked. Her breasts were heaving and her nipples were poking through the thin t-shirt she wore. I had to have her.

Adrienne pretending not to want me turned me on even more. I think she wanted me to beg. She knows she likes it rough. Sex with Adrienne is always good. She's the best I've ever had which is why I married her. Which is why most men get married. And that night, I came so hard I could feel it in my toes. Until she slapped me. I've been trying to figure out a way to get her back in my bed ever since.

"Hey, man. Sorry I'm late." Michaels slides into the seat across from me.

"No problem," I say. "I started without you. Grab a plate. The prime rib is delicious."

Michaels orders an Arnold Palmer from the mystical Todd and goes to the buffet.

"This is my first time in this club," Michaels says between bites of food. "Very nice."

I knew this would impress him. "You should join. There are some great networking opportunities."

Michaels nods. "Yeah, I was a member of a group like this in New York. I believe it's under the same umbrella."

Before I can respond, the mayor stops at our table.

"Christopher 'Money Making' Michaels," his voice booms. "Glad to see you took me up on my offer."

Michaels stands and shakes his hands. "Brian 'Born Ready' Bradley. When the mayor calls, you move. Thanks for the heads up on the new development."

"That's what frat brothers do. Surprised you gave up running Wall Street though."

"It was time," Michaels says. "Running a few businesses now. In fact, this is my attorney. Logan Rutherford."

"Mayor Bradley." I stand to shake his hand. "Nice to meet you."

"Are you related to the late Logan Rutherford?" he asks.

"Yes, sir. That was my father."

"Good man. I was sorry to hear of his passing. He was instrumental in my first campaign. He helped me get the vote."

I remember Senior going on about needing to help make history and get the first Black mayor elected. I wasn't interested in politics then. With this new introduction, maybe it is something I need to explore.

Bradley turns back to Michaels. "Give me your number. I could never beat you on the court, but I have an improved golf game. We could settle our bet on the links."

"If your swing is as weak as your jump shot this should be easy money. My number is still the same, but here is my card."

"Good to see you, man," Mayor Bradley says. "And bring Mr. Rutherford along. I can take his money too."

The mayor leaves to greet another table.

"How do you know the mayor?" I ask, picking up my fork.

"We went to undergrad together at the university," he says. "We were roommates for a couple of years. Line brothers after that."

I nod. I knew getting Michaels would be advantageous to the firm. I already have a golf invite from the mayor.

Michaels tells me more about the relationship he has with Mayor Bradley. They were thrown together by chance as roommates. Bonded over a shared interest in business and being only sons of single women. Competed in everything from grades to girls.

"We kind of lost touch when I moved to New York. I reached out when he won his first election. He came to New York for business and we met for drinks. He's a good person to know."

"Looking forward to the golf game," I say.

Michaels drains the last of his drink and pushes his plate away. "You have those papers for me?"

I wipe my mouth and toss the napkin on my plate, pulling out the folder. Todd reappears to clear the dishes. That man gets an A+ in customer service.

"Here you go," I say and explain the documents establishing Michaels' business in the state.

He signs the papers and his phone vibrates. He grabs it and starts typing.

"Text message from the ex," he says. "I'm getting my daughter for the weekend. Hey, do you know of a fun spot a five-year-old would enjoy?"

I shake my head. "Adrienne handles those things."

"Speaking of your wife, I want to thank you again. Adrienne was a great help and I enjoyed her company. You got a good one there, man."

"I know," I say, wondering for the tenth time what happened between my wife and this man.

"Did she get the job at the school?" he asks.

It takes me a second to remember Adrienne's mention of the teaching position.

I wave my hand. "No. I told her she doesn't have to worry about working. I have our finances under control."

"That may be true. But I don't think she wants to teach for the money. It seems to be something she loves."

I raise an eyebrow. "What do you know about my wife?"

Michaels raises both hands. "Hey, no disrespect, just some unsolicited advice. You ever heard the saying, 'Happy wife means a happy life.'"

"That work well for you?" I ask.

He chuckles. "Not at all. I didn't make my ex-wife happy."

I drop my defenses. "Why not?"

"Let's say, I let the right one get away and married the wrong one for the right reasons."

I ponder that for a second. "What's the right reason to marry the wrong woman?"

Michaels shrugs. "A pregnancy. We all good here?"

"Yes. I'll file these and send over the copies when I get back to the office."

"Thanks for lunch." Michaels hurries out the restaurant.

I sign the check, leaving a generous tip for Todd and stand to put on my suit jacket. Michaels was in a rush to go spend time with a kindergartener. I can't relate. I have serious concerns. Business has picked up, but I still have the pressure of carrying all Mother's affairs. Not to mention my agreement with Sheila to keep her quiet and available. I don't have the time or patience to deal with kids.

And then a thought hits me. Thanks to Michaels, I know how to fix things with Adrienne.

CHAPTER SIXTEEN

ADRIENNE

Am I happy? I don't want to think about it. The next week plods along at a slow pace like pouring cold syrup from a glass bottle. I enroll Nicholas in school and he settles in. Every morning he is eager to get to class. His energy is barely contained, and I worry that all the excitement will bring on a crisis. Every afternoon when I pick him up he is full of stories and ready for bed after dinner. He has stopped asking for his father who continues to work late.

Logan and I have an unspoken truce. I sleep in the guest room each night and we pass each other in the mornings. Polite words exchanged if necessary. He continues to send flowers and one day I find diamond earrings on my pillow. The flowers go into the trash and the earrings are returned to the store. He can't buy his way out of this mess.

I spend another evening alone. Nicholas is asleep and I am showered and sitting in the middle of the bed. My constant companions are beside me: the remote control, an unfinished novel, and a bag of Pecan Sandies. I flip through the channels and try to convince myself that the five extra pounds I notice have nothing to do with scarfing down cookies every night. A random commercial comes on showing a happy family sitting down for a chicken dinner and I have what Oprah would call a moment of clarity. There is no such thing as a happy family. It's all a myth. My mom dies when I'm young. My dad soon after. Not a happy ending. I marry Logan thinking I could live happily ever after and I sleep alone every night. I have been striving for an ideal that exists in movies.

I am drowning in self-pity so when my phone rings I reach for the lifeline and answer.

"Hey," he says surprise registering in his voice. "How are you doing?"

That simple question of concern almost brings me to tears. "I'm okay."

Christopher pauses. He could always detect my moods. I'm relieved when he changes the subject. "I'm glad you answered tonight. Did you get my message?"

"Yes, I did."

"And you can't call a brother back?" he teases.

"Busy being married, I guess." I know the comment wasn't called for, but I can't resist. Christopher mumbles something I don't catch. When I ask him to repeat it, he doesn't.

"What do you want, Christopher?"

"I want to be there for you, Ms. Adrienne. If you'll let me, I'll be your friend. We were good friends once."

That's true. Truth be told, he was my best friend besides Kim. I could use a friend. I can't discuss marital woes with Vanessa. She lives in the world of fairy tales and happy endings. I lean against the pillows.

"A friend would be welcomed," I say.

"So, friend, what have you been up to this past week?"

"The usual." I tell him about Nicholas starting school and how excited he is.

"It's a big adjustment, isn't it?"

"Nicholas jumped right in with no problems."

"I was talking about an adjustment for you."

And there it is. Someone who acknowledges my feelings. He gets me. Always has. But choices have led us down separate roads. Still I hear myself confessing.

"The truth is I'm bored. Everything has revolved about Nicholas and now he is moving into a new phase. What do I do with myself?"

"Go back to what makes you happy. Go back to teaching."

Sounds simple enough. Logan and I aren't speaking, but I hear his familiar arguments run through my head. Even as I repeat them to Christopher, I feel sick.

"That doesn't sound like you talking," Christopher says. "I get it. Ol' boy doesn't want you to work. He doesn't want you to have a life outside of him."

Christopher has summed up the state my marriage in three minutes when it has taken me three years to figure it out.

"Why?" I ask. "Why does he hold on so tight?"

His voice is a whisper. "Maybe he's afraid if he lets go, he'll lose you forever."

"That's ridiculous," I begin before I realize the conversation has shifted. We are not talking about Logan anymore.

"You didn't lose me," I tell Christopher. "You left me. There is a difference."

"Doesn't feel that way. You're with another man and I'm left feeling like a dumb ass."

"Don't be too hard on yourself. You were always dumb, but you still have a nice ass," I tease. As soon as the words are spoken, I want to snatch them back. It is so easy to fall into the familiar comfort zone with Christopher. But I don't want to lead him on.

"I was kidding," I rush to explain. "I hope that wasn't out of line."

Christopher's voice deepens. "Not at all. I think you have a nice ass too. I miss the feel of it. I miss the taste of your lips. I miss you, baby."

I can't respond. Everything in me screams out for this man. But I remember who I am. I should stop the reminiscing before it leads to something more. I swallow down the desire that is trying to bubble to the surface. "How is Logan coming along with your paperwork?"

"Damn, girl. You know how to bring a brother's high to a halt."

"Just two friends talking, right? This is all I can offer, Christopher." I forget how to breathe in the heartbeat before he responds.

"Friends, huh? I'll have to accept that. Anything so long as I get to talk to you."

I smile. "Is the deal almost done?"

"I wish. We hit a snag and have another technical issue to iron out. Hopefully next week we'll have signatures on an agreement. I got my first statement from the Rutherford Law Firm. Logan has been working hard it seems."

"He's been working late," I say. "He wants your company to be satisfied."

"Yeah, well, he seems to be a decent attorney. But is he a decent husband? Does he make you happy?"

"Why would you ask that? Should you even be asking me that?" My stomach clenches.

"We're friends, right? Then answer the question. Does he make you happy?"

"First, answer me. Why do you ask?"

Christopher pauses. The television, which was a low hum in the background, goes silent. "I know a thing or two about being a bad husband. Logan is just like me, working all the time. All he talks about is work. And outdoing his old man."

I cringe. "He told you about that mess with his father?"

"For like an hour. He has some serious issues with that. I guess he never got daddy's approval."

"You don't know the half."

"Bottom line, he doesn't seem like your type of guy."

"And what's my type? I would guess someone like you, huh?"

Christopher laughs. "Not someone like me. Me."

"Okay, I can see where this is going."

"I understand if you don't want to talk about it. No man could ever measure up to me."

"Now you really are tripping." I smile and my heart sings. "It's okay to admit it. It'll be our secret."

"You need to stop."

We both hold the phone for a minute. Content to listen to each other breathe.

"Hold on a second," Christopher says. "I'm getting another call. It's my mom."

"Tell her I said hello."

He clicks over and I turn off the television. I look at the clock and notice it's after 10 p.m. Still no sign of my husband. And no call. I choose not to dwell on that and walk down the hall to check on Nicholas. He is sound asleep on his back with one arm thrown over his head. The covers are kicked into a pile at the bottom of the bed. I adjust his sheets and head back to my room.

"I'm back," Christopher says. "Mom says hello."

"How is she doing?"

"She's great. Called to tell me she plans to come visit in a couple of weeks."

"That would be nice. I hope I get to see her."

"She wants to see you. I told her we were on the phone and you know what she said?"

Curiosity gets the best of me. "What?"

"She said, 'Baby, that's the woman you should have married.'"

I love Ms. Michaels. It's how I envisioned my own mother would be.

"Hey, remember that time we took Mom and Kim on vacation with us?" Christopher asks.

"How could I forget?" It was the first time in long time that I felt like part of a family.

"I bet they still have a sign banning us from that restaurant. That was the first time I was asked to leave an establishment."

"No," I add. "That was the first time I ever saw someone, that someone being your mother, go back in the kitchen to tell the staff her secret to frying chicken."

"Momma can fry up some good chicken."

We share more laughter and more stories of our times together. I settle under the covers and let the smooth baritone of Christopher's voice caress me. We talk for another hour or so until I can no longer stifle a yawn.

"Alright, Ms. Adrienne. Let me let you go."

I turn to look at the clock. The time is creeping toward midnight and still no husband. This has been the pattern all week, but tonight I don't feel alone.

"Let me say this before I go," Christopher sounds serious. "I hope you don't mind me calling. I told myself not to bother you, but I find myself picking up the phone anyway."

"You're not bothering me."

"And I'm not trying to break up your marriage. I've been through it and it doesn't matter what the reason is. It still hurts."

"I know."

"I want you to know I'm not leaving you this time. You need me, I'll be there."

"Okay." It's the one word I feel safe to utter. Christopher is the balm to soothe my soul.

"Goodnight, baby."

"Goodnight," I say. Somewhere between consciousness and sleep I have a revelation. I love that man. Still.

I fall asleep with dreams of Christopher. I wake to the smell of alcohol and sweat. I sense a presence in the room with me. My eyes focus in the darkness.

"Logan." I startle, fully awake now. He is standing over me. "What are you doing?"

"How long are you going to do this?"

"Do what? You're drunk. You really need to stop all this drinking." It is three in the morning and this man is looking unstable. Did he drive home like that? I sit up and flip on the lamp. Logan blinks at the sudden brightness and rubs his red eyes.

"I had a few drinks after work. I'm fine. Now come to bed."

"I'm already in bed."

"No. Come to our bed."

"Why?" I yawn and lean against the headboard.

"Because you are my wife and that's where you belong."

I raise my eyebrows. This man has lost his mind. They say alcohol kills brain cells. From the odor coming from Logan, he is working on losing some vital parts that make up common sense.

"Are you serious?" I ask. "After what happened the last time we shared a bed?"

Logan looks defeated and collapses on the edge of the bed. "How many times do I have to apologize?"

"Once. I got your flowers and other trinkets. I didn't hear any of them say a thing."

Logan looks at me in surprise. He takes a moment to regroup and clears his throat. I brace myself for this mess by crossing my arms.

"Come on, Adrienne. You know I got a little carried away. You can't fault me for wanting my wife. You are always so busy with Nicholas that I don't get anytime. I'm working hard for us, and all I get from you are demands to go back to work and what Nicholas needs. What about what I need?"

I slide under the covers. "You need some sleep. Can you get out of my room now?"

Logan hangs his head. "I'll make it up to you," he mummers. "I'm sorry, baby. Let me make it up to you. Baby, please."

I look at my husband and almost give in. He looks defeated. I can see the frightened little boy he must have been, constantly seeking his father's approval and failing.

"I need you," Logan reaches out his hand.

I hesitate for a second then pat the space beside me. I move over and Logan lays down fully clothed. I wrap my arms around him. He mumbles incoherent promises until he falls asleep. I turn away and stare into the darkness wondering why I feel trapped.

CHAPTER SEVENTEEN

ADRIENNE

I wake up the next morning to the sound of Nicholas's laughter and bolt upright. Why hasn't he come to wake me up like every other morning? Then I hear Logan's voice and notice he is no longer in the bed. I throw on my robe to go investigate. I find them in Nicholas's room.

Logan is rummaging through the dresser drawers. On his head sits one of Nicholas's baseball caps. The sight of the small cap on his father's head makes Nicholas giggle. He is sitting on the edge of his bed with a pair of shorts on.

"Think I can wear this, man." Logan turns and holds up a Spiderman t-shirt

"No, Daddy. It's for me. You're too big."

"Guess you'll have to wear it then."

Nicholas is enjoying the attention. My heart softens at the sight. I start to back out of the room, but Logan looks up and sees me.

"Like my new hat." He starts to bob his head. The hat falls and Logan catches it in one swift move and returns it to the perch on top of his head. Nicholas howls with laughter and I smile.

Nicholas runs and wraps his arms around my legs. "Hey, Momma." He puckers his lips for a kiss and runs back to put on the t-shirt Logan is holding.

"Daddy and Nicholas go to the zoo today," Nicholas announces with a flourish. "Need shoes."

I retrieve Nicholas's tennis shoes from the closet and bend down to help put them on.

"For real?" I ask Logan.

Logan nods, but before he can respond Nicholas pipes in again. "Momma can't come. No girls allowed. Right, Daddy?"

"That's right, son. Only us guys."

Now this is a first. I can't remember a time that Logan has ever expressed an interest in Nicholas let alone take him somewhere without me. I sit and cross my arms waiting for the angle.

Logan's smile fades. "I said I would make it up to you."

I hold up a hand to stop him and look at Nicholas. He is standing between us taking in every word. I send Nicholas on a quest to find his daddy's sneakers and he skips out of the room.

"Tell me what's going on?"

Logan sits on the bed. "I thought I would spend the day with our son. Give you a weekend day to yourself."

I'm still skeptical. "You mean, you don't have to work today?"

The man has the nerve to look hurt. "It's Saturday."

"That's never mattered before."

"You know what they say about all work and no play."

When I don't respond, Logan reaches for my hand. I sit down beside him. "Don't worry, Momma. I can do this."

Nicholas rushes back into the room cradling his dad's Nikes. He carefully sits them at his father's feet.

"Let's go," he chants.

Logan laughs. "Okay, okay."

I gather Nicholas's backpack and make sure his supplies are there. I never leave the house without an extra jacket.

"You need to make sure he stays hydrated," I tell Logan. "We always travel with a couple of water bottles."

"Stop worrying, Momma. We'll be fine."

"Okay, but if he starts to look tired then you need to make him take a break. Sometimes he wants to keep going."

"Stop okay. You do need a break. Let me take Nicholas out and you try not to worry for a while." Logan stands in front of me and caresses my face. "I can handle it."

I make myself relax. Why am I worried? Nicholas will be with his father.

"Let's go," Nicholas pulls on Logan's leg. "Let's go, Daddy."

"One moment."

Logan stands and looks back at me. "I'll pick up dinner on the way home. That way you won't have to worry about doing anything today."

"When did you plan all this?" I stand too.

"This morning. I was watching you sleep and I could see the stress on your face. I know I put it there. And I want you to know that I'm sorry for being a jerk."

This is the Logan I fell in love with. Could my husband be reborn in one night? Nicholas continues to jump around and chant. I see the excitement on my baby's face, and I appreciate Logan for doing this for our family. I consent and kiss Logan full on the lips. He pulls me close.

"Maybe I should stay here," he nibbles my ear.

"Don't start," I say. I appreciate Logan's efforts to make amends, but I'm not sure I'm ready to have sex with him again. I try to step back but he holds me tighter.

"I've missed you," he says. "You feel so good."

"Later," I say. "Nicholas is waiting."

Logan doesn't stop. He continues to grind against me and kiss my neck. Nicholas stands beside me.

"Hug me, Mommy," he says and tries to worm in between Logan and me.

I reach for my son, but Logan twists us so that he blocks Nicholas.

"Move, Daddy," Nicholas says.

Logan continues to ignore Nicholas and presses up against me.

"What are you doing?" I hiss in Logan's ear.

Nicholas sees me struggling to get free and clamps onto my leg. He tells Daddy to let Mommy go. My heart races. Logan's eyes focus on my face and he steps away; the look of shame replaced with something I can't else.

"Hey, little man," he reaches for Nicholas. "You need to get your own girl."

Nicholas buries his face in my leg and I rub his back. I'm not sure I want to let Nicholas go anywhere with Logan right now. I kneel in front of Nicholas.

"Mommy is fine." I comfort my son and look up at Logan. He is adjusting his clothes but stops when he sees me watching. He sits on the bed and puts on his shoes.

"Ready to go," he says.

Nicholas squirms out of my embrace. "Can we feed the giraffes?" he asks.

That is his favorite exhibit in the zoo. The last time we visited, we spent almost an hour and all the change in my purse feeding the long neck mammals.

"Sure, little man," Logan says. "Whatever you want to do. It's all about you."

Nicholas misses the sarcasm, but I don't. "I don't think—"

"You don't think what," Logan cuts me off. "Now I can't take our son to the zoo?" Logan puts emphasis on the word son and my stomach clenches.

"Not at all," I stammer. "Are you sure you're up to it? He can be a handful."

I smile and try to ease the tension that invades the room like smoke. Logan studies me for a second and then stands and slips on Nicholas's jacket.

"For the last time, don't worry."

I walk them to the garage and watch Logan take the car seat out of my vehicle and put it in his Benz. He makes a comment about his leather seats getting damaged but manages to secure it in place with minimal instruction from me. I buckle Nicholas in and give him a kiss. He'll be fine, I tell myself as I shut the car door.

"What are you going to do with your free time?" Logan blocks the path between the cars.

I shrug. "Take a long bath and relax, I guess."

"Going anywhere?"

"I don't know. Why?"

He clears his throat and shrugs. "You make sure you're ready when we get back. We still have to finish making up."

When I don't respond, Logan takes my hand. "I know I messed up and I'm trying, okay. But you have to meet me in the middle. You are everything to me."

I sigh and start to reply, but Logan stops me with a kiss.

"I need you, babe. You know I love you, right?"

"I know."

"I need you," he says. "In every way."

Logan kisses me more passionately this time.

"I'll see you later," I tell him. He picks up on the promise in my words and smiles.

"Later." Logan walks around to the driver's side of his car.

I watch them back out of the driveway and wave as they pull off. I head in the house for my bath and try to convince myself that I am looking forward to making love to my husband.

CHAPTER EIGHTEEN

ADRIENNE

With the guys gone, the silence closes in on me. No distractions mean I can't hide from the annoying feeling of dread. I go into the kitchen and start to run water in the sink. Logan's attempt at making breakfast resulted in a mess of scattered dishes on the counter. The physical labor narrows my focus but the thoughts return to buzz around my head like a gnat. What did Logan mean by that son comment? Was he being an ass with the way he said it or is there some hidden meaning? I tell myself to relax as I wring water out of the dishtowel.

I go upstairs to the bathroom and run water in the tub. I check the temperature and add vanilla musk scented bath beads. The smell reminds me of Christopher.

I undress and ease into the water. The water caresses me and I let out a sigh of contentment. I rest my head on the pillow and close my eyes. The smooth sounds of old school R & B whisper through the speakers and I hum along. My thoughts return to Christopher and the feelings I can't deny. If I am honest with myself, I will admit that my feelings for the man never left. A part of me wishes he was Nicholas's father. But I know who the father of my child is. His condition ensures me that Logan is his father. We both have the defective gene that made our baby sick. Christopher doesn't have sickle cell. Mystery solved.

A bigger mystery involves why Logan thinks we can resume our sex life as if nothing happened. I still can't comprehend what went on between us or rather what was going on with Logan. I'm doing good being able to look at him. I guess he is trying to make amends, but I'm not sure if it is enough.

The next song that comes over the speakers brings sex immediately to mind. The piano chords sing, the horns swell and I am back in Christopher's apartment the first time we made love. I settle further against the tub and let the sounds of Earth, Wind & Fire's *Loves Holiday* take me back in time.

Christopher and I had been dating for a few weeks and I was starting to fall for him. He was smart, good to his momma and funny in a goofy way. And it was a bonus that the man was so fine I had to pinch myself to prove he was real. That we, as a couple, were real. The man was into me too. He got me. I trusted him with my dreams and more importantly, my fears. He may not have understood all my hang-ups, but he didn't mock them. He made me feel safe. I hadn't felt that way with a man since my dad died.

Chemistry was crazy between us. The sight of him made my heart pound. And when he smiled at me, I was mesmerized. We resisted the urge to follow through on that desire. We both were enjoying the anticipation too much. But when Christopher invited me to his place for dinner that night, I knew we wouldn't be able to wait any longer.

I sing along with the radio. I take the towel and run it over my body imagining it is Christopher's touch. I let out a contented sigh as my body comes to life.

I picture Christopher that night. After a dinner of Salisbury steak, we moved to the living room. Christopher hit play on the cassette player and took my hand. He danced with me while he sung the words into my ear.

"Would you mind, if I touched, if I kissed, if I held you tight, in the morning light?"

Our kiss lasted throughout the song and when it began to play again, he led me to the bedroom. There were candles lit around the bed and Christopher promised to take his time. He did. He undressed me with deliberate details and lingered longingly over my every body part.

I toss the towel and put my hands between my legs and stir. Sensations awake and I continue to touch myself the way Christopher made my body hum.

I recall the scent of the candles that night and the way Christopher looked in that light. There was a hunger in his eyes that equaled the desire in mine. I am reminded of the heat. The way my body was on fire and when I was about to be consumed, Christopher would slow it down. He would let me smolder and then stroke the flames anew. He continued that sensational tease until I was begging for release. Then he went even deeper. I remember the way he tasted, the smell of his skin and the weight of his body pressed onto mine.

My moans are so loud I am brought back from my trance, but I am too far gone to stop now. I continue to stroke myself. The orgasm is so powerful when it comes that my thrusts splash water on the floor. The ripples of pleasure flow down my body and my back arches causing me to slip underwater. I sit up spewing water and Christopher's name from my lips.

I wipe the water from my eyes and look around. Everything in the bathroom looks the same. Except for my reflection in the mirror. I look exactly as I feel. Guilty. I wash away all evidence of my fantasy and stand up to towel dry. I pause when I hear the front door beep. Someone has come in. Did Logan come back so soon? Did he hear me get myself off to a memory?

I wrap the towel around my body and walk out the room onto the landing. I call out for Logan, but Marilyn appears at the bottom of the stairs.

"Hello, darling," she says.

I almost drop my towel. "Marilyn," I say. What is she doing here and why is she walking into my house? Do I need to flash the woman again?

Before I can articulate my questions, Marilyn turns to a man that appears at her side. A man wearing dirty jeans, a sweaty t-shirt and hair that has never met a comb. A man carrying a box marked 'fragile.'"

"Please sit that box here," Marilyn points to a spot near the table in the foyer. "The boxes marked 'books' can go into the study."

I start down the stairs. "What is going on? Why are you bringing boxes?"

"Didn't Logan tell you? My house is being renovated and I'll be here for a few weeks."

Of course, Logan didn't mention a thing to me. No wonder he got out of here so fast this morning.

I fake a smile. "Was that today?" I say through clenched teeth.

"The workers start Monday," Marilyn says. "The job should last—"

Marilyn is interrupted by the return of the dirty man. He is carrying three large suitcases one of which he drops with a loud thud.

"Careful, Winston," Marilyn says.

Winston? The name does not fit the man walking toward me. His mother had lofty ideals for her son. I know she taught him to wash. I wonder why he forgot.

"Adrienne, can you show Winston the way to the guest room." Marilyn's request focuses my attention back to the intrusion on my afternoon. Why did Logan set me up if he knew his mother was moving in? Why didn't he tell me?

"Sure," I tell Winston and turn to go back up the stairs.

"After you get dressed, of course," Marilyn adds.

I'm glad my back is turned to Marilyn. She doesn't need to know how embarrassed I am. I clutch the towel in a death grip and point Winston to the guest room. I pretend I don't see him leering at me.

In my room, I throw on some clothes, an old pair of jeans and a university t-shirt. I dial Logan's cell phone, and he answers on the first ring like he is expecting my call.

"Hey, babe," he says.

I ignore the formalities. "Why didn't you tell me your mother was moving in?"

"What?" he stammers.

I repeat the question louder this time. Logan clears his throat. "I guess it slipped my mind. We just started speaking to each other late last night."

"And you couldn't remember to mention it this morning before you left?"

"I'll make it up to you, okay? The work on her house shouldn't take long. A week or two."

"Then why is she moving in with boxes, Logan?" I am pacing back and forth.

Instead of answering my question, he calls to Nicholas. I hear Nicholas laugh in the background and then he is on the phone.

"Hey, Mommy," he says. "Ms. Sheila said I could feed the giraffes. They have a baby giraffe. Bye."

He is gone before I can respond. Sheila? When Logan returns to the phone, I ask. He does the throat clearing thing again.

"Um, Sheila. You know, from the office. We ran into her out here."

"What is she doing at the zoo?" It sounds contrived. What are the chances she's out there today?

"Yeah, she's here with her nephew. We figured the boys would be good company for each other, so we started walking around together."

I don't have time to dwell on this coincidence. My more immediate concern is the woman bringing suitcases into the guest room.

"About your mother, Logan?"

"Babe, we'll talk about it tonight. Got to go." He clicks off despite my protests. Now I am pissed. And I have to get out of here.

I grab my bag and go look for Marilyn. I find her in the kitchen.

"There you are, dear," she says. "Do you mind if I put this here?"

She is holding a pot. One in a set of pots that she is unpacking. She has already cleared a spot in the cabinet by stacking my pots and pushing them into a corner.

"Why are you unpacking dishes?" I ask.

"I told Logan I would cook dinner tonight."

"Logan is picking up a pizza."

"That's not a suitable meal for my grandson." Marilyn reaches into a bag and pulls out bottles of spices. "I figure since I'm staying here I can help you with meals."

"That's nice, Marilyn, but you don't need to go to all that trouble." I fight to maintain a calm demeanor. I will not be baited into a fight with this woman.

Marilyn waves her hand. "No trouble. I've missed cooking for a family." Her eyes mist up. Okay, time to exit.

"Make yourself at home," I say as if I had any doubt that she will. "I'll be back in an hour or so."

Marilyn says something, but I don't hear her. I am already out the door. I call Kim from the car.

"What has Logan done now?" Kim asks as soon as I say hello. She picks up the stress in my voice. She is as shocked as I am.

"Come on over," she says. "Brother-in-law is seriously tripping."

I am pulling into Kim's driveway when my cell phone rings. I assume it is Logan calling about me leaving his mother alone at the house. I am ready to explode, but the voice on the other end makes my breath catch.

"Ms. Adrienne," he says. "I hope I didn't catch you at a bad time."

"Christopher," I say and smile.

"Can you talk?"

"Yeah, what's up?"

"I need someone to talk to. Before I do something stupid."

I cut off the ignition. "What's wrong?"

"Let me ask you a question. Would you ever keep Nicholas away from his father?"

That gives me pause. I hope he's not bringing up the issue of paternity again.

"What do you mean?"

"If Logan wanted to see Nicholas, spend time with him, would you deny him?"

"No," I say my heartbeat slowing. "In fact, Logan is with Nicholas at the zoo right now."

There is silence on the other end of the line. I look at the phone to make sure the call didn't drop. "Are you still there? Tell me what's wrong?"

Christopher's voice is tight with emotion. "I was supposed to get my daughter today. This morning I drive to their house to pick her up and Lisa meets me at the door and says Mya can't go with me. She tells me that Troy's mother is sick and has to have surgery. They are booked to catch a flight out to Florida."

"Why couldn't Mya stay with you?" I ask.

"Same thing I said," he continues. "I'm like, okay no problem. Mya can stay with me until you get back. Lisa says she's not comfortable with that. That she hasn't had a chance to see where I'm living and that she's not sure how long they will be gone. That Mya needs to be with family during this time."

Christopher's voice raises. "I'm her goddamn family."

"I know."

"Of course, now I'm getting angry. Lisa could have told me all this before I drove two hours thinking I'm going to pick up my daughter. You know what she said to me."

"What?"

"Well, I figured you would at least want to see her for a few minutes." Christopher blows out a frustrated breath.

"What did you do?"

"I'm on the porch talking to my baby while they are loading luggage in the car. I'm trying to cram weeks of parenting into fifteen minutes. Mya lost her first tooth, you know. I wasn't there to play tooth fairy. She's gotten taller and more beautiful. So many things I've already missed out on."

"I'm so sorry Chris," I say. I can hear him struggling to hold it together. The man is torn up about this.

"You know what the worst part is? Mya asked to come with me and I had to tell her she couldn't. The disappointment in her eyes…" Christopher's voice trails off. "I wanted to grab her and run."

We both hold the phone. I try to think of words to comfort him and fall short.

"I'm standing there like a fool while Troy drives off with my family. The man has the nerve to look at me like he's better than me. But if this is how Lisa wants to play, I can play. I've tried to be reasonable and she still wants to use Mya to get back at me. I'll deal with her in court. My lawyer already has the paperwork ready to go."

"So, what are you doing now?" I ask.

"Heading home," he says like he's not sure where that place is located.

"I'm at Kim's. Why don't you come over here?" As soon as the words are out of my mouth, I get nervous. Flashback to my little rendezvous in the tub.

"Are you sure it's okay?" he asks. The underlying question is if my husband will find out.

"I have the afternoon free. My guys are at the zoo."

"Yeah, about that…" Kim comes out of the house and stands on the porch. She makes a gesture asking why I am still in car. I get out and walk toward the house.

"Are you coming over? Kim would love to see you." I don't think he needs to be alone. Kim and I can take his mind off his trouble.

Who is that? Kim mouths. I mouth back his name and her eyes dance with delight.

"I'll see you in a few," Christopher says.

"Do you remember the way?"

"How could I forget?"

CHAPTER NINETEEN

LOGAN

Operation get my wife back got off to a promising start but thirty minutes into this zoo trip I am ready to abort this mission. I should at least get points for trying. Who can keep up with this kid? As soon as we walk through the gates, he takes off.

"This way, Daddy," he calls over this shoulder. "I want to see the giraffes."

I know Adrienne has brought him here a few times, but I do things differently. I corral Nicholas and we move between the habitats in a civilized manner. The zoo is designed in a circle and we start at the beginning and follow the proper layout. I stop and read the plagues to Nicholas. He should learn something while we are here.

"Listen, Nicholas. Did you know gazelles can run at high speeds for long periods? The males are called bucks and the females are called does. Do you know what baby gazelles are called?"

The kid gives me a blank stare. I shake my head. I thought Adrienne was teaching him something.

"They are called a calf or a fawn," I tell him.

"A baby giraffe is a calf," Nicholas says.

I raise an eyebrow. The kid does know something. "What else do you know about giraffes?"

"They are the tallest in the whole zoo. Mommy giraffe takes care of the babies. It has a long tongue." Nicholas stretches his arms out wide to illustrate. "And it tickles when they lick your hand. Can we go feed the giraffes now, Daddy? Please."

"Sounds like a good idea."

I turn at the sound of Sheila's voice. She is leaning against the opposite railing. I'm surprised to see her. I called her this morning to give her the day off. We had planned to meet at the office to work on a couple of cases. How did she know I was here?

"How long have you been here?" I ask. I don't want her to think I am surprised by her presence.

"Not long. I figured you could use some company."

"Some company or your company?" I appraise Sheila's attire. She has on a pair of tight jeans with heels, a low cut white blouse that shows off her ample cleavage and a blue blazer.

"Looks like you are happy to see me," she says and hooks her arm through mine. "Nicholas, which way are the giraffes?"

He points the way and Sheila and I follow behind. I look around, but no one seems to notice us. I pay for a cup of pellets and Sheila helps the kid stand on a log behind the fence and feed the animals. He calls to me, but I sit on a bench and watch them. I'm glad Sheila is here. Let her deal with the kid. Well, I'm happy she is here until Adrienne calls.

I started not to answer, but I must get my wife back in my bed. She starts going off about Mother moving in. It's not so much that I forgot to tell her. I didn't want to deal with her questions about it. Mother is moving in and that is that. I try to distract her by letting her speak to Nicholas but then the little dude goes and mentions Sheila. I can't catch a break. I promise to talk later tonight and end the call.

After the kid lets a giraffe slobber all over his hands, we make our way through the rest of the zoo. We don't stop to observe the animals until we get to the Bird House. We are in time for the penguin feeding and the kid goes and presses his face against the glass.

"You know the best thing about penguins?" Sheila slides up behind me.

"They are formally dressed." My joke falls flat.

Sheila takes my hand. "They mate for life."

She wants to have this conversation now. I look around the room. Most people are minding their business but one Black lady looks at me with disgust. A look I've seen many times, mostly from my own mother. The look that says a Black man has no business loving a White woman. I snatch my hand and step back.

"This is not the place," I say through my teeth.

Sheila's face flushes. "Then where is the place? Let's go there now because I can't do this anymore."

I have to diffuse this situation before Sheila makes a scene. I grab her hand and pull her into an enclave.

"What's wrong now? I thought we were good."

Sheila burrows her face in my chest. "I'm lonely, Logan. Here you are playing family man and I'm pushed aside again. Do you want me or not?"

I rub her back. "Of course, I do. But you know the deal."

"I know."

I chance a stroke of her hair. "I need some time, okay? Just give me some time to figure things out."

She settles against me. My stomach churns from the stress. I am juggling too many situations right now. The law firm is getting an infusion of funds to keep the lights on and salaries paid. I can't afford to keep Mother's house and need to sell it. And I have to get my wife to get past her silly tantrum and act like my wife again. Sheila was the one person I could count on to stay in her place. Now she wants something more.

"Maybe I should quit." Sheila says.

I stiffen and step back. "This again? You know I need you at the firm."

"And I need the man I love to make me a priority for once. I know you're married, but you don't have to stay that way."

She had me on that point, but I wasn't leaving my wife. I like my life the way it is. I have to protect my reputation. How would it look for me to leave my family for another woman? What would my Mother think if I brought home a White girl?

I clear my throat. "Listen, baby. I know you deserve more than I can give right now, but I need you to be a little more patient with me. We have a history and I don't want to lose you."

Sheila's face softens. I keep talking. "Can I count on you, baby?" I glance around and pull her close to me.

"I'm not going to wait forever, Logan." Sheila peers up at me with watery eyes. "Either you make me and us a priority or I'm moving on. From the firm and from you."

"What are you saying?" I know she isn't talking about leaving me. Is she crazy?

"You think I can't get another man? I turn down advances from men all the time." She turns and scans the area. "See that man over there. I could get him if I wanted too."

She is pointing at some dude in khakis with a camera strapped around his neck. He is the lone adult at the feeding exhibit without a child.

I laugh. "You think he can compete with me? Stop being silly and listen to reason."

"I'm done listening to your lies. Make a choice, Logan." Sheila walks over to the khaki dude and touches his shoulder. I watch her flirt with him and he starts pointing out different birds as they walk away. Sheila glances back at me and winks.

When did I lose control here? I'm going to make Sheila pay for that little stunt. She'll come back to me. She always does.

I look around for the kid. He is still watching the workers feed the penguins. It's time to get out of here. I think I've put in enough time playing daddy.

We head toward the exit and I check my phone. Adrienne hasn't called. I stroll through work email. This is what I need to focus on. Spending time at this stinking zoo isn't going to generate a billable hour.

"Hey," a lady pushing a stroller yells in my direction. I keep walking but she gets louder. "Yeah, you, asshole. You're leaving your kid."

I follow the end of the flabby finger and see that she is pointing about twenty yards back. Nicholas is running to catch up. "Daddy, wait," he calls.

"Some father." The lady rolls her eyes before stomping down the walkway.

That's what I need. I can't let anything happen to this kid. Adrienne would never forgive me. When he catches up, I lean down to make sure his is okay. He is sweaty and out of breath but seems fine.

"Daddy, can we get ice cream?"

I study Nicholas's face. This child bears my family name, but I don't see any similarities to the Rutherford men. From the shape of his eyes to the curves of his lips, all I see is Adrienne. The woman I love.

"Sure, kid," I say and take his hand this time. Now everyone can see we are the perfect father and son. I want to bring the boy back to his mother, get her forgiveness and get her back in my bed. Maybe then I'll be able to think straight. Maybe then I can keep up the charade of a man in control. A man that isn't afraid of disappointing his father.

I can still hear his deep baritone voice that made my stomach clench. "You are messing up, son. Are you a man? A Rutherford man is always in control. Handle your business and handle your woman."

A new game plan forms. I head home.

CHAPTER TWENTY

ADRIENNE

I fill Kim in on the events of the morning. She is equally disgusted with the way Logan moved his mother in and sympathizes with Christopher's situation.

"Do you know what you are doing?" she asks.

"We're just friends," I tell her. "And he needs a friend."

She pretends to be convinced of my motives. So, do I.

When Christopher arrives, we settle into an easy rhythm. Kim resumes her role as annoying little sister, Christopher teases her and I relish reliving past memories. Before we realize it, the sun is setting and Logan has been calling me for the past hour. We are dissecting the merits of Kim's DVD collection (what self-respecting person owns a copy of "Howard the Duck") when my phone goes off again.

"Brother-in-law will not quit," Kim says.

"Yeah," I sigh. "I better take this. It could be Nicholas."

I leave the couch and walk down the hall into Kim's office. "What is it now, Logan?" I snap.

"You're still at Kim's?" he asks. "How long are you planning to stay over there?"

As long as your mother stays there, I think. Instead, I ask about Nicholas.

"He's fine. Mother is giving him a bath."

Great. She's taken over my kitchen and my son.

"When are you coming home?" Logan asks.

"Why? Your mother seems to have everything under control."

Logan clears his throat. "I know you are upset I didn't tell you mother was moving in today."

I remain quiet. I'll give the man a chance to explain.

"You want me to apologize for that, okay. But it's for a couple of weeks, babe. It's not like she'll be living with us indefinitely."

"That's not an apology, Logan."

"You have to be reasonable about this. This is my mother. What was I supposed to do?"

"You could have talked about it with your wife first. I'm asking for some consideration here."

"You're right, okay. But we weren't really communicating and—"

"Why was Sheila at the zoo?" I blurt out the question that has been nagging at me all day.

Logan chuckles. "Is that the real issue? I told you. It was a coincidence. We ran into her and her nephew out there. We let the boys run around together. Nicholas had a good time."

I listen to him make his case of the accidental meeting which seems plausible. Before this morning, I wouldn't have believed that Logan would volunteer to spend time with Nicholas so anything is possible.

Logan stops rambling and calls my name. "I'm still here," I say.

"Thought I lost you," he chuckles.

"Maybe you already have," I mumble and turn toward the door. Christopher is leaning against the doorframe.

"What did you say?" Logan is calling my name again, but I can't focus on his words. I tell him I'll be home soon and end the call.

"I wanted to check on you," Christopher says. He gestures toward the phone in my hand. "Is everything okay?"

I nod.

"Guess I'll head home," he says. "Wanted to tell you thanks. Being here was good. Felt like old times."

"Yes, it did," I agree.

Christopher looks into my eyes and I feel the mood shift. "Maybe we can do this again? I would love to see you tomorrow."

And I know I should say no. I should keep a respectable distance from this man. Friends are okay but to start planning to see him feels like something else. I am a married woman with a child and a mother-in-law living in my house and I can't sneak away to see a former boyfriend. I open my mouth to tell him all this.

"I'll make time," I say.

Christopher's smile is the reward I didn't know I needed.

"So, we'll talk tomorrow," he says.

"I'll call you."

Christopher ushers me out of the room with a hand in the small of my back. The electricity from this simple touch makes it hard to walk straight. I manage to make it back into the living room without embarrassing myself. Kim is clearing our glasses and greasy napkins from the coffee table.

"Is Nicholas okay?" she asks.

"He's fine. Marilyn is giving him a bath."

"Didn't take her long to take over." Kim voices the thoughts that have been strumming along my conscience. I should be taking care of my own child instead of going back down memory lane.

"Who's Marilyn?" Christopher sits on the couch to slip on his shoes.

Kim fills him in while I take the empty pizza box into the kitchen and grab my purse. He stands when I return.

"Dealing with the in-law 24/7, huh?" Christopher takes my hand. "I feel your pain."

He puts my hand on his chest and fakes an attack.

"Stop playing," I snatch my hand away. I don't need to touch the hardness of his body. It's already a struggle to keep my thoughts in the friend zone.

I tell Kim that I will talk to her tomorrow and Christopher follows me out.

"Listen," he says. "Earlier you said Logan took your son to the zoo."

I unlock the car door and sit my purse inside. "Yeah, why?"

"Maybe it's nothing, but Logan called me this morning and said he would be working on my business all day. We have our final meeting with the buyers on Tuesday."

"And?" I turn to face him.

"I'm wondering how he was working on my case when he was at the zoo."

The anger is sudden and startles me as well as Christopher. "Are you saying Logan can't take a day off to spend with Nicholas? You of all people shouldn't have a problem with that."

Christopher steps back and holds up his hands. "Hey, take it easy. You know what I meant."

He looks wounded and I feel like a jerk. I'm guilty of enjoying my day without my son, but it doesn't mean I need to twist the man's words. "Sorry."

Christopher gives me a sly smile. "Defending your man, huh?"

"I guess so." I turn to get into the vehicle. Christopher shuts the door and motions for me to roll down the window.

"You'll call tomorrow, right?"

My emotions are all over the place. I'm unsure if I can or should continue to rebuild a relationship with Christopher. I don't trust myself to speak.

"I don't want you to feel weird, but I'm glad you allowed me back into your life." He leans in and kisses me on the cheek. His lips are soft and my stomach flips. I feel warm. I try to think of a response to diffuse the tension I feel but Christopher winks and walks to his car. I blow out a deep breath. Strictly friends, I tell myself. Who am I fooling?

CHAPTER TWENTY ONE

ADRIENNE

It's amazing how something can start off innocent and grow into something beyond your control. For the past few weeks, I see and/or talk to Christopher every day. The meeting place is Kim's house. It is there where we can pretend the past three years apart never happened. And although I try to fight it, I find myself comparing Christopher to Logan. And Logan is losing.

The arrangement with his mother is not working well. Marilyn has made herself at home and has taken over the preparation of all meals. She claims I don't clean or dust often enough and goes behind me to rescrub everything. Logan keeps claiming it is temporary but we are going on a month and I don't see an end in sight. To keep my sanity, I escape. Every morning I take Nicholas to school and hang out at Kim's until it is time to pick him up. Christopher comes by with lunch from one of the many restaurants in his development.

Kim pulls me aside one afternoon after Christopher leaves. "Do you think this is a good idea?"

"What?" I pretend I don't know what she is talking about and fluff the pillows on the couch.

"Don't play. You know you are close to crossing a line here."

I take a deep breath and turn to her. "Don't worry, little sister. Nothing's going on I can't handle. And I need this."

These secret afternoons are the highlight of my day. The evenings are spent avoiding a confrontation with Marilyn and not having sex with my husband. The first night Marilyn moved in, Logan tried to get frisky. I told him I couldn't with his mother down the hall.

"You're joking, right?" he asked.

"I'm tired, okay," I said through a yawn and turned my back to him in the bed.

"Come on, babe," he whined. "We're supposed to be making up."

"Consider us made up."

"Are you going to deny me? I thought we were going to work on making a baby."

I ignored him and snuggled further under the covers. Logan grabbed me by the arm and twisted me around. He pressed his lips hard against mine. When he came up for air, I asked, "Are you going to rape your wife again?" My tone was calm and even. He wasn't drunk that night.

That stopped him cold. He hasn't touched me since.

This is part of the reason I find myself currently locked in a passionate embrace with Christopher. We are in our usual spot on Kim's couch. Most visits are chaperoned. Kim may be in her office working but she was always in the house. Today, she had to meet a new client. She makes a big production out of leaving us alone, but I assured her we were adults and could handle things without her. Christopher gives me a look that says he is aching to get me alone, but I shrug it off. We are just friends.

Friends who kiss. One moment we are having a serious discussion about the merits of social networking and the next we are engaging in a kiss that makes me lightheaded. This kiss leaves no doubt that my body was designed to respond to his.

I know I should stop but it feels so good. I lay back and let his hands roam under my shirt. He massages my breast and a cry escapes my lips.

"I want you," Christopher whispers and trails fiery kisses down my neck.

I can't deny that I want him too. My hands show him what I am afraid to vocalize. They touch places on Christopher that I have fantasized about. I stroke him and he moans deep in his throat. He swells with my caress and my mouth waters in anticipation. My skin tingles with energy and I am no longer thinking. My body reacts and I am caught up. Damn, the consequences.

"Maybe we should go in the back." Christopher stands and reaches for my hand.

I follow him down the hall. At that moment, I am not thinking about my husband or my marriage. I am not concerned about Kim coming home and finding us locked away in her guest room. All I see is Christopher. And then I make the mistake of looking in the mirror.

That's another thing about Kim's decorating tastes. She has lots of candles and pillows and an overabundance of mirrors. She has a fascinating collage of mirrors over her sofa. A local artist created the piece for her, and Kim has been obsessed with them ever since. In addition to the huge piece in the living room, Kim has mirrors placed randomly down the hall. I avoid looking directly into them.

Chris pauses at the doorway and kisses me. "I've been waiting for this for a long time."

I don't respond. I pull him close and bury my face against his neck. I want this so bad; my legs are shaking.

"Are you okay with this?" Chris strokes my face. His eyes search mine. I know he can see the evidence of love and lust. He grins and kneels in front of me. One hand goes under my shirt and the other unbuttons my jeans. I close my eyes to savor the anticipation of his lips on my most delicate places.

I am about to tell him yes. Hell yes, when I make the mistake of opening my eyes and staring into a mirror. Chris has started to nibble on my breast, but I am fixated on my reflection. Damn, if Kim isn't right. You can't hide from yourself. I back away.

"I can't."

Chris looks up at me and stands. He takes my hands. "The marriage thing, right?"

I nod. What I saw in the mirror was a cheater and I can't go down that road again. I can't deal with anymore guilt.

"It's okay," he says and kisses my hand. "I can wait until you are ready."

I breathe a sigh of relief. I'm glad he understands. I can't imagine not talking to him every day. Now that he is back in my life, I don't want to lose that connection.

"I can't make any promises," I say.

"I'm not asking for any."

"Logan is a good man and—"

Christopher cuts me off. "A good man, huh? He has you fooled. He has everyone fooled."

"What are you talking about?" I drop his hand.

"I can understand you wanting to work on your marriage," he says. "I've been through a divorce and I know how painful it can be no matter who is at fault. But I can't stand how you put him on a pedestal. Like he can do no wrong."

"I don't do that," I say. "I know better than anyone that Logan isn't perfect."

Christopher adjusts himself and sneers. "You don't even know half of the story."

"Why don't you tell me? I know Logan finished your case. Did he do something wrong?"

Christopher starts to say something and then stops. The tension leaves his face, and he tries to reach for my hand. I pull away.

"Tell me," I repeat.

Christopher stuffs his hands in his pockets and looks at me with such tenderness, I want to hug him.

"Is it that bad?" I ask.

He avoids my gaze. "No, no. I shouldn't have said anything."

"Shouldn't have said what?"

"Nothing. Look, I was out of line. I know your situation and I got caught up in what I wanted."

"Don't try to change the subject."

"This is the subject. No matter how bad I want you, I have to respect your marriage."

I turn and walk away. There is something he isn't telling me and his constant reminders of my marriage make me feel worse. He hurries behind me.

"Where are you rushing off to?"

I stop abruptly and Christopher wraps his arms around me. Being in his arms makes me relax.

"What is going on here? You know you can tell me anything, right?"

Christopher pulls me closer. "I promise to tell you when the time is right."

I settle into his embrace and then the meaning of his words hit me. I shove him away. "You are doing it again."

Christopher tries to maintain his balance. "Doing what?"

"Deciding for me. Why the hell do you assume you can get away with that?"

He looks confused for a second then stands up straight. "This isn't the same thing."

"It is the same. Like you decided to leave me and go be a daddy without giving me a choice."

Christopher throws his hands in the air. "I thought we were past all that."

"Obviously not."

We stand staring at each other, neither one of us backing down. I'm usually the one to give in during disagreements. Try to reach some compromise. It's not happening today.

"How long do I have to pay for leaving you? I think I paid that debt by spending three years without you and being married to the wrong woman. Having a child that I don't get to see often." Christopher collapses on the sofa, the weight of his words too heavy to carry.

"You think your debt is paid in full? Then tell me what you know about Logan." I stand in front of Christopher with my hands on my hips.

"Logan is stealing from me." Christopher's statement deflates my anger.

"What?" I feel behind me for a place to sit.

Christopher looks pained. "I got suspicious the other day when you mentioned Logan was at the zoo. I got an invoice from the Rutherford Law Firm for all these billable hours, which seemed excessive. I asked for further details and got a list of hours and dates. One date was for that zoo trip."

"What does that mean?"

"It means if Logan wasn't married to the woman I love I would have turned him into the Bar Association yesterday."

Whoa. What has Logan been up to? Would he do something so un-ethical?

"Are you sure?" I ask. "Maybe it's an accounting error."

"It wasn't an error," Christopher crosses his arms.

"There's got to be an explanation."

"There is. You don't want to hear it."

"Hear what?"

"The truth. Logan is not the good guy you want to believe he is."

"And I suppose you know my husband in a few weeks better than I do." Christopher is starting to piss me off again.

He nods. "It didn't take long for me to see what kind of man he is."

My voice rises. "And what kind of man is that?"

"You know." Christopher leans back.

"What do I know?" I shout.

"Come on, Ms. Adrienne. Aren't you tired of playing games?"

"What the hell are you talking about?" I explode. Christopher is giving me a headache with this cryptic conversation. "Tell me what you know."

He shakes his head.

"This is what I'm talking about. There you go deciding for me again. Like when you decided to leave me."

Christopher sits up straight. I know I have tested his patience when he says, "All right. Time out for throwing that in my face. I admitted I was wrong, and you need to let it go. Besides, for all your talk about being allowed to make your own decisions, you seldom do it."

"What?" Now it's my turn to lean back in the chair.

"Yeah, you want to make decisions so bad. What happened with the job offer at Harrison Hall?"

My mouth opens to respond, but nothing comes out.

Christopher doesn't have that problem. "Logan *decided* that his wife didn't need a job, right? He told me all about how his wife doesn't need to work. How he likes it that she doesn't work. How he refuses to let her work. He says a man should take care of all the business and a woman should focus on taking care of him and the kids. The man bragged about how he has his wife in check. He calls all the shots."

Having Christopher throw my life back in my face renders me mute. He might as well have hit me with a stun gun. I force myself to look in his eyes expecting smug satisfaction. What I see is worse. Pity.

I jump up and grab my purse. "You know what I can make a decision on? Not seeing you anymore."

Now Christopher looks stunned. "What? Why?"

"What was it you said earlier? You have to respect my marriage. I am married and I can't keep sneaking around to see you."

"But nothing has happened between us. We're just friends." Christopher stands and reaches for me. I step away. The hurt on his face strips me to the core, but I have enough pride to maintain my stance.

"Friends?" I ask. "We both know we could never just be friends. Not when we used to be so much more. Logan isn't perfect and neither is my marriage, but it is what it is. We keep meeting like this and it's a matter of time before we end up in bed. I can't do that to my family. I have Nicholas to think about."

"So, now it's about Nicholas?"

"Yes."

"And you would use your child to stay?"

"Why not? You used your child to leave."

Christopher takes the verbal slap but shakes it off. "Why stay with a man you know isn't right for you?"

"How do you know he isn't right for me?"

"Because he isn't me."

I am about to respond but pause mid-sentence. We stand there looking at each other, both of us struggling not to reveal the true emotion behind this. After a moment, I ask the question I have wondered about for years. "Why didn't you stop me?"

"Stop what?" Christopher rubs his hands down his face.

"The day of my wedding, you were there. Why didn't you stop me?"

"It wasn't my place," he shrugs. "I messed up. I guess a part of me didn't think I deserved you."

I think about that response. Wonder how things could have been different if he had stood up in the church that day. Would I have gone with him?

"Why didn't you stay with me that morning? We could have left together."

Now it's my turn to shrug. "I was getting married. I couldn't hurt him like that. I know what it feels like to get left."

Christopher throws up his hands in disgust. "Arghhh," he growls. "Why can't you let that go?"

I am so furious that my chest heaves up and down. "You know how I can let it go? By leaving your ass this time."

And with my final retort, I walk out the door.

CHAPTER TWENTY TWO

LOGAN

I open the billing software and start entering my billable hours against various cases. This quarter has been a good one thanks to the connections with Michaels. The guy came through with the golf invite with the mayor. I lost on the greens but gained the acquaintance of the mayor and his promise to throw some contract work my way.

I click the tab for New Moon Landscaping & Construction and pull up the task code for Project Administration. I add up the hours I spent researching regulations for construction permits and environmental protections. It totals three and a half hours, but I round up to four. Always round up is my motto. The client can afford it.

Michaels, Inc. can afford it. I looked into some of the man's finances and his personal net worth rivals some professional ball players. I pad his invoice with charges for overhead and use the paralegal rate for delivering documents to the court. I even bill him for time spent talking about him to other clients.

I need the extra cash. The Rutherford Law Firm is in the black, but my personal expenses have increased. Adrienne put the kid in some school, and now we have a weekly fee. Why can't she see that I am trying to make her happy? I thought we were back on track, but she still refuses me. I stopped asking. Let her have some space. But I still have needs.

I save the billing report and send an email to Beatrice to print and mail invoices. I email Sheila an assignment for case research on a bankruptcy we are handling. She replies that she is on it.

And she has been, in more ways than one. After our discussion at the zoo that day, Sheila tried to show out. She didn't show up for work that Monday. No call or anything. After work, I went by her place. I turned down her street and who do I see in her driveway? That square from the zoo.

I watched while she hugged him goodbye. She waved at him as he drove off. By the time she returned to her condo, I was out the car and pounding on her door.

"Open the damn door, Sheila," I shouted.

She peeked around the door with wide eyes. "What are you doing here?"

I pushed past her and started looking around. She regained her balance and closed the door. "Logan, what are you doing?"

I ignored her and marched to the bedroom. The bed was undisturbed. I went back into the kitchen and saw the remnants of dinner and two wine glasses.

"What is going on?" I demanded.

"What are you talking about?" Sheila looked everywhere but at me. "I had dinner with a friend."

"That's the dude you were all over at the zoo. You don't waste any time."

Her nostrils flared. "Why should I? I've wasted enough time with you."

"So, you sleep with some cornball to get back at me."

"Not everything is about you, Logan."

"Did you sleep with him?"

Sheila threw her hands up and walked into the living room. "Maybe you should go home to your wife."

I was in her face when she turned around. "Answer me. Did you fuck him?"

She tried to step away, but I caught her wrist.

"Are you crazy?" she asked.

"Yes." I buried her face in fiery kisses. "You are driving me crazy."

I pressed against her. I wanted her to feel me.

"Logan, stop," she said.

I wrapped my arms around her and pulled her close. "Can he make you feel like this?"

She tried to resist but gave in and kissed me back. We fumbled with our clothes.

"This is what you want," I said and took a breast in my mouth. I sucked her nipples until she moaned.

I ripped her panties pulling them aside. I had to show her that no one could take my place. "Can he make you feel like this?"

She tried to say something, but I didn't wait for a response. I bent her over the sofa and rammed myself into her until she screamed my name.

I wanted her to know she was mine. She didn't get to decide to move on with someone else. By the end of the night, I had her back on my team. I sexed her from the living room to the bedroom. All you have to do is give a woman a screaming orgasm and she will forgive you.

I lean back in my chair and shake the memory of that night. I was out. I could have been free to remain faithful to my wife. I look at the picture of Adrienne that sits on the corner of my desk. This is my favorite picture of her. I took it during a weekend getaway at a bed and breakfast. The wind was blowing through her hair, the water behind her and she was laughing. She looked happy to be with me. I could make her happy then. Now I can't get a smile. And forget about sex. Nothing is happening in the bedroom. I come home after working all day to find my wife curled up in the fetal position with the covers up to her ears.

That makes me wonder if she is giving up the goods to someone else. *No way*, I think. *She would never betray me like that*. To make sure, I pull out my cell phone. Pull up an app and click on the icon for Adrienne's vehicle. It gives me the status and history of her movements.

I smirk. She is where I thought she would be. Kim's house. My predictable wife follows the same routine. She takes Nicholas to school at 7:30 a.m. She goes to the gym and then to Kim's. She leaves there by 2:00 to get the kid and then it's back home.

Which means Adrienne is holding out on pure principle. I admire that. But she'll eventually tire of this game and come back to me. The best thing is not to push her. I can wait. Sheila is a suitable stand in for an unwilling wife.

I work for another hour and then stop to take a breather. I stand and walk around my office, the office that used to belong to Senior. I've changed the furniture, but one remnant of my father remains, a self-portrait that hangs behind the desk. It shows Senior at his best. Shirt sleeves rolled up, tie askew with a permanent scowl on his face. If I stare at it too long, I can feel the disappointment. *You are a Rutherford man, son. You must carry on the family legacy. You need to focus on what's important. Settle down and have a family like a real man.* And then... *You'll never measure up, Junior. Maybe you're not good enough. Not good enough.*

With my father's voice in my head, I turn away from the picture. I pace back and forth to shake the cloud of failure that tries to settle over me. The long hours are starting to stress me. I remind myself that I am winning. The firm is prospering under my leadership. I am the one that brought in a major client. I am the one that networked with the mayor's office. I am the one that will hire a new lawyer and paralegal this month. Would that make my father proud?

I stretch and rotate the muscles in my shoulders.

"Let me help you with that." Sheila has come in without knocking. I start to say something about the need to keep it professional at the office but she starts massaging my back.

"You're tense," she says. "Sit down."

I sit and she stands behind me. Her fingers push and prod the muscles and I feel them start to loosen up.

"Have you told your wife about us yet?"

My muscles coil like a boa constrictor and I swivel in the chair. "What are you talking about?"

"The other night. When you came by my place. You said it was me and you. You said we would be together."

I don't remember what I said. All I know is I wasn't about to let some other man step in and take what's mine. I'm an only child. I don't like to share.

I clear my throat. "I know, babe…I'll tell her soon."

Sheila crosses her arms.

"No. I will. But Mother is staying with us now. I can't end things with Mother there."

She throws her hands up. "Here you go with more excuses."

"Not an excuse. How would it look if I ended things with Adrienne and moved you in with my Mother there? I don't want to put you in that situation."

Sheila considers what I've said. "You're right."

I smile. Relieved I've bought more time. "Can we get back to that massage?"

Sheila starts kneading my neck again. "Are you coming over tonight?"

I've been to Sheila's every night to tuck her in. The woman is insatiable.

"I'm not going to make it. I have a deposition to prepare for. You know we have a client that's being sued."

"I think you're coming by," she says and swings the chair around.

"How are you going to change my mind?"

Sheila thrusts her breast in my face. I nuzzle them and grab her thigh. The form fitting black skirt she wears gives me easy access.

"I've locked the door. How about an appetizer to get you motivated?" She reaches for my belt buckle and licks her lips. "Does your wife do it like this?"

I shake my head and let Sheila do her thing. I love a blowjob in the office. I lean back and look up at the picture of Senior. I bet he never got off in the office. Wouldn't he be proud of his son? I imagine his peering glare as a smirk of approval. I close my eyes and enjoy the moment. I'm going to miss this when I have to end things.

CHAPTER TWENTY THREE

ADRIENNE

I sit outside of Nicholas's school fuming. I was in such a hurry to leave that I didn't think about locking up Kim's house. Christopher will have to sit there until she gets back. I know I'll hear about it later. But I am done with whatever this thing is with Christopher. I don't want to dwell on what that means.

By the time Nicholas gets out of school, I am calm enough to remember the errands I need to run today.

"Hey, baby," I buckle Nicholas into his car seat. "What did you do today?"

We chat about the wonders of preschool and the joys of eating lunch as I drive to the local grocery store. Once there, I lift Nicholas into the shopping cart and we swing by the bakery. The complimentary cookie helps keep Nicholas occupied while I shop. Our first stop is the pharmacy to get Nicholas's prescriptions filled. I called in the refill earlier so I give the clerk his name.

"That'll be $267.34," the clerk says and teases Nicholas for a piece of his cookie.

I am no longer shocked by the monthly total. I am shocked when I slide my debit card and watch the screen go from saying 'transaction processing' to 'transaction declined.' The clerk stops talking to Nicholas and gives me a look before asking if I have another form of payment.

"No," I stutter. "Can you try it again?" This time I choose credit but get the same result. Denied. Embarrassed, I stuff the useless card back in my wallet. I have about $30 in cash. Enough for either the penicillin or the folic acid that Nicholas need to take every day. No way can I afford the pain medicine that I keep on hand in case of a crisis. The clerk shows no sympathy as she casually tosses the drugs back into a bin behind the counter.

"Wait." I dig out the credit card I keep for emergencies and swipe. I get the package and flee the store. I sit in the car and think.

"Momma, we forgot to get juice," Nicholas calls from his booster seat in the back of the car.

That's not all we forgot, I think. I checked the account last week, and we had enough money to cover the monthly expenses. I drive to the nearest ATM and do a balance inquiry. Our account shows a balance of $27.13. I stare at the slip wondering what is going on. Logan insists on handling all the bills but I am aware of our expenses. At least, I thought I was.

"Momma," Nicholas whines. "I'm thirsty."

I look back at him in the rearview mirror. His mouth is smeared with cookie crumbs.

"I know, baby." I put the car in drive. "Let's go get you some juice."

I park in front of the law firm and shut off the car. It's been over a year since I've been here. Things still look the same, including the familiar sight of Ms. Beatrice.

"Well, hello there," she greets us. "It's been a while since you've come by to visit."

"Is Logan in?" I skip the formalities.

Beatrice cuts me a look that tells me she doesn't appreciate my lack of manners.

"I'm sorry," I say. "How have you been?"

"Just great, baby. And how is my little handsome man today?" She turns her attention to Nicholas. He grins and tries to get free from my hand. Beatrice gives him a treat of some sort, but today I don't have time to let them play. I tighten my grip and repeat my earlier question.

"Yes, he's in," she says and begins digging in her desk. "Let me see what I have for my little man here."

"We'll stop back by on the way out." I am already moving toward the stairs. Nicholas tries to protest, but I pick him up and march up the stairs. Logan's office is at the end of the hall. We make it to his door without seeing any other employees. How many employees does Logan even have now? It is unusual not to see at least a paralegal on this floor. I put Nicholas down to open the door to Logan's office.

"Let's go see Daddy," I say. I reach for the doorknob, but it opens before I can grab it. Sheila backs out. I move to avoid being knocked over. I'm not fast enough because when she turns we are kissing distance.

"Oh," she jumps. "Mrs. Rutherford. I didn't see you there."

"Didn't mean to startle you," I say.

Sheila lets out a nervous laugh and pats her hair in place. "Oh, no. You didn't. I wasn't expecting you. Are you here to see Logan? Of course, you're here to see Logan."

I shoot Sheila a look. Why is the woman acting so weird?

"Are you okay?" I ask.

"Okay? Yes, I'm okay. What brings you by?" Sheila fiddles with her hands. She looks back and forth between me and the door.

"Is Logan busy?" I motion toward the door.

"Umm, no, go on in. I'm sure he'll be surprised." Sheila tugs at her skirt and smooths her blouse.

We walk into Logan's office and see him leaning back in his chair with a contented smile on his face. I've seen that smile on two occasions. The first is after one of his mother's fried chicken, macaroni and cheese, and collard green dinners. The other time is after sex. And I don't see any chicken bones on his desk.

"Daddy," Nicholas shouts and runs around the desk.

Logan almost falls out of his chair. "Hey, hey, um, little man." He looks up at me. "What's going on?"

"You tell me."

Nicholas climbs on Logan's lap. "Daddy, can I work with you?"

"Maybe later." Logan turns back to me. "What are you talking about?"

I push aside my suspicions and focus on the most immediate need. "I stopped by the store to pick up Nicholas's prescription, and my debit card was declined. Why don't we have any money in our account?"

Logan looks confused for a second but recovers by clearing his throat. "I forgot to transfer some money over. I had the mortgage come out yesterday and it drained the account."

"That's never happened before."

Logan turns away from me without responding and begins typing on his laptop. Nicholas reaches for the mouse.

"I can do it, Daddy," he says. "I know how." Nicholas is beaming, but Logan is not amused.

"Would you get him?" He slides Nicholas off his lap. Nicholas starts to whine, but I distract him with a notepad and marker I swipe off the desk. I position him on the floor and return to Logan's side. I try to get a look at the screen.

"You know, it wouldn't hurt you to be more patient with him," I say. I thought I would see some improvement in Logan's parenting after the zoo trip, but he has fallen back into his usual routine.

"Maybe I would if you didn't barge in here during office hours."

"Barge in? Now I need an appointment to come visit my husband?"

"Would you lower your voice? I don't want the entire office to hear you."

I put my hands on my hips and get ready to unleash. What office? I didn't see a soul working when I came up the stairs. Before I can get a word out, Sheila pokes her head in the door.

"Logan," she says so sweetly I can see the high fructose corn syrup drip from her lips. "Don't forget your five o'clock conference call."

"Thanks, Sheila. We are about finish here." Logan watches her until she leaves. Would he cheat on me this way? I picture him and his secretary carrying on in the office like a bad soap opera. I shake the thought out of my head.

With a final click of the mouse, Logan leans back in the chair. "There."

"Where did you get the money from? I need enough for groceries and Nicholas's medicine." I checked our savings account at the ATM and it has an even lower balance than the checking.

"My business account. And don't worry. I put more than enough for you to spend."

"Are you implying I spend too much money?"

The smirk on his face deepens. "I don't see you contributing any funds."

"And why is that? You are the one that insists I don't need to work. You're the big man who can handle it all, right?"

All amusement is gone when he stands. "Look, Adrienne, I don't have time for this."

I start to continue but glance at Nicholas. He is watching us intently. I don't like to argue in front of him. Besides, this is not the place to get into it with Logan.

"Fine," I say. "We can finish this conversation at home later."

"I'll be late," Logan says. "Meetings."

"Big client?" I ask.

Logan clears his throat. "Yeah, remember that guy that came by the house, Michaels? I'm still trying to wrap that up. These high rollers are a pain to work with."

I know he is lying. Christopher told me the deal was done. Something else is going on with my husband.

I take Nicholas's hand. "Tell Daddy bye."

Nicholas grabs Logan around the legs. "I want to stay with Daddy." He looks up at Logan. "Wanna stay with you."

"Got work to do," Logan says and tries to pry Nicholas's arms loose. I watch him struggle to remove his son and my heart breaks.

"Adrienne, can you get him? I don't——"

"Have time," I finish the sentence. "Come on, baby." I stoop down and reach for Nicholas. "I need you to help Mommy. You will see Daddy later."

Nicholas looks at me with the saddest eyes, but he takes my hand. When I stand, onr look at Logan, and my earlier suspicions are confirmed.

"Your fly is open," I say and walk out the door.

CHAPTER TWENTY FOUR

ADRIENNE

My husband is having an affair. I turn the sentence over and over in my mind. Brand the betrayal in my brain. Now it all adds up. The late nights. The accidental meeting at the zoo. And I know we haven't been having sex. I shake my head. What a cliché my life has become. Logan is sleeping with his secretary. His white secretary. And I've been feeling guilty about spending time with Christopher?

I reach for the cell phone to call him but remember our fight. I can't call him now. And I'm not ready to tell Kim. I need more concrete evidence. Maybe this is all some crazy coincidence. I'm sure there is an explanation for everything. I don't want to believe it. Logan wouldn't cheat on me.

We return to the store and pick up a few grocery items. I know Marilyn has already cooked dinner. It's the one benefit of having her stay with us. And I must admit, she's a better cook than me.

On impulse, I turn down the street that leads to Marilyn's house. It's after five o'clock, but if there are any renovations going on there should be some indication of it. I pull into the driveway. A For Sale sign is perched in the yard. A woman in a nice suit and sensible heels is locking the door. Nicholas is starting to doze off so I leave the car running and get out.

"Is this house for sale?" I ask the agent as she approaches me.

"It sure is," she tosses her brown hair and extends a hand. "Sharon Bouknight."

"Nice to meet you. I was driving by and saw the sign."

"Are you in the market for a home? This one hasn't been on the market long and the owner is extremely motivated to sell."

"A motivated seller?" I don't have to fake the surprise in my voice. Why is Marilyn's house being sold instead of renovated?

"We're planning an open house tomorrow, but I can give you a quick tour now," Sharon pulls out her keys.

"Now isn't good." I motion toward the car. "My son is asleep."

Sharon glances at the car. "He's adorable." Her focus returns to me. "You know this house is great for a family. I would love to sit down with you and your husband."

"That would be great."

"Here is a flyer for you. I hope to see you tomorrow."

I take the flyer and Sharon's business card. Evidence to build my case. I make the short drive home with my heart racing as fast as the car. What else could Logan be lying about?

I carry Nicholas into the house. He feels a little warm, which I attribute to the warmth of the car but make a mental note to check on him later. I put him down on the couch and follow Marilyn's voice into the kitchen.

I find her in an animated conversation with one of her many visitors. Another reason I tend to stay away from the house during the day. This one is Mrs. Clover or Carter, one of Marilyn's church members. The woman always has a pinched look on her face like she smells something. Must be her funky attitude. She and Marilyn get along great.

Marilyn greets me when I walk in the room. "I didn't hear you come in." She moves from the table to the stove. She lifts the lid to stir and the scent of tomatoes and oregano fill the air. Marilyn's spaghetti sauce is legendary. Normally, the sight of it makes my mouth water. Right now, it makes me want to gag.

I nod in greeting and grab a bottle of water from the fridge. The liquid does little to cool the anger I feel.

"Where's my grandbaby?" Marilyn looks toward the entrance for Nicholas to appear.

"He fell asleep on the ride home. He's on the couch."

"You shouldn't let him sleep long during the day. He'll be groggy at dinner," Marilyn takes a box of spaghetti out of the pantry.

"These young mothers today need to listen to their elders," Mrs. Clover/Carter says. "Why I remember when my Milton was the age of your grandbaby, the boy wouldn't sleep unless I lay down with him. Well, I had to break him out of that quick when the Mister started to complain about his lack of quality time."

I interrupt her before she goes into detail about her love life and makes me sick to my stomach. "Nicholas needs more rest than the average 3-year-old. His illness makes him tired."

Marilyn rejoins her friend at the table. "She fusses over that boy so. I've been here almost four months and Nicholas is fine."

"I'm sure your being here has helped," Mrs. Clover/Carter pats Marilyn's hand.

I slam the refrigerator door. "And how much longer will you be here, Marilyn?" I strain to keep my voice neutral.

Marilyn glances at her friend and turns to me. "Um, they ran into some delays with the work."

"Is that right?"

"Yes, dear. Are you trying to get rid of me?" Marilyn laughs. She does a nervous dance in her chair.

"You're welcome to stay as long as you need to." I manage a smile.

Marilyn relaxes and starts to say something. I walk over and put my hand on her shoulder. "Of course, you may want to talk to the workers. I rode by your house on my way home, and it doesn't look like they are making much progress."

Marilyn's eyes plead with me to back off.

"You should have Logan stay on them," Mrs. Clover/Carter volunteers. "I never trust those contractors. They try to take advantage of elderly women, you know."

I leave them to their gossip and go check on Nicholas. He seems to have cooled off so I collapse beside him and stroke his face.

This is a lot to process. First, the fight with Christopher, the situation with Logan and now to find out that Marilyn's stay with us was an elaborate cover up. I'm surrounded by liars.

My eyes get heavy and I sink into the cushions. I wish I could rewind the day. Start over and still have Christopher as a friend, the illusion of a marriage and a mother-in-law that hadn't taken up permanent residence. The truth is overrated.

I'm awakened by Marilyn standing over me with her hands on her hips.

"What?" I look around to get my bearings. Nicholas has crawled onto my lap. I try to stretch without disturbing him.

"You heard me. What were you trying to do? Embarrass me in front on Eunice Carter? You know that woman is the biggest gossip in the church."

"Marilyn, you need to calm down. I don't know what you are talking about." I don't like her standing over me. I maneuver Nicholas's head and stand. Marilyn backs up.

"Asking questions about the house in front of that woman. No one knows we are selling the house."

"I didn't know either." I put my hands on my hips.

Marilyn sits. "It's nothing to worry about."

"What shouldn't I worry about?"

"Logan has everything under control. He went through a rough patch during the transition at the firm."

"What are you talking about?" I blow out a frustrated breath.

Marilyn fiddles with her skirt and avoids my stare. "Maybe I should put the baby to bed."

"Nicholas is fine. Please tell me what is going on."

Her face struggles to maintain a hard stance but then she takes a deep breath. She motions for me to sit.

"Logan was having some money issues," Marilyn explains. "He lost some clients when his father passed and then that man took most of the rest."

"What man?" I ask. Then I remember Logan complaining about his former partner. "Greg Atkins?"

Marilyn twists her lips as if she can't bring herself to say the man's name. "Yes, him. Spreading vicious lies around town." She mumbles something I can't make out.

"Are we broke?"

Marilyn shakes her head. "Of course not. My Logan has everything under control. He got a major client."

"Then why is your house for sale?"

"I needed to downsize. That house is too big for me to manage. We decided to sell it. I'll get a condo or something."

"And when did you two decide that?" I am starting to get angry all over again. I know Logan discusses everything with his mother, but now he is totally leaving me out of the conversation.

"Don't get upset," Marilyn says. "Logan didn't want you to worry."

"Really? I find that hard to believe. Besides, I've been telling him I could go back to work."

Marilyn cuts me off. "See, that's why he didn't tell you. You have to let a man be a man. He has to feel like he can provide for his family."

"It doesn't make him less of a man if I have a job."

"Logan wasn't raised like that. His father always took care of us, and Logan is expected to do the same." Marilyn sits back in the chair like she has proclaimed the eleventh commandment.

It's pointless to argue further. Logan is expected to take care of his mother, and I know I am the last person that can come between that.

Nicholas stirs beside me. I ask him if he had a good nap and he climbs in my lap.

"How's my grandbaby?" Marilyn reaches for Nicholas. "Are you ready to eat?"

I stand to follow them into the kitchen when Marilyn pauses. "Let's keep this conversation between us. Okay." Her eyes plead with me.

"Sure," I agree. "No need to stress out Logan."

She smiles confident that she has settled the situation. Nothing is settled in my mind. It's time to do a little investigating.

I wait until the light dims under Marilyn's door. Ten o'clock on the dot and the woman is out. Nicholas has been down since 8:30.

I enter Logan's office and switch on the light. The room is typical man cave complete with hardwood floors, dark mahogany desk and leather chair and sofa. One entire wall has built in bookcases and the other has a huge flat screen television. In keeping with appearances, Logan has a stocked wet bar. He claims it is to entertain clients, but he is the only one who drinks in here.

Maneuvering around the desk to avoid several boxes of Marilyn's things isn't easy. Seems as if the woman has taken up residence in every part of the house. I settle in front of the desktop computer and power it on. Logan likes to handle all of the finances but when I was sitting in the dark one afternoon because he had forgotten to mail the check for the electric bill, I made him show me all the accounts. I set up electronic payments for all the major bills. I hope he hasn't changed the passwords.

I log on the bank website and click on the past month's statement. My eyes widen at the numbers in front of me. We are broke. I can see that Logan has been doing some a lot of transferring but our savings has dwindled from a nice five figures. I pull up a few more months and see several deposits from Marilyn's account to our joint one. No wonder he moved his mother in with us. Logan has handled all of Marilyn's finances since his father passed. Did he spend all of his mother's money trying to maintain the firm and two households? And why wouldn't he ask for help?

I print out eight months worth of statements. I study those sheets like a junior accountant. There are several deposits from a foreign account showing deposits of varying amounts. Counting the deposit from today, I can guess that Logan is taking funds from his business account. The firm pays Logan a salary, and I'm no CPA but I know he shouldn't double dip.

Earlier today when Christopher insinuated Logan had billed him for work he didn't do, I was quick to jump to his defense. Factoring in Logan's weird behavior and it seems as if I was way off base. Christopher is right. I don't know my own husband.

That thought makes me shiver, and I rub my hands up and down my arms. I check the time and log off the computer. I gather the papers I printed and open the desk drawer to find a clip. What I find instead brings a smile to my face.

Logan and I had been dating for three months when he surprised me one day and picked me up from school. He already had our bags packed and drove us to the beach. We spent the weekend in a bed and breakfast with oceanfront views and homemade biscuits that would make you forget your diet. It was perfect. We played in the surf, went for walks exploring the surrounding neighborhood, and made love all night. Our last night there, we were relaxing in the parlor. I was reading a book and Logan was sitting at the desk across from me doodling in a drawing pad he found. The man had a real talent that he considered a hobby. I looked up when he slid a drawing on top of the pages I was reading. It was something out of a comic book. It showed Logan as a super hero complete with huge muscles and a cape. He was flying after having rescued me from some unseen danger. When I looked at him he was on one knee in front of me with a ring.

"Let me take care of you forever," he said. "Marry me?"

The most overwhelming emotion, greater than the love I felt for him in that moment, was relief. Relief that I didn't have to carry the burden anymore. Maybe in letting someone rescue me, I lost myself.

I take the picture upstairs with me and check on Nicholas. I tuck the papers in my nightstand drawer and get ready for bed. Once I am settled under the covers I return a call to Kim. I fill her in on the fight with Christopher.

"Are you sure you want to end things like that? That man loves you," Kim says.

"Maybe, but I am married. Everybody seems to forget that." Including me, I think.

I hurry to end the call with Kim telling her we'll talk more tomorrow. I focus on Logan's picture. It is best I don't see Christopher anymore. That situation is too much temptation because I will always be attracted to the man.

My husband is a different matter. Maybe I didn't see what I thought I saw. I'm going to give him a chance to explain things. He rescued me once. Maybe he can prove to be that man again.

CHAPTER TWENTY FIVE

ADRIENNE

I hear Logan tip into the room. It is dark so I listen as he goes into the bathroom and shuts the door. The time illuminates from my alarm clock, 12:46 a.m. I turn on the lamp and sit up.

Logan walks out in a pair of white boxer shorts, a blue t-shirt and a look of surprise that is priceless.

"Sorry, babe," he stammers. "Didn't mean to wake you."

"Where were you?"

"What?" He looks at his feet as if they are glued to the floor. "I told you I was working late."

"This is awfully late. Don't you think?"

Logan remembers how to walk and crosses the room. He pulls back the cover and gets in bed turning his back to me. "Can we do this later? I have another long day tomorrow."

My good intentions evaporate as anger surges through me. I've been waiting all night to talk to him, and he dismisses me.

"Are you having an affair?" I ask. When he doesn't respond, I push him in the back. "Answer me."

Logan turns to me. "Woman, what is wrong with you?"

"It's a simple question, Logan. Are you having an affair?" I hold my breath waiting on his response. I want to hear him deny it.

"Don't be ridiculous. I was working, okay? Working hard for our family."

I cross my arms. I need an answer that is better than his standard line about work. Logan sees that I am not satisfied so he sits up. "Since this is something that is keeping me from getting to sleep I'll play along. Who am I having an affair with?"

"Sheila."

Logan's eyes widen, but he composes himself making me wonder if I imagined the reaction.

"What would make you think that? She's my secretary. I would…I mean…I wouldn't," Logan rambles. "Is this about earlier today? There is nothing going on with that woman." He raises a hand. "I swear on everything. I wouldn't do that to you. To us. Maybe you need to get some rest because you are talking crazy."

"I'm crazy now, huh?"

"Yes, you are. My mother would have a fit if I messed with a white woman." He laughs and pulls me down beside him. He kisses my fore-head. "Now get some sleep."

I push away from him. "It's about your mother having a fit. What about your wife?"

"You know what I mean. I love you and only you, babe. Don't you trust me? Even though you haven't been giving me any. Nothing's going on. If Sheila is a problem, I'll get rid of her."

I raise my eyebrows. "Get rid of her how?"

"I'll hire someone else. I plan to expand the staff anyway. I can let her go, if it will make you feel better."

Logan pats my leg and takes a deep breath. He turns on his side. I want to let it go, but I can't.

"I need to tell you something," I whisper.

Logan's eyes are closed, and his breathing has slowed. "What?"

"I know you are selling Marilyn's house, and I want to help with our finances."

Logan rolls over on his back. "How did you find out?"

"I rode by there today. Saw the sign in the yard. Why didn't you tell me?"

"Nothing to tell. The house got to be too much for Mom to handle. We decided to sell it, and we'll get her something smaller."

"See, that's the whole problem in our marriage. You don't talk to me. Why the whole charade about her moving here being temporary for renovations? I can understand you helping your mother. And besides, if we are having money problems, I can get a job."

"Are you trying to say I can't support my family?"

"No. I am saying I can help."

Logan is getting worked up. He kicks off the covers and tries to stand but the sheets get tangled. "How many times do I have to tell you I can handle things? I am handling things."

"I know you are handling things. Look…" I reach for the picture to show him. I want to explain that I want to rescue him back. "Remember when you gave me this?"

Logan snatches the picture from me. "Where did you get this?" He doesn't give me a chance to respond.

"This is about this afternoon, right? There is nothing for you to worry about. I forgot to transfer some money into our account."

"But where did that money come from?"

He studies my face for a second. "I transferred money from the business account."

"Can you do that?"

He nods. "It's my company."

"Okay, but I still want to help. Like in that picture."

Logan considers the picture in his hand and then rips it into two pieces. "Child's play. This doesn't put food on the table or pay the bills. Now drop it and cut off that damn light so I can get some sleep."

I stare at him like he has two heads. He takes my hand and kisses it. "I'm sorry, okay. About everything. But I'll fix it. Can I please get some sleep now?"

I turn off the light, but it's a long time before I fall asleep.

CHAPTER TWENTY SIX

ADRIENNE

Nothing changes over the next few weeks. Nicholas continues to enjoy school. Thankfully, we haven't had any crises to speak of. Marilyn continues to take over my kitchen. And Logan continues to work late, though it's not every day. I take a job as a substitute teacher. I will be starting the next semester at Harrison Hall. But when I told Logan about my employment, he stopped talking to me.

Not that he was home much to have any interaction with me. Nicholas saw his dad on the weekends, and those were brief encounters at best. Logan would eat breakfast with his son and Marilyn and then disappear for most of the day. It was either golfing with a client or schmoozing at the club. On Sundays, he would take Marilyn to church and then stay holed up in his office. A visit from Nicholas or me was not appreciated.

This particular Sunday, I am trying to drown my thoughts in bad acting dramas on television. Nicholas and I are sprawled across my bed. When he falls asleep watching Nickelodeon, I switch to a movie. The women on the screen are getting more action than me.

The phone rings and I am glad for the distraction before the pity party can set in.

"Hey, sister," I say. "How was your date?"

"Great. I'm just getting in from it."

"You didn't?"

Kim laughs. "Yes, I did. Spencer has potential. We did the dinner thing and hit up a couple of clubs for drinks and dancing. Then it was back to his place for dessert."

"You nasty," I tease.

"Not nasty. Single and free. You know you wish you were me."

"No way. And be considered a fast tail like you."

Kim laughs loud at that one. "I haven't been called a fast tail since we moved out of Uncle Raymond's house. Aunt Joyce was quick to call somebody fast."

"All you had to do was mention a boy's name and she started preaching."

"It's a wonder we even like men the way she went on. Although, I wonder about Monica sometimes."

Kim never misses an opportunity to tease our cousin Monica. Those two never got along. Monica didn't welcome us into her only child family, and she especially resented Kim who was younger.

"Nobody paid Joyce any mind. As much as she and Uncle Raymond got off. Those walls were thin, and she was loud."

"Ugh. Don't remind me. I couldn't believe Monica always slept through that."

I stop the laugh that tickles the back of my throat. "That's because she was at home. I always felt like a visitor."

"Me too," Kim adds.

"You know when I miss our parents the most?"

"When you need some advice?"

"No, when things are going well." I stroke Nicholas's face. "I miss not being able to share good things with them. Like their grandson."

"You know Dad would have spoiled him rotten. Finally, another man in the house."

"And Mom would have been so proud of you," I say. "Independent businesswoman."

"She would have been prouder of you. You took care of me and got that degree. You know how to handle your business."

"Yeah, well, what happened to that woman?"

Kim knows the conversation has changed from our parents to the state of my marriage.

"Brother-in-law still tripping, huh?"

"If by tripping you mean still not speaking to me then the answer is yes."

"He is serious about you not working."

"The man told his mother like always. Marilyn tried to convince me to quit because I didn't need to challenge my husband's authority. She was preaching some 1960's mess."

"Marilyn is definitely old school."

"But I'm not trying to hear that. I never asked Logan to be my savior."

Kim pauses before she says, "In a way, you kinda did."

"What are you talking about?"

"Why did you marry Logan? I mean, he seemed like a decent guy, but you jumped into a relationship so soon after Christopher, and the next thing I know we are planning a wedding."

"He made me feel safe." The realization hits me like a body blow. Is that enough to base a marriage on?

"You thought he wouldn't leave like Christopher?"

"Christopher left. Mom and dad left."

"You can't blame our parents. It wasn't intentional."

"I know that, Kim. I'm not crazy. But it left a void. And then with Christopher."

"He says that is his only regret."

I sit up. "When did you talk to him?

"The other day. I ran into him at the mall."

"And you are just now telling me." I thought Christopher would call after our fight, but he didn't. I picked up the phone to call him a few times. But I figured it was for the best that we didn't speak.

"Thought you were done with him, remember? I am married, you said."

"Shut up and tell me what he said. Did he ask about me?"

"That's all he talked about. He wanted to know if you were okay. Were you happy? That man loves you, girl."

I smile and bask in the warmth of that knowledge. Hold it close.

"Oh, and I met his daughter. She is adorable," Kim says.

"I bet."

"He said he had her for the weekend. He is fighting for custody."

I remember the situation with his ex-wife. I should be helping him through that. Strictly as a friend, of course, I tell myself. "I know how bad he wanted to spend time with Mya," I say. I pump Kim for more information. How did he look? What else did he say?

"Do you think I should call him?" I ask. "We could still be friends?"

"The type of friends that hang out with you and your husband?"

I groan. That would never work. Logan would pick up on the attraction between us immediately. And there is the fact that I never told him about our history.

I answer my own questions. "I guess not."

"Sister, I know Christopher loves you. And you still love him. But the timing is all wrong."

I agree.

"But let me say this, I don't know how much longer Christopher will be single. The women at the mall were checking him out. A good-looking man taking care of his kid. And he's rich. That's sexy as hell to a lot of women."

Kim and I talk a few more minutes. We make plans to get together soon. Nicholas needs to visit his favorite aunt. When we hang up my thoughts return to Christopher. What if he meets someone else? Of course, I would be happy for him. I want him to be happy. And I need to find my own happiness.

I go in search of my husband. He is sequestered in his study. The door is ajar and I hear Logan raise his voice.

"They can't tell me how to run my business."

My hand is posed to knock, but I wait to hear more.

"What are they accusing me of? Who is behind it? Is it Greg? He's been bad mouthing me ever since he left."

And then I hear, "You're right he's jealous. I brought in more influential clients than my father ever dreamed. I grew the Rutherford name."

I roll my eyes. Still competing with a dead man.

"I need your help on this," he says into the phone. "I know I can count on you."

His voice lowers and I lean in closer. I am hoping to hear a name so I'll know who he is talking to.

"You shouldn't eavesdrop," I hear from behind and jump. Marilyn stands there holding a dishtowel. I am caught so I stand there defiant. She looks as if she is about to challenge me and then her stance relaxes. She looks from me to the closed door. Marilyn lives here so I'm sure she has sensed the tension between Logan and me. Or maybe she remembers a similar situation with Logan Sr.

"You shouldn't eavesdrop," she says. "Because you may hear something you don't want to know."

Before I can respond, she turns and walks back into the kitchen. Marilyn's advice is sound, but I need to know what is going on. I open the door without knocking. Logan is smiling into his cell phone, but when he sees me he ends the call without another word.

"Am I disturbing you?" I ask.

His phone immediately starts buzzing. "No," he stammers. "What's up?"

"We need to talk," I say.

"The phrase no man wants to hear," he jokes.

I sit in the chair in front of his desk, which is littered with files and legal documents. Logan still has on the suit he wore to church earlier. His jacket is thrown across the couch and his shirt sleeves are rolled up. His phone begins to vibrate again.

"Do you need to get that?" I ask.

He glances at the screen and turns it off. "Nothing important. What do you want to talk about?"

"Us. What is going on with us?"

Logan picks up a drink I didn't notice he had and takes a swallow.

"I know you were upset when I took the job, but can't you see I did it to help us? You don't have to shoulder the financial burdens for this family alone. I'm not the enemy here."

At the mention of the job, Logan stiffens and takes another gulp of drink.

"You're right," he says. His eyes soften, "I've been stressed out at work and taking it out on you. I know you mean well."

It's the closest thing to an apology I'll get. I raise my eyebrows and Logan laughs. A sound I haven't heard in ages.

"I know you're doubtful. But I agree that you having your own spending money is a good thing. I'm still paying all the bills. You can depend on me."

I see him struggling to make peace with it and still come out as the man in control. Logan finishes his drink and comes around to the desk to kneel in front of my chair.

"I can make it right," he says. "I can fix us."

This is the Logan I fell in love with. The sweet vulnerable man that feels he must prove how tough he is to the world, the man competing with his father in a one-sided race. Logan takes my hands and kisses them. His eyes ask for permission. I take his face in my hands and kiss him.

Logan hungrily kisses me back. He sucks my tongue with such need that it takes my breath away. His hands are everywhere, but when he lifts my shirt I stop him. Images of the last time we were together threaten to ruin our reunion.

"Please," Logan whispers the word. "Please, Adrienne." A plea for atonement.

I stand and lead him to the couch. Undress for him as he watches. Logan sheds his clothes and touches me like it is the first time. He slows it down and we explore each other bodies. Reacquaint ourselves with familiar territory.

Logan pauses above me. He tells me he loves me. "I'll give you anything," he says.

And I think, this is the man I chose. He is not perfect, but he is my husband. He is the one that didn't leave me.

I open wide and pull him in. With each thrust, I give it right back to him. It has been so long that my body is on fire. I push away thoughts of Christopher and suppress suspicions of infidelity and grip my husband tighter. He moans my name and moves faster. I pull him even closer. Lock my legs around him with reckless desire. I reach the peak in a heartbeat and take Logan along with me. The release is a cocktail of pleasure and promise. We stay attached like that until each spasm has run its course. Until all that is left is a tangle of limbs and sweat drenched skin.

Wow," Logan says after a moment to catch his breath. "That was intense."

"Well, it has been awhile," I squirm underneath him.

He rises on his elbows. "I guess it has been. I almost forgot how good you feel. Damn, woman, you got the good stuff."

I smile at the compliment, but a nagging thought wonders if he is comparing me to someone else.

"I need to go check on Nicholas," I say and try to sit up.

"Don't worry," Logan doesn't move. "Mom will hear him if he needs anything."

"I should still go check," I say.

Logan moves against me. "I got you back. Can I have some more time before you start worrying?"

I am about to protest when he whispers, "I need you too."

I no longer resist. If I want to get us back on track, I have to focus on him. I get Logan to sit up and straddle him. I ride him with fervor until he calls out my name. I sing his name in response. We take turns whispering words of passion and promises of love until another orgasm erupts. I hold my husband tight and convince myself that we will be okay.

CHAPTER TWENTY SEVEN

CHRISTOPHER

I think I've lost her. For good this time. Maybe I was wrong to come back here. I'm not sure what I thought would happen. I would show up and Adrienne would run into my arms, happy to see me after all these years. That she would leave her unhappy marriage and we would live happily ever after like a damn fairy tale. What a joke.

I overplayed my hand and went too far. Things were going great. We were rebuilding our friendship. I could feel her letting her guard down. And then we kissed.

I could sense she wanted me as much as I wanted her. We were in the hallway headed to the bedroom. All I could think about was my need. I wanted to make love to the woman that is the beat in my heart. But she couldn't do it. She isn't a cheater.

Her husband is one though. I've dealt with lawyers for years. I know there is some padding in almost every bill, but Logan is excessive. I've delayed dealing with it because of Adrienne. I don't want to hurt her by suing him.

It's my fault she's even married to him. I left her out in the world unprotected. I thought I was doing the right thing letting her go. I didn't want her in the middle of my mess with Lisa. It was my mistake. I'll have to deal with the consequences alone.

"Daddy," Mya calls.

"Coming." I put the finishing touches on our lunch of grilled cheese and orange slices. I pour a cup of milk and a glass of iced tea. I put everything on a tray and enter Mya's room.

"Finally," she says. "We're starving." Arranged around the table are a teddy bear, Minnie Mouse and a Barbie doll missing an arm and a chunk of hair. I love teatime with Mya.

My baby is no mistake. She was meant to be here no matter the heartache. "Tea is served, my ladies."

I have Mya for the weekend, so I am in full daddy mode. We eat our lunch and gossip about the happenings in first grade. She likes her teacher but not the gross boy she sits beside. We play a quick game of Uno. After that, she picks out a Disney movie with a princess. I sleep through most of it with Mya curled next to me on the couch.

Later, I cook dinner and then we go for a walk around my development. I buy Mya some outfits to keep at my place and we get ice cream for dessert. I run Mya a bath, tuck her in bed and read her two bedtime stories.

"Love you, Daddy," Mya says and snuggles under the covers.

"Love you back, Mya Papaya." I kiss her forehead and cut off the light.

I've had a great day with my daughter.

I lay in the bed at night happy but incomplete. My thoughts return to Adrienne. I'll never get over that woman. I thought I could live my life without her, but I was wrong. I need her in my life and I'll take her anyway I can. I tried calling her tonight but it rings straight to voicemail. I know I should fall back but I can't control myself. If all I can get is the sound of her voice, then I'll take it. If being married to Logan makes her happy, then I'll celebrate with her. Respect her marriage. For now. Logan is a bigger fool than I was. He'll make an unforgiveable mistake. And I'll be that safe place where she can land. I've waited four years. I can wait a little longer.

ADRIENNE

Logan sits at the head of the table holding court. His mother waits on him. She is ecstatic that he has made it home for dinner the last two weeks. Marilyn's meals get more elaborate as she tries to please him. Tonight, she has prepared lobster tails, salmon with a sweet and sour glaze, baked red potatoes and broccoli. There is another workday in this week. I wonder how she can top this meal.

"Mom, you have outdone yourself." Logan wipes his mouth with a napkin, his linen napkin. I didn't know I had linen napkins, but Marilyn dug them out.

"Someone has to prepare the meals around here," she says and cuts her eyes at me. "Since both of you work, I mean."

I don't respond. I continue to eat my salmon. It's good. If Marilyn wasn't being such a witch, I would tell her so.

"Well, we both appreciate having you here to help us out," Logan says and winks at me. I wink back.

Things have been good between us. Logan makes it home for dinner, no more working late. We are talking again, and we make love every night. Things are so good I'm afraid something will implode at any minute.

"Good new, ladies," Logan says. "I signed a new client today. Got the Dingle Brothers, Inc."

Logan has been talking about these guys for the last week. The Dingle Brothers are a pair of twins that played college football at the local university. After graduation, when the NFL didn't pan out, they opened the first of several businesses. They now own a restaurant, several fast-food franchises and a movie theater. The local news mentioned they were purchasing a strip mall to revitalize the downtown area. According to Logan, they are major players.

"That's great," I put my hand over his.

He pushes his empty plate to the side. "Thanks for fine-tuning my proposal. I think that helped seal the deal."

Marilyn looks back and forth between me and Logan. "I think it was your hard work, Logan, networking at the club. I knew good things would happen for you. Your father would be proud."

Logan slides his hand from mine. "You're right, Mom. The Brothers heard about how I negotiated that Michaels deal and knew they had to call me."

"That's right, dear. Now we have something else to celebrate."

"Something else?" I ask.

"We have a buyer for the house," Marilyn proclaims. She misses the look on Logan's face. I don't. Still telling Mommy everything, I see. I give Logan a questioning look.

He clears his throat. "The paperwork was completed this afternoon."

Marilyn nods. "I am sad to see it change hands. Are the buyers a good Christian family?"

"I don't know about their religion. I know their money is green." Logan and his mother banter back and forth.

This is good news, but it serves to make me more apprehensive. I tune them out and turn to Nicholas. He has eaten a few potatoes and is picking the fish apart with his fingers.

"Come on and eat some vegetables," I coax. Nicholas scrunches up his face and turns away from my fork.

"No, Mommy," he says. "No veggie tales."

"Just a little bit."

He shakes his head and crosses his arms. I lose all patience. "Nicholas, you are going to eat your broccoli."

His eyes widen at my tone, but he shakes his head again. "Don't want it."

"You are going to sit there until you eat some," I say. Potatoes are not enough fuel for his body.

"How about if Grandma puts some cheese on it," Marilyn is already at the refrigerator before I can protest.

"How about if you cook a meal a three-year-old would actually eat?" The words are out of my mouth before I can stop them.

Marilyn turns from the microwave and looks as if I slapped her. She clutches her chest in shock. "How dare you speak to me like that?"

Logan pipes in. "Adrienne, what is wrong with you?"

I throw up my hands in surrender. "Sorry."

Marilyn puts the melted cheese over Nicholas's broccoli. Of course, he smiles and eats it. Marilyn returns to her seat with a smug look on her face. I excuse myself and escape to the bathroom. I splash water on my face and look in the mirror. I have good news to share too, but I can't tell anyone. I dealt with Christopher and declared my full commitment to my marriage. Logan and Marilyn would be proud.

I had been avoiding Christopher's calls for weeks. Today, I called and asked him to meet me outside of Nicholas's school. Kim's house holds too many memories and would make this harder.

"Ms. Adrienne, how are you doing?" he asked after parking his car beside mine and walking around to the driver's side door.

"I'm fine." My words were clipped and direct.

"I know that. But how are you doing?"

I don't fall for his clumsy attempt at humor. Or linger on his face. "You kept calling me. What do you want?"

"I see you are still upset with me. I wanted to apologize again."

"Okay."

"Okay? Is that it? Is something the matter?" He asked.

I take a deep breath. "What do you want, Christopher?"

"Damn, baby. Why so cold? I thought we were friends."

I chanced a glance. "Friends? You know good and well we can't be friends. We have too much history." A parent walks in front of my vehicle and waves. I wave back but couldn't manage a smile. She looks puzzled but turns into the building.

"I know I love you, Adrienne," Christopher said. "I've never stopped and as much as I tried to turn that shit off, it won't go anywhere."

I forced myself to deliver the next blow. "That's not my problem."

"What?"

"You come back to me after all this time expecting a relationship. Am I supposed to welcome you back and forget I'm married?"

"No."

I ignored him and continued before I lose my nerve. "Or is this some sick game between you and Logan? You get me caught up in an affair and show everyone you are the better man."

"Adrienne, stop. Where's all this coming from?"

I hear the hurt in his voice, but I pushed ahead. Christopher is my past. Logan is my present and future. I had to fully invest in my marriage to make it work.

"Stop, Christopher," I said. "Stop calling me. Stop telling me you love me. Stop trying to have a friendship with me. I need you to stop."

He put his hands in his pockets and stepped away from the door. When he spoke, his voice was so low I strained to hear.

"Ol' boy is lucky. Hope he doesn't mess it up like I did. I'll back off, okay?"

"Good."

"Remember one thing. If you need help with anything, you have my number. And you know where I am. I'm not leaving this time." I watched him walk back to his vehicle and drive away.

I head back to the kitchen and pass Logan on the way to his study.

"Are we okay?" he asks.

"Sure."

Logan hugs my waist. "I won't be long." He nods toward his office.

I say okay and try to continue on, but Logan pulls me close and kisses me. "Maybe we can work on making that baby tonight."

He has been dropping hints all week so I shouldn't be surprised. "Maybe," I say and kiss him back.

I walk into the kitchen and see that Nicholas still hasn't eaten his food. All he has done is smear cheese all over his face and hands. Marilyn is clearing the table.

"Need help with anything?" I ask, already knowing the answer. Marilyn has taken over the kitchen to the extent that I no longer know where the dishes belong. The other day I went to the cabinet for a glass and the woman had moved them.

"Thank you, but I have it," she says. She starts running water in the sink.

"Why don't you use the dishwasher?" I point to the square door I haven't seen her touch once.

"Dishes should be washed by hand. How else will they get clean?"

"It will save time," I point out.

Marilyn shakes her head. "Young women are always in a rush." She puts the dishes in the sudsy water and starts humming.

I turn to Nicholas. "Let's get you into the tub."

Bath time with Nicholas is one of our special times. Since he is now in school all day, I look forward to our one-on-one time. Usually, I sit and watch him play with his toys and we talk about his day. When I announce the soak is over, Nicholas will grab the washcloth and wash himself. He'll take the soap and lather up his stomach until there is a layer of white covering it, proclaiming that he is clean. We have been working on him washing other areas too.

Tonight, Nicholas is quiet. I ask what he did at school today.

"I colored. I drew a picture of you, Mommy." He pushes a toy boat in a circle.

"You did? I can't wait to see it."

I try to get more out of him, but he nods or shakes his head to my questions about his teacher and his buddy, Parker. Something isn't right and I find out what it is when I tell him the soak is over. He barely stands before he cries out.

"Mommy, leg hurt," he says.

"Are your Spidey senses tingling?" I ask.

Nicholas nods. This is my fault. While I was distracted, the monster has returned to attack my son. I wash Nicholas and scoop him into my arms, wrapping the towel around him like a cocoon. I retrieve his pain medicine from the cabinet. Nicholas takes a dose without a word. I carry him to his room and dress him in pajamas.

"Here, baby. Drink some of your water." I keep a water bottle by his bed. He probably didn't get enough fluids today. I know he didn't at dinner. Nicholas takes a couple of sips. I tuck him in and crawl in beside him, stroking his forehead as I check for fever. A fever would mean an infection and a trip to the emergency room. I am hoping to avoid that and decide to call Dr. Payne in the morning.

The medicine makes Nicholas sleepy, but I stay with him and massage his leg until he dozes off. I sit there awhile longer and watch him sleep. My entire world rests along with my son. And I bargain with God. I would give up everything as long as Nicholas is okay.

I head to my room to take a shower. Logan stands at the sink, skin still moist from his shower.

"There you are," he says and smiles with a mouth full of toothpaste.

"Nicholas had a pain episode," I tell him. "I'm going to keep him at home tomorrow." Good thing I don't have a substitute assignment.

I shrug off my clothes and get in the shower. No time for a soak tonight. When I step out, Logan is still at the sink. He leans against it clothed in a pair of boxers, holding a single rose is in one hand and my pack of birth control pills in the other.

Before I can ask a question, he says, "I think we should celebrate."

I turn away from him and towel off. "Celebrate what?"

"The good life."

I look at Logan like he has bumped his head and lost all good sense. He shakes my pill compact and tosses it in the trash.

"I think we should have another baby."

I put my hands on my hips. "What?"

Logan presents the flower as a peace offering. "It's time we work on having a baby." He tries to kiss me and I move away.

"I don't think now is a good time."

"It's the perfect time. Business is picking up. Mother's house just sold. Money shouldn't be an issue. You can stay at home again."

"Is that what this is all about? You want me to stay at home."

"No. I mean…you would have to stay at home with the baby. But, it would be okay because your husband is the man."

I don't comment. He thinks this is a good thing. I can tell by the tent in his shorts.

"Did you and your mother discuss this? Did she tell you she wanted another grandchild?" I take satisfaction in watching him deflate.

"That is not fair. Mother is not the issue."

"Okay, but there is the issue of having another sick baby. Didn't you hear what I said? Nicholas had another pain episode."

"We won't have another sick baby."

"How can you say that to me? I've done the research. The percentage of us having a baby with sickle cell is 25%. We both have the trait, remember? Even if the baby doesn't have the disease, she or he will still have the trait. I don't want to take that chance."

Logan remembers the flower in his hand and put it on the counter. "Won't happen."

I can't believe his arrogance on this issue. I know he thinks he is "the man" but even he can't beat science. I dry off and walk to the dresser for a pair of pajamas. Logan follows pleading his case.

I whirl around. "Why are you so set on having another child? You weren't exactly thrilled when I told you about Nicholas."

He is caught off guard. "What?"

I remind him of the things he said. The words imprinted on my heart like a brand. The sense of abandonment still fresh.

"How could you,' you said. When I told you I was pregnant, that's what you said." The tears threaten to come, but I hold them back.

"I didn't," Logan begins.

"You took something that was special and good and threw it back in my face before you walked out. The entire nine months you treated me like I was a stranger instead of your wife. Did you go to one doctor visit?"

Before he can answer, I continue. "No, you didn't. And let's talk about the here and now. I told you Nicholas was sick. Did you even go check on him? Did you even think to go tell your son good night?"

I go back into the bathroom and retrieve my pills from the trash. "I don't know why you want another baby. You don't want the one you already have."

Logan stands there with his mouth open. I take pleasure in rendering the great debater mute. The thought of sharing a bed with Logan at this moment is sickening. I put on my slippers and grab my robe. I'll go bunk with Nicholas. I walk past Logan, and he growls, "You selfish bitch."

I stumble. Logan is so close I feel his breath on my neck. He grabs my arm and repeats it. "You selfish bitch."

And the real Logan is back. I face his venom head on. "How am I the selfish one? Because I would rather take care of the child I already have instead of bringing another one into the world?"

"Why do you get to decide this in a vacuum? I've given you every-thing. Why can't you give me this?" He looks more confused than angry.

"Everything?" My voice softens. "I appreciate how hard you work for this family. I do. But all of this," I indicate the house, cars, the jewelry. "I never asked for it. That was all about you."

Logan squeezes my arm. "I've given you everything." His eyes bore into mine like lasers, and I wince in pain.

The verdict is in. This man is crazy.

"Logan," I say. "You are hurting me."

He gathers himself and steps back. "I'm sorry. I'm sorry, okay."

I massage my arm. Logan sits on the edge of our bed and hangs his head. I start to say something. Offer him forgiveness or give him hope that one day we can try to have a baby. But then I realize, I'm the crazy one. I need to stop giving in to this man. I have nothing to feel guilty about.

"Don't leave me."

The words are spoken softly. I stop at the door. Logan repeats it. Three words that convey all the pain I carry around like a backpack.

"Don't leave me," Logan looks up with red tinged eyes.

I go to him and envelop his head into my chest. He clutches me.

"I'm going to check on Nicholas, okay." I rub his back.

"I need you too," he says. But Nicholas needs me more. Is he asking me to choose? I try to step away, but he continues to hold on as if he'll lose me forever.

"I'll be right back," I say. He nods but doesn't release me. I am starting to lose patience when I am saved by the bell. Logan's cell phone buzzes and skims across the nightstand where it is charging.

"Are you going to get that?" I ask. I look at the clock. It is late for a business call. Logan reaches for it and hits ignore after a quick glance at the number. It starts humming again.

I step back. "Maybe it's important."

"No, not important." Logan powers off the phone. "Not more important than this."

He sits on the bed and stares at me.

"What do you want from me?" I sigh.

Logan clears his throat. "Things have been so good between us lately. I know before things were tense, but the last few weeks have been good, right?"

I nod.

He continues, "I want us…" The house phone interrupts Logan.

"Who could that be?" I ask and walk toward the phone on my side of the bed.

Logan lunges across the bed to grab it. "What is it?"

This does sound important. I stand there with my arms crossed watching him.

"Why are you calling at this hour? I asked you to respect my family time." Whatever the person says on the other end causes Logan to turn his back to me.

"Are you sure?" he asks.

Enough of the mystery, I walk over to Logan and touch his shoulder. "Who is that?"

He covers the mouthpiece with one hand. "Don't you need to check on Nicholas?"

I raise an eyebrow. It's like that now. I do need to check on my baby, but I'm not going anywhere. I walk toward the door but stop there.

Logan still has his back turned and lowers his voice. I can barely make out the words until he sits on the bed. "Can we talk about this tomorrow? You know why. Listen, you need to be reasonable."

He senses me behind him and turns. "I have to go," he snaps and hangs up the phone.

"Who was that?" I ask and go to stand over him.

He walks pass me without a word and goes into the bathroom. I check the caller id. It says private. I still have the phone in my hand when Logan walks back out.

"What are you doing?"

"Trying to find out who is calling my house this time of night."

Logan takes the phone out of my hand. "That was Sheila."

"Sheila? Why is she calling here?"

Logan pulls the covers back on his side of the bed. "She had some business to discuss."

The suspicions of an affair return. "What kind of business could she want to discuss that couldn't wait? I thought she wasn't an issue."

Logan gets in the bed and reaches for me. "Nothing, babe. Come here."

I shake my head. "What is going on with you and that woman?"

"Don't start that again. She works for me. She's worked with me for years."

"Then tell me what she wanted."

He reaches for me again. "Come here."

"No." I walk out and check on Nicholas. I feel his forehead, rearrange the covers that he has kicked off and kiss his face. The pain medicine should let him sleep comfortably through the night.

I go back in the room and ignore Logan. I get in the bed and show Logan my back.

"Alright, babe. Here is the deal. Sheila called to tell me some news she found out." Logan clears his throat. "I'm being sued by one of my clients."

I turn to face him. "What?"

"Yeah, one of my clients is suing me. Said I didn't represent him well and charged for services I didn't provide. It's all bogus."

I immediately think of Christopher. He was complaining about Logan. Would he sue him to get back at me? "Do you know who it is?"

He shakes his head. "Doesn't matter because it's not true. The charges won't stick."

"What are you going to do?"

He shrugs. "Make love to my wife if she stops talking and kisses me."

I push his hand away. "You aren't worried? What if you lose your license?"

"Not going to happen, babe." He rubs my arm. "Good to know you care though."

"Of course, I care, Logan."

"Sometimes I wonder," he says and smiles. There is a touch of sadness in his eyes.

"Is there something else going on?" I ask.

He shakes his head and pulls me closer. His hands stroke my body. He kisses me so tenderly that all my resistance melts away.

"I love you so much," Logan says. "Promise you'll always remember that."

I promise and wonder why my husband holds me as if it will be the last time.

CHAPTER TWENTY NINE

ADRIENNE

"Okay, kiddo," Dr. Payne says. "You did a good job today." Nicholas manages a smile. He looks so small sitting in the middle of the examination table.

"Mom, you get your little web slinger dressed, and we'll talk in my office." Dr. Payne washes her hands and leaves the room. I help Nicholas slip back into his shirt, and we walk down the hall to the office.

The bright fluorescent décor on the walls is made to disguise the nature of the business here. Sick children. I wonder if the colorful rainbows, puppies and a mural of a playground scene help parents cope with the unimaginable. None of it is working on me today. Even the antiseptic smell of the place seems to be an overpowering presence. The smell of dread clogs my nostril. I know that Nicholas's diagnosis will not be a good one.

Dr. Payne is scribbling in a chart when we come to the door. She removes her glasses and stands.

"Come on in. Look what Dr. P has for you today." She takes Nicholas's hand and escorts him over to a nook in her office. She has a little play area furnished with children's books, a toy chest and oversized pillows. She hands Nicholas a new action figure. His eyes light up. Dr. Payne sits with Nicholas for a minute and makes sure he is comfortable. She gets him a juice box from the dorm size fridge and returns to her desk.

"Now, Momma. Tell me how you are doing?"

I'm exhausted. I couldn't sleep last night. After Logan was snoring, I went back to Nicholas's room. He was sound asleep, but I sat there watching him. My thoughts were a jumble of emotions between worrying about Nicholas and wondering about Logan.

"I'm doing fine. How is Nicholas?"

Dr. Payne raises an eyebrow but is kind enough not to call me a liar. She puts on her glasses and reads Nicholas's chart.

"I'm concerned about his low blood count. We ran the usual full labs and Nicholas is anemic. His hemoglobin is in the moderate borderline to severe range. That explains the frequency of the last few crises you called me about. You said he hasn't been as active?"

I nod. Nicholas has been usually quiet and tired the last few days. His teacher remarked that Nicholas didn't participate in playtime yesterday.

Dr. Payne removes her glasses and looks at me. "I suggest we do another blood transfusion. It will raise the amount of normal hemoglobin in his blood. It will also decrease the chance of blockage or crises."

"Okay," I say. Anything that will decrease the odds of my baby going through the pain is a good thing. I know this is a temporary solution. This will be his third transfusion.

"We can schedule the procedure before you leave today. Like last time, it takes a few hours and Nicholas can go home feeling a lot better. We can do it here at the clinic or at the hospital, whichever you prefer."

"Sounds good. We can do it here."

Dr. Payne makes notes in Nicholas's chart. "How are his meds? Do you need any refills?"

"They're fine," I say.

Dr. Payne closes the file and sits beside me. "Have you thought any more about a bone marrow transplant?"

When Nicholas was diagnosed as a baby, Dr. Payne discussed our options. The bone marrow transplant seemed extreme for a baby. And

Nicholas was relatively crisis free for years. Now the events are becoming more frequent. Maybe it's time to explore this defense.

"We have had success with the procedure. In fact, I have two patients that came through it. Their labs show they are disease free."

"Isn't it hard to find a match?" I ask. I would donate today if my blood weren't the reason we are here in the first place.

"It can be. The National Marrow Donor Program lists more than six million donors. If this is something you're considering, it would be good to do it now. We have a greater success rate with young children whose organs haven't been damaged yet by the disease."

I feel a sense of relief I haven't experienced in years. This may be the answer to my prayers.

"The best match will come from a sibling. Have you considered having another baby?" Dr. Payne asks.

Has she been talking to Logan? I shake my head. "No. Wouldn't that child have sickle cell too?"

Dr. Payne knows our file. When Nicholas was diagnosed, I got tested here at the clinic immediately. When it showed I had the trait, I insisted Logan get tested.

"There is a chance the child might. But an infant sibling can donate cord blood rather than bone marrow. The umbilical cord is rich in stem cells and offers the best chance of a successful transplant and a cure."

"But I can't risk a pregnancy and find out that child has sickle cell too." Surely the good doctor is not suggesting I become a baby factory and keep reproducing in the hopes one child is disease free.

Dr. Payne smiles and goes over to a file cabinet. "No need for that. We could do genetic screening and in vitro fertilization instead. We would ensure the fetus is a disease free genetic match."

I turn toward Nicholas who is running a car back and forth in a small circle. I see a future of doctor's visits and pain wondering when the disease will strike again. And Dr. Payne is offering hope. My mind races with the possibilities. I imagine Nicholas disease free and the brother or sister that can save him.

Dr. Payne hands me the brochures and I want to hug her. "Now, this process can be expensive. A single cycle can be around $15,000 and it will probably take more than one cycle to get a genetic match. We could be talking in the neighborhood of $300,000 to $400,000 for everything. Some insurance plans cover some part of it."

I am no longer listening. The cost doesn't matter. We'll figure out a way to pay. I see a future for my son.

I get Nicholas settled in the car and call Logan. His cell phone and office line go straight to voice mail. Maybe Beatrice knows if Logan is in court this morning.

"Hi, Ms. B," I say when she answers. "This is Adrienne. Is Logan available?"

"Hello there. How's our little man doing today?"

I look in the rearview mirror at my son. "He is going to be fine."

"Now that's good to hear," she says. Mrs. Beatrice begins to ramble about her grown daughter. I think she lives in New York or some other big city. I interrupt her before she gets going.

"I can't reach Logan on his cell. Is he in court this morning?"

Beatrice hesitates. "No, baby. He came in this morning and left. Said he was taking a personal day."

"A personal day?" I repeat. Logan didn't mention anything to me last night. "Maybe Sheila knows. Is she in?"

"Humph. Little Miss Thing called in sick." Beatrice mumbles something that I think is Jezebel. I smile. She doesn't like her either. I knew something was going on with that woman.

I start the car and head to Kim's. Why are Logan and Sheila out of the office at the same time? Is this another coincidence or something more? I tell myself there is nothing going on. My husband is devoted to me. He wants to have another baby and that is the answer to my prayers for Nicholas.

I have to stop Beatrice's rant again. "You see everything that goes on at that law firm my father-in-law built."

I can see her sitting up straight. "That's right. I helped him build this practice up from having one client, me, after my Sherman died. You know Logan, Sr. handled the estate for me."

I've heard the story of how Logan, Sr. helped the young widow get back on her feet by offering her a job when the creditors her husband left behind wiped out all of their assets. I don't want to hear it again.

"Is everything okay there?" I ask. "Logan has been acting weird and working long hours."

"Baby, that boy is trying so hard to outdo his daddy that he is starting to lose his way. He is here all hours of the night. I try to talk to him, but he doesn't think an old secretary knows anything. He'll figure it out," she says. I hear the affection she has for Logan in her voice. She considers him a son since she has literally watched him grow up.

I hear several phones ring at once. "It was great talking to you, Adrienne. You bring that baby by to see me now. Let me get these phones. Bye, now."

I hang up the phone with even more questions. I try Logan's cell phone again but still no answer. Seems my answers will have to wait. Logan will have some explaining to do when he gets home.

"You're saying this could be a cure," Kim rocks Nicholas on her lap.

I look at my child curled up on his aunt's lap like the baby he is outgrowing. "Yes, he could have a chance at a normal childhood. No more transfusions, no more pain."

"That's great, Sister."

I nod in agreement. It is great.

Kim tilts her head. "But…I sense there is a but coming."

She knows me well. "I'm wondering how Logan will take the news."

"You haven't told him yet?"

"Tried to reach him but…"

"Let me guess. Brother-in-law is working and won't answer your call."

"Something like that. Supposedly, he's taking a personal day that he neglected to tell me about."

Kim stops rocking. "What does that mean?"

"I wish I knew." I bite back the urge to tell Kim what I feel is going on. I have my doubts, but if I tell Kim that I think Logan is having an affair with Sheila that will somehow make it real. If it's real, I'll have to deal with losing my husband. And I need him now to save my baby.

"He is under a lot of stress at work," I tell her. "Last night he said a client was suing him."

Kim looks alarmed. "A lawyer getting sued. For what?"

"Something about inadequate representation. Logan claims the client didn't like the outcome."

"Okay."

"And I told him I didn't want to have another baby."

"So, you think he is ignoring your call to punish you."

"At this point, I have no idea. All I know is that I must get my husband to agree to have a baby after I told him I didn't want one. I want a baby to save the child I already have. What kind of parent does that?"

Kim kisses the top of Nicholas's head. "A good one," she says. "A good, loving parent will do anything to save her child."

I hold on to Kim's statement as I go through the rest of the day. Nicholas and I run some errands and then return home. Marilyn has dinner ready, and we sit down to eat without Logan. By the time I give Nicholas a bath and put him to bed, Logan is still missing. He hasn't even returned a call to his mother. I don't know whether to be angry or worried.

Later that evening, I am sitting on the bed in complete "Al Green" mode when my cell phone rings. Thinking its Logan, I answer without checking the caller id.

"Where are you?"

"I didn't know you missed me," he laughs.

My anger dissipates to be replaced with something else. I turn down the CD player.

"I thought it was someone else," I stammer.

"Does that mean you don't miss me?" Christopher teases.

I don't bother to answer that question. "Why are you calling?"

"Damn, girl. Still mad at me I see," he says.

"I thought I made myself clear."

"Trust me you did. You're married. I get it. I come in peace, okay."

"Then what do you want," I say.

"I thought I would give you a courtesy call to see if you were cool with me coming over tomorrow."

Now, I am confused. "Why would you be coming over here?"

Christopher laughs. "That's what the invitation says. A drop-in for the Rutherford Law firm. A celebration of the employees and clients that helped make the business a success."

My silence spurs Christopher to continue.

"I mean it sounds like a nice event but if you aren't comfortable with me being there, I can RSVP my regrets."

"No, don't do that," I say. I don't want to hear Logan go on about being spurned for this event that he neglected to tell me about.

"Whew, for a minute there I thought you didn't want to see a brother."

"Don't get the wrong idea, playboy. You are a client." I refuse to admit I wouldn't mind seeing the man.

"That's okay, Ms. Adrienne. You can try to fight it, but I know you still got a thing for me."

"Whatever, man." I smile at his silliness.

"At least I have someone that still loves me. I can't wait for you to meet my date."

That statement makes my stomach clench. "Why would I want to meet your date?"

Christopher chuckles. "Because she is smart and cute. I think you'll like her."

I swallow the nasty retort and give myself a self-check. I have no right to be upset. "How long have you known her?"

"Almost five years."

Five years? Is this some old girlfriend he neglected to mention when he was confessing his undying love for me?

"Where did you two meet?" I ask.

"Believe or not, we met through my ex-wife."

Christopher seems amused by my questions, but I plow ahead trying to gauge how long this woman has been in the picture.

"Is it serious?"

"She has my heart, if that's what you want to know." Christopher tries to suppress his laughter but fails. He is laughing so hard he has to catch his breath.

"What the hell is so funny?" I ask.

"You are."

"You are bringing a date to my house, and I'm the one that's funny?"

"Are you jealous, Ms. Adrienne?"

I catch myself before a "Hell, yes" escapes and I embarrass myself. Instead I say, "Why should I be jealous? You are a single man free to do or see whoever you want to."

"Yeah, you're jealous," Christopher says. I can see his smug smirk through the phone.

"Whatever. Listen, I have to go."

"Don't hang up. You know you want to know my date's name?"

Why would I care? But I play along. I can show him that he has no effect on me at all. "Alright, tell me her name, Christopher."

"Mya."

The realization hits me. "As in your daughter, Mya Michaels?"

"The one and only," Christopher says. "I got my baby for the weekend."

He goes on to explain that he got his ex-wife to agree to regular weekend visitations, though he still plans to seek full custody.

"Sounds as if things are working out. I'm happy for you," I say. I know how much it means to him to have his daughter. A father's love is important for little girls. And little boys.

"Seems that way. Too bad my love life isn't working out so well."

"I'm sure you have a lot of suitors. Some even over the age of five."

"Maybe," Christopher says. "But I can't help but wait on this one special lady."

I pull my legs up and wrap myself in a hug. Christopher is tempting, but he is my past. I have to save my son. And that means having another baby with my husband. I know Christopher won't continue to wait on a pregnant woman who is not leaving her marriage. But I don't say any of that. I leave open the door of possibility.

"I can't wait to see you and Mya tomorrow."

CHAPTER THIRTY

LOGAN

Momma's boy. Weak. Not good enough. Disappointment. Words that cut deep. All of the things I heard from my father. Seems as if Senior had me pegged since birth. I swallow that grain of truth along with my scotch.

Today started out an ordinary one. I pull up to the firm and get out of the car with thoughts of the legal brief I had to file. He was in my face when I shut the car door.

"Hey, I'm glad I was able to catch you," he said. "I need your help with something."

"Do I know you?" The guy was non-descript. Khakis, polo shirt, gelled down hair.

"Yeah. You're Logan Rutherford? The attorney." He stuck out his hand.

Thinking he could be a potential client, I returned the handshake. "How can I assist you?"

"You've been served." He slapped the document in my palm and retreated to his vehicle. A pickup truck I didn't notice, parked three spaces away.

I look up from reliving that nightmare and signal the bartender for another drink. The club prides itself on being discreet, and I am grateful that the libations are served without condescending looks. I clutch the cool glass in my hand and toast myself in the mirror behind the bar. Here's to me, the guy that ruined his father's legacy.

A client is suing me. Me. Hell, I've been playing loose with billing hours, but no one ever questions their invoices. I'm worth every dollar. No one understands the pressure I'm under.

Mother is counting on me to handle her affairs. The small insurance policy Senior left was drained in the first year. I've been subsidizing her lifestyle. Moving her in with us made good financial sense. Mother doesn't question my decisions.

Adrienne does. My beautiful, dutiful wife is full of questions. I miss the days she would stare at me with those hazel eyes like I was her hero.

My cell phone buzzes again. It has been a constant hum since I disappeared. Adrienne has called a few times. Mother once or twice. I ignored them all. The problem with being a superhero is that you always have to be a superhero. I can't manage those expectations right now. But this call is from Sheila.

"What?" I slur into the handset once I figure out how to answer the damn thing.

"Where are you?"

"Why?"

"You blew off a meeting this morning. Your Mother called looking for you. And Beatrice said you flew out of the parking lot after some guy approached you."

I grimace. It figures that Beatrice saw my humiliation. She is always there. I fill Sheila in on current events.

"You're drunk," she says.

"Seemed like a good plan when everything is falling apart."

"A minor setback, right? We can figure something out. Let me come and pick you up."

Every superhero needs a place of solitude. I throw back the last of my drink and stand with some help from the bar.

"Alright. Come and get me."

CHAPTER THIRTY ONE

ADRIENNE

A thud, followed by an expletive, jolts me awake. Logan hobbles to the bathroom and cuts on the light. I look at the clock. 12:14 a.m. When he comes out, I snap on the lamp. His bloodshot eyes look surprised.

"Sorry I woke you," he mumbles.

"Where the hell have you been?"

He holds up a hand like a stop sign and limps around to his side of the bed. "Not now, okay?"

"Yes, now." He will not dismiss me that easily. "Why haven't you returned any of my calls? That is so inconsiderate. You could have been dead for all I knew. Your mother even said she couldn't reach you. So, I repeat. Where the hell have you been?"

Logan sits on the bed and winces. "You could keep your voice down."

"You could answer the damn question," I reply.

He pulls back the covers and fluffs the pillows. "It's been a long day. I can't do this with you now."

I stare at his back in disbelief. All the anger and frustration I feel bubbles up and spills over with my hand slapping the back of Logan's head.

"What the hell is wrong with you?" Logan jumps out of bed and rubs his head.

"You," I scream. "You are what's wrong with me."

I throw the covers aside and face him. My breath quickens, and I am ready for a fight.

Logan hangs his head. "I'm sorry, okay. I have a lot going on with work. I should have called."

His apology throws me off stride and takes some of the edge off my words.

"Yes, you should have called. But let's talk about work. Why weren't you there?"

He clears his throat and now I hold up a hand to stop him. "Don't lie because I spoke with Beatrice, and she told me you were taking a personal day."

Logan sits on the bed and takes a deep breath. "I wish she hadn't told you that."

I sit beside him. "Why?"

"I didn't want you to worry."

"Worry about what?"

"The Dingle Brothers account fell through. They decided to go with another firm."

I ask what happened, and he continues. "They heard I was being sued by a client, that's what. I went by their office this morning, but they already signed with another firm."

"I'm sorry to hear that."

Logan reaches for my hand. "Thanks," he says and gives me a smile that doesn't reach his eyes. After a moment, I can't resist probing further.

"Where were you all day?"

He eases his hand from mine. "I don't know. I mean, I drove around. I got this devastating news and I had to get my mind right, you know? I kept thinking about what my dad would do. I had to come up with another plan."

"And you didn't once think about calling your wife?"

He looks at me, and I can see the thought never entered his mind.

"You wouldn't understand. It's my responsibility. I have to work this out."

"And you have to do it alone? With a bottle? This drinking has to stop."

"Yes. My dad built this business from the ground up and he didn't bother my mother with the details. You shouldn't have to be concerned either. I'll work it out, okay?"

"How? By drinking yourself to death. Where were you all day? And don't lie to me."

He rubs his hands down his face. "I was at the club, okay. I needed some time alone. I was there until they called an Uber for me."

I search his face for the truth. He clears his throat but maintains eye contact. "I'm sorry I didn't call."

"Okay, but we really need to have a conversation about your drinking," I say. "And your terrible communication skills. I guess you're sorry about not telling me about your get together tomorrow, either?"

Logan groans. "I forgot all about that. It's too late to cancel now." He tells me he planned it a couple of weeks ago.

"Everything is taken care of. I have an event planner that handled everything. Someone will be here in the morning to set up the patio and deck. The food will be catered. They'll even clean up afterwards, so you don't have to do a thing."

"Then what do you need me for?"

Logan wraps an arm around me. "I need you here. A reporter will be here to interview me for an article. The newspaper is doing a section on small businesses. The Rutherford Law firm will be profiled. They will want to photograph my family."

"All the more reason you should have told me about it."

"Slipped my mind. I know it's short notice, but we better get some rest." Logan moves to get back under the covers. I return to my side of the bed. Now I need to focus on what we need to agree on for Nicholas.

"There is something I need to discuss with you."

"Can it wait until the morning, babe?"

"Technically, it is the morning. If you had come home at a decent hour," I begin.

Logan rolls over. "Okay, what is it?"

I settle under the covers and turn his face toward me. "I think you were right. We should have another baby."

I think my declaration will make my husband happy. Instead, his eyes flash with anger.

"You picked a hell of a bad time to come to that decision."

"It may seem like it, but—"

He cuts me off and sits up. "You are unbelievable. When I tell you I want a baby, you shut the option down. Now that I have all this stress on me, you come out the blue with this."

"No, listen. I took Nicholas to the doctor today, and Dr. Payne explained how we could ensure that we have a healthy baby." I talk fast and tell Logan about the procedure and the child that could save Nicholas.

Logan kicks off the covers. "I tell you I lost a major client, I'm being sued by another and you want us to incur some major medical expenses to have a baby solely to be a donor for Nicholas. What are you thinking?"

"I'm thinking about saving Nicholas."

"That's all you think about, isn't it? Doesn't matter what I want? Doesn't matter that you would manufacture a baby, not one made out of love, but made to be donor."

"Of course, I'll love the baby. We'll both love the baby."

Logan stands and grabs a pillow.

"Where are you going?" I ask.

"Downstairs to get some sleep."

"Don't walk out. We need to discuss this."

"There's nothing to discuss." He opens the door and pauses. "You are a piece of work to hit me with this shit now."

"Logan, please. I thought you wanted a baby." My voice chokes.

He looks at me with contempt. "I don't know why you would want to have a baby with me, babe," he sneers. "I don't want the one I supposedly already have, remember?"

And with that, he slams the door shut on my hopes to save Nicholas.

CHAPTER THIRTY TWO

MOMENT OF TRUTH

ADRIENNE

I toss and turn all night but at some point, I must have dozed off because I am awakened by Nicholas prying my eyes open.

"Wake up, Momma," he says. "We having a party."

I sit up and grab Nicholas in a hug. He pats my back before squirming away. He slides to the floor, and I see he's already dressed in navy blue slacks, a white shirt and tie. I rub my eyes and kick off the covers.

"How are you feeling, baby?"

Nicholas jumps around in a circle. "Good."

"Who helped you get dressed?"

"Grandma. Daddy says we having a party and I have to be a good little man."

At the mention of Logan, the anger returns in a flash. I have to get out of here. I can't stay with a man that won't do everything to save our son. I flick on the television and plant Nicholas on the bed.

"Stay here and wait for Momma."

Nicholas nods, lies on his stomach, and props his head on his hands. I rush into the bathroom and brush my teeth. I hunt in the closet for some jeans and a shirt. I throw clothes in a bag and walk over to Nicholas's room to do the same. I pull out my cell phone and dial Kim's number.

"Listen, Logan is tripping. Nicholas and I need to stay with you awhile," I say when she answers.

"What did he do now?" Kim doesn't sound surprised.

I give her the quick and dirty details of our fight.

"Bring my baby over here. We'll figure something out."

I hang up the phone and feel better. Kim and I will take care of Nicholas. Now that I have a plan, I need to execute it. I go back to my room to retrieve Nicholas, but he has deserted the bed. I pick up the duffel bag of my things and head downstairs.

Logan meets me at the bottom. "Hey, babe," he says as if nothing has changed between us. "I was about to come wake you up."

"Where's Nicholas?"

He nods his head to indicate the kitchen. Then he notices the bag I am carrying.

"What's that?"

"What does it look like? I'm leaving."

"You can't leave," Logan sets his mug on the table in the foyer.

"Oh yeah? Watch me," I call for Nicholas.

Logan grabs my arm. "Why are you doing this? You know I need you here."

"That's not my concern," I shake my arm loose. "Nicholas is."

"Typical," Logan says through clenched teeth. "Nicholas is all you ever think about."

"And the law firm is all you think about," I reply.

We stare each other down until Nicholas skips between us. My heart pounds in my chest, but I stand my ground. I have given in to Logan too many times. On this issue, there can be no compromise.

I reach for Nicholas's hand. "Come on, baby."

"No, Mommy," he backs away. "Want to stay for the party."

"Nicholas, come here," I reach for him again.

He grabs onto Logan's leg. "Want to stay with Daddy for the party."

I am losing patience and my nerve. "Nicholas, if you don't come with me this instance…"

"The boy doesn't want to go with you. Why don't you calm down and we can talk about this later?"

"You don't want to talk, Logan. You want me to play along with your show today."

Marilyn appears in the doorway. "Logan, I… Is everything alright?"

Logan puts on a smile before he turns. "It's fine, Mother. Simple misunderstanding. Will you take Nicholas and let him help you in the kitchen?"

Marilyn takes in the scene but doesn't question it. "The caterers have some questions."

"Tell them I'll be right out," Logan says. "Nicholas, go with Grandma."

I watch Nicholas skip into the kitchen. For the first time, I notice all the activity going on. People are going in and out of the kitchen carrying trays of food, chairs and tables. I can see the beginnings of a tent being erected in the back yard.

I swallow hard. "I am leaving, Logan."

He turns to me and smiles, "Now why would you want to do that?

"You know why."

Logan leans in so close, I smell the coffee on his breath. "A better question is, what makes you think I will let you leave?"

I try to step back, but Logan grabs my arm and squeezes. "You will not embarrass me today. You will stand by my side like a good wife. Because don't think for a minute that I will let you take Nicholas away. I will go to court and allege that my son was removed from the home without my consent. The family law judges I know frown on that type of behavior. And if you decide to leave anyway thinking you'll get Nicholas later, I will file for abandonment. What do you think your chances of getting custody will be?"

The threat hangs in the air and paralyzes me. I look in Logan's eyes and see someone I don't recognize. I am trapped, and he knows it. The doorbell rings and breaks the tension. Logan takes a step back.

"That would be the newspaper reporter. You may want to go get changed before the interview."

I make it through the newspaper interview by not saying a word. The interviewer, a young no nonsense junior reporter whose name I don't catch, only has questions for Logan. After introductions and the requisite compliments, I am treated as an accessory. I watch as the reporter recites Logan's bio and tells him that he has grown the firm to surpass his father's legacy. The man is easily impressed, I think. He clearly has fallen for Logan's act. And Logan can't resist the opportunity to brag about his many accomplishments.

"Through my efforts, the Rutherford Law firm has grown into a prestigious business with unlimited growth potential. I plan to expand the services or areas of law covered and recruit more attorneys," Logan boasts.

My stomach churns listening to it.

The photographer places lights around Logan's desk and takes a 'working' shot with Logan posed at the computer. His tie is loose and he has a pen poised above some documents. Nicholas and Marilyn are corralled into the room for the requisite family portrait. When the final bulb flashes, I bolt from the room like I heard a starter's pistol and my name is FloJo. My mood gets worse when I run into Sheila standing in my foyer.

"What are you doing here?" I ask the question with such force that Sheila takes a step back.

"I…" she stammers and then recovers. "Logan invited me."

"Why?" I ask, but Sheila ignores me and starts to look around.

"You have a beautiful home. I've never been here, you know. But this is nice. Did you decorate it yourself?"

What is this woman talking about? I suspect her of having an affair with my husband, and she stands there sizing up my home like she can envision her furniture up in here.

"Why are you here again?" I ask through clenched teeth.

Sheila meets my challenge. "Like I said, Logan invited me."

"For what?"

Sheila starts to respond, and then her demeanor softens. "Logan," she says.

He comes up behind me and slips an arm around my waist. "Sheila is here to work. I need someone to greet the guest and escort them to the back."

Sheila turns a shade of pink. "But that's not what you said—"

Logan cuts her off. "Maybe you misunderstood. You are here to work."

Sheila looks crestfallen, but I don't take comfort in her being put in her place. Something is going on between these two. I step away from Logan. "I need to check on Nicholas."

"Mother has him. I need you beside me."

Sheila's mouth opens, but she covers it with her hand as if she has to physically keep herself from speaking. Logan ignores her and glares at me. He dares me to defy him. I feel Sheila's piercing stare as well. I turn and walk into the kitchen with Logan close on my heels. The irony of not being able to take the heat and going into the kitchen is not lost on me.

CHAPTER THIRTY THREE

ADRIENNE

The cookout/party has been in full swing for about forty minutes, and I am tired of smiling. Logan introduces me to everyone, and I stand beside him like a supportive wife and laugh at their weak jokes. He keeps a firm grip on my arm, but I manage to break free when some local city councilman takes Logan aside to discuss a personal issue. I go in search of Nicholas. I've seen him running around the backyard, and I need to make him rest for a few minutes.

When I spot him, I pause. Christopher is kneeling to give Nicholas a high five when I approach.

"I was asking Nicholas where I could find his pretty momma," Christopher stands.

I remind myself to breathe. The man is a vision. He has on a pair of cream linen pants with matching button down shirt, soft butter cream loafers massage his feet and a diamond stud sparkles in his ear. He smiles at me, and I can't help but smile back. I want to hug him but settle for the handshake he offers.

Still holding my hand, caressing it, he places his other hand on the head of his daughter. "This is Mya."

"Hello, Ms. Adrienne," Mya says like she rehearsed it. She looks to her dad for approval. He gives it to her with a wink.

"It's nice to meet you, Mya," I say. She grins at me with two missing teeth, and I fall in love. She has on a yellow sundress with matching ribbons in her hair and a cute pair of white sandals. If I had a daughter, this is how I would dress her. "Have you met Nicholas?"

Nicholas steps forward and takes Mya hand. "Wanna play?" he asks. She nods, and they run off.

"I guess they hit it off," I say.

"My daughter has that effect on all the boys," Christopher jokes.

"Is that so?"

Christopher turns serious. "How have you been, Ms. Adrienne?"

"I'm fine."

"I can see that," Christopher looks me up and down. "But, how are you?"

"Still using those corny lines."

"The classics work every time."

"Are you sure about that?"

"Can't blame a brother for trying." His gaze pierces mine. "Are you okay? You have that look."

I tug at my blouse. "What look?"

"I can tell something heavy is on your mind. I always could."

I look at this man, and he has so much compassion and worry on his face that the truth springs out before I can censor it. "Nicholas is sick."

Christopher searches for the kids. They are on the swing set, and Nicholas is trying to push Mya on the swing.

"Sick? What do you mean?" He steps closer to me.

I watch the kids play. "He doesn't look it, does he? But he is. Has been since he was born. He has sickle cell anemia and a bone marrow transplant can save his life." I tell him everything. I stand there on my patio surrounded by people I don't know and don't care to impress and unburden myself.

"I'm tired, Christopher," I add. "I'm tired, and I'm afraid all the time. If something happens to Nicholas…" I fight back tears.

Christopher strokes my arm. "Hush, baby. We'll figure out something, okay. Whatever you need, I got you."

And like that, I know it will be okay. This man will help make it better. I take a deep breath and resist the impulse to fall into his arms right here.

Christopher looks at the kids again. "What does Logan plan to do?"

I roll my eyes. "I am not worried about Logan."

"You saying he isn't stepping up?" His hands ball into fists.

I shake my head. "I don't know who he is anymore. What type of man won't do everything to help his child?"

We stand and watch the children play for a moment. Words aren't needed. Christopher stands close without touching, but I still feel him. I feel something I haven't felt in a long time. Protected.

Christopher flexes his fingers and glances at me. "Ms. Adrienne, I have to tell you something."

I turn away from Nicholas and Mya who are now holding hands and whispering in each other's ear. I look at this man I must admit I still love. Hell of a time to have that emotion.

Christopher looks at me and hesitates. His body language changes. "Logan," he says.

I wrinkle my brow. Before I can ask what he is talking about, I feel an arm slide around my waist and pull me close. Too close.

"Michaels. Glad you could make it," Logan says his voice amplified in my ear. He reaches to shake hands.

"Wouldn't miss it. Thanks for having us. My daughter seems to have made a new friend," Christopher waves to the kids who wave back.

Logan doesn't even glance in their direction. "That's nice. What have you two been talking about?" He looks at Christopher, but the question is for me.

"I'm welcoming your guests," I say.

"Looked like more than that. I'm over there talking to the judge and you two seem cozy. All huddled up."

I can't believe this. The man is jealous. I try to step away, and he squeezes me tighter. Christopher eyes the grip.

"I was asking your wife about summer camp programs. I'll have Mya when school ends. I remember you saying that she's a teacher."

Logan nods and loosens his hold.

Christopher continues. "You have a beautiful family here, man."

"My family is the most important thing. It's the reason for all my hard work." Logan starts in on the history of the Rutherford Law firm. Christopher has heard it before, but he listens politely. When he chances a look my way, I apologize with my eyes. Logan can rave about his pseudo success all day.

"You know, I have some people here you should meet, judges, councilmen and a few bankers. Networking is the name of the game, right?"

"Sure, Logan," Christopher says and ask if I would like to join them.

Logan remembers I am there and drops his arm. "I'm sure Adrienne has more pressing matters."

I know when I have been dismissed but welcome the respite. Christopher looks back and forth between us but doesn't comment.

"You guys go ahead. I'll check on the kids."

"You do that," Logan says and leads Christopher away. I survey the yard and see groups of people clustered together like grapes. Each circle engaged in conversation, food and drink. The speakers pipe jazz tunes mixed with instrumental old school R & B tunes.

The kids are sitting close on the ground. Nicholas shows Mya one of his toys. They seem content for the moment so I decide to go inside and get them something to drink.

I walk into the kitchen to find it empty. The caterers have left no evidence of their appearance. Marilyn made it clear she did not want them in her kitchen. I open the refrigerator to find some juice boxes for the kids when I hear raised voices coming from the foyer.

"Lady, I don't care about a list. If you don't move out of the way," Kim says.

"I'm sorry. You don't have an invitation," Sheila says. "I am going to have to ask you to leave."

I go into the foyer and see my sister in full attack mode. Her hands are gesturing wildly, and I can tell she is about three seconds from kicking off her sandals and knocking Sheila to the side. Sheila either isn't easily intimidated or naïve to the threat of a physical altercation.

"If you don't move your bony body out of the way and let me in," Kim threatens.

I forgot all about Kim after the mess with Logan on my way out. I rush to save Sheila from a beat down.

"What's the problem?"

"This woman is not on the list," Sheila looks relieved to see me.

"This woman is my sister."

Kim rolls her eyes at Sheila, but she is busy flipping through some papers in her hand.

"Logan gave strict instructions not to let anyone in that's not on the list."

"And I said this is my sister. She doesn't need an invitation to come into my house," I emphasize the words my house.

Sheila opens her mouth to say something but backs down. She folds the papers. "Fine."

Kim walks past and can't resist one last comment. "The hired help needs to learn their place around here."

I nod in agreement. Something flashes across Sheila's face. Her cheeks turn red, and I chalk it up to embarrassment.

We leave her there, and I take Kim into Logan's study so we can talk.

"What the hell is going on?" Kim asks and slings her purse on the couch. Before I can answer she continues, "You had me waiting on you and you don't show up. I've been blowing up your cell phone and no answer. I didn't know what to think. Then I show up here and you're having a party with security at the door."

I take Kim's hand. "I'm sorry I scared you."

She calms down enough to give me a hug. I hold on tight and try to sap some of her energy for the battle ahead.

"Alright, I forgive you this time. Now what is the deal?"

We sit. "Logan wouldn't let me leave."

Kim leans back and raises an eyebrow. I hold up a hand to pause her reaction and explain. I tell her about the interview and party he told me about last night and the threat when I tried to leave.

"He threw me with his stance that I can't take Nicholas and leave. He does know judges. In fact, a couple of them are in my backyard now."

"Brother-in-law is showing his ass today," Kim says.

"I need to regroup and make sure I do this the right way. Because there is no way I am staying with a man that won't try everything to save his son's life."

"And where is my baby?" Kim asks.

"Out back playing with his new best friend, Mya. On top of everything else, Christopher is here."

Kim almost jumps off the chair. "Chris is here. How did that happen?"

"Logan invited all his clients."

"Well, there you go. Christopher will help you get up out of here. I'm sure he knows people too. He can help you get an attorney."

I shake my head. "I don't want to drag him into this mess."

"And why not? The man still loves you."

"I know."

"And he'll help you if you ask."

I smile. "I know that too."

"Then what's the problem?"

"I can't, okay?" How can you verbalize that it doesn't seem fair to ask one man to help you leave the man you married? "I'll figure something out."

"No, we'll figure something out," Kim says with a determination that makes me tear up. Me and Kim against the world. We have always been able to conquer anything life throws our way. For a moment, we are those orphan, homeless children again. I hug Kim tight until I am able to be strong.

I pull away and wipe my face. "You might as well stay and get something to eat."

Kim pulls out a compact mirror. "I'm not dressed appropriately for some bougie law firm shindig."

"Girl, you look great and you know it. It's a fancy cookout." Even in my sister's frazzled state, she never leaves the house looking as she puts it 'any kind of way.' She has on a pair of dark blue skinny jeans, a black blouse that exposes one shoulder and silver accessories to match. Her high heel sandals expose perfectly manicured feet. She freshens her makeup and stands.

"At least now I'll have someone to talk to," I tell her as we walk through the kitchen. "It's mostly men and the few that brought their wives, have formed some sort of club. Obviously, I'm not old enough, rich enough or politically connected enough to join." I grab juice for the kids, and we step onto the patio.

I look around. Christopher is in a group of men showing them a golf swing. They seem to take whatever advice he is offering as gospel. Nicholas and Mya are chasing each other up and down the slide. Marilyn is instructing the caterers on the proper way to serve food to a line of guests at the buffet. And Logan is standing close with Sheila. They are away from the crowd. Sheila is giving Logan an earful. I assume reporting that Kim has crashed the party. When Logan looks our way, I turn and go toward the kids.

"Hey, Aunt Kim," Nicholas runs and hugs Kim around the knees.

"How is my favorite nephew?" she asks.

He takes her hand and says, "This is Mya. She's my sister."

My stomach clenches. "Nicholas, baby. Why would you say that? Mya is your friend."

He turns his light brown eyes to me. "Uh huh, Mommy. Mya says I'm her little brother, so she is my sister."

"No," I say with more force than the comment warrants. "Mya is your friend."

Kim laughs. "Chill, sis. I think it's cute they want to be related."

Nicholas looks to me for approval. "I'm sorry, baby." I kneel for a hug.

"Here, you and Mya drink your juice. Are you guys ready to eat?"

Nicholas shakes his head and sits on the ground beside Mya. They race to see who can drink their juice the fastest.

Kim turns to me. "What was that all about?"

"Nothing," I say.

"Look at them. They have hit it off."

I do look at them, and I am startled at the resemblance. They could pass for siblings. Same eyes, same nose and when they both look up at me, I see the same smile. The secret I have kept hidden all these years threatens to be exposed right here in my backyard. Could it be true? Can everyone see my transgression?

"Sister," I say and take Kim's hand. I have to tell someone what I did that night. I have to imagine the possibility that the thing I have been denying all this time because of Nicholas's illness could be true.

"Daddy," Nicholas calls, and I turn half expecting it to be someone else.

Logan walks up. "Kim, what brings you here?"

"Hello, to you too, Logan," Kim puts her hands on her hips.

Logan tries to laugh it off. "Yeah, hello. I was wondering what brings you by today?"

"Are you saying I'm not welcome?"

He turns to me for help. I leave him on that island all alone. "Are you trying to say my sister isn't welcome at your party?"

Logan puts his hands up and looks back and forth between us. "No, no. It's,…this is a work function for me and—"

"Your guard, Sheila told you someone crashed the party," I finish for him.

Logan looks surprised and clears his throat. "No, that's not it."

"So, let me get this straight. I can't leave, and I can't have company either. Is that the new rule, Logan?"

Now he looks angry. "Don't be silly. Can I talk to you for a second?"

I let him simmer for a moment before I give Kim the eye to watch the kids and pull Logan to the side. "What is it?"

Logan takes a deep breath. "It's about time to wrap this up, and I need my wife beside me."

"Why should I keep up this charade? When I need you to stand with me, you refuse."

We stand there at a standstill. Neither of us wants to back down. Logan blinks first and looks around. He softens his stance. "Babe, I know we have some issues, but it's nothing we can't work out."

I raise an eyebrow. "I've heard that before."

Logan ignores my attitude and continues. "I know it hasn't been easy these last few months."

"Can't you come up with something original," I say and start to walk away.

"Please, babe," he says. "I need you."

Something in his voice stops me. A hint of the old Logan. So many conflicting emotions race through my head that I am unable to move. But, he is my husband. I won't let him look bad in front of the people he works so hard to impress.

"Nicholas," I say. He knows that is the deal breaker.

"Whatever you want to do," he pleads.

"Okay," I relax my shoulders and relent. "I'll follow your lead, but as soon as we get these people out of here, we have to talk. I mean it."

"You got it, babe," Logan smiles and reaches for my hand. I take it and try to shake the feeling that I have made a deal with the devil.

I stand beside Logan as he gives a "state of the Rutherford Law firm" speech. I watch the reaction of the participants, and they seem to hang on every word. The free food and drinks make for a captive audience.

Kim and Christopher are off to the side. They have settled the kids down with some food, and I am grateful that Nicholas is eating something. That is where I should be.

Logan raises his glass in a toast. I continue to scan the crowd of his admirers. They seem to believe Logan is the hot shot lawyer he tries to be. And then I see Sheila. She stands in the back, staring lasers into Logan. When she sees me looking, she flips her hair and takes a swig from her glass. Someone else is not happy with Logan. I wonder what reason she has for that look.

Afterward, I am mingling with guests, thanking them for coming, when Christopher comes over.

"Mya and I are getting ready to go," he says.

"I don't know if you'll be able to tear those two apart." I gesture toward Nicholas and Mya who are standing hand in hand.

"Yeah, it's amazing how they've connected. We'll have to set up a play date."

I nod, and Christopher's eyes turn serious. He starts to reach for my hand and pauses. He looks around and leans in close.

"I need to talk to you. When can I see you?"

"I'm not sure. I have a lot going on right now."

He insists. "Tomorrow. What about tomorrow?"

Tomorrow, I think. I am still trying to figure out what to do with the rest of the day. I would love to spend the day, the week…hell, the rest of my life with this man. But there is the matter of my marriage and I don't want to get Christopher mixed up in my craziness. I look into his eyes and see an urgency that I can't place.

"It's about Nicholas. I need to talk to you about Nicholas."

Now, I am puzzled. Before I can ask Christopher what he means, Logan is there.

"Michaels," he says loudly. "So glad you could make it. Hope you had a good time."

Christopher steps back. "Certainly did, Logan. Thanks again for inviting us."

"No problem. I look forward to us working together again. If you need anything, let me know."

"Sure. I'm going in another direction with my business, but I'll let you know." Christopher turns and calls Mya over. She is followed closely by Nicholas.

The departure is not as tearful as I imagined. After a long hug, Mya tells Nicholas she will see him tomorrow with all the certainty a five-year-old can muster. He nods and smiles at her.

When they leave, Nicholas turns to me. "Can Mya come play tomorrow?"

"We'll see," I tell him. He skips off and goes to Kim who is having a conversation with the newspaper reporter.

"Did Michaels blow me off?" Logan asks. He looks pissed.

"What?"

"I offer my services, and he says he is going in another direction. What does that mean?"

"Why are you worried about one client?" I ask. "I think you have schmoozed a lot of other clients today."

"Yeah, but he was the biggest. Having him on my roster would attract more of the big boys. I need more corporate clients."

I look at Logan and see the insecure man out to prove to the world, or specifically his dead father, that he is a good man. But he gets no comfort from me.

"Guess you'll have to do better next time," I say.

He pushes me away. "You think I can't keep Michaels on board?"

"I didn't say that."

"But you think it. I saw you looking at that punk. You must think I'm stupid."

"No, I think you're acting crazy." I remain calm. I will not be drawn into another fight.

Logan looks around. All of the guests have gone. "No, I'm crazy for trying to be a success. To try to give you everything."

"We can stop that lie right now. All of this is about you trying to impress a ghost."

Logan looks as if I punched him in the stomach. "You don't get it, do you? You never did."

He walks away, and I shake my head. I can't worry about Logan and his bruised ego right now. I go over to Kim to check on my son.

"Excuse me," I say to the reporter who is leaning over Kim. She is sitting on a bench with Nicholas curled up on her lap.

"No problem, Mrs. Rutherford," he says and slips his cell phone in his pocket. "I'm leaving, Kim, I'll give you a call."

"Seems a little young," I tease Kim as we watch the reporter walk away.

"He's twenty-five. Old enough."

"What is his name anyway?"

"Rodney. And he is a big fan of brother-in-law."

I roll my eyes. "You should have been in the interview."

"I'll give him a chance anyway."

I change the subject and rub Nicholas's head. "Is my baby all tired out?"

Nicholas nods and snuggles closer to Kim.

"I think he is all played out," Kim says and pats the space next to her. "Thought anymore about what you are going to do?"

"I don't know, Sister. I'm not sure if my marriage will survive."

I watch Logan across the yard. He gives some instructions to the caterers and says something to his mother. He checks his watch and hurries into the house. It's probably some important phone call he needs to make.

"Whatever you decide, you know I got your back," Kim takes one arm and pulls me close. I rest my head on her shoulder. Nicholas dozes in his aunt's arms. We sit that way for a few minutes longer. The caterers pack up, and Marilyn follows them out the side gate.

I look at Nicholas and tell Kim that I'm not going anywhere today. "Let me put this boy to bed. I worry about him getting over tired."

"I'll take him up," Kim says. We walk into the house and pass Marilyn in the kitchen. She is mumbling about having to get her kitchen back in order.

At the bottom of the stairs, Kim pauses. "Hey, do you know where I left my purse?"

"Maybe in the study," I glance at the closed door. I'm sure Logan is sequestered inside. "I'll get it."

I walk into the office without knocking and see Logan standing with his back to the door. It takes a few seconds for my brain to process what I am seeing. My husband's pants are around his ankles, and he is humping someone like he is trying to ram something through the desk. He keeps repeating, "Is this what you want?"

Once the fog clears, my first thought is that I knew I wasn't crazy. I knew he was having an affair. That emotion is replaced with something else.

"Logan," I choke out.

He turns, and his face is a mixture of pleasure and horror as he reaches his climax at the same time he sees me standing there.

He steps back from Sheila and holds up his hands, "Adrienne. It's not what it looks like."

CHAPTER THIRTY FOUR

ADRIENNE

"**D**on't you dare tell me it's not what it looks like when your semen is dripping on the carpet," I say.

Logan almost trips as he pulls up his pants. "Babe, listen."

My eyes tighten, and I cut him off. "Don't you dare. You are such a fucking cliché. I catch you banging your secretary and you have the audacity to do it in our home." My nails bite into my palms, and my nostrils flare. I grind my teeth to keep from screaming.

"We didn't want you to find out this way," Sheila says and smiles.

"What did you say?" I clench my fists and take a step toward her.

Logan steps in between us. "Hold on, Adrienne."

I take two steps back and take a deep breath. No need to catch a case behind this woman.

Logan looks over his shoulder at Sheila. "I thought you said you locked the door."

"You were never going to tell her, were you?" Sheila crosses her arms.

"Tell me what?" I ask Logan. "How long has this been going on?" I think back on all those late nights supposedly working and his disappearing act from yesterday.

Logan clears his throat. "Babe, it's not like that."

Before I can call him on the lie he is about to tell, Sheila pipes in again.

"Logan, why don't you tell her the truth? Why don't you tell her we have been together for five years?"

I do the math. They have been carrying on before we were even married. That revelation renders me mute. Logan looks pained.

"I broke it off," he says.

"But you came back like always," Sheila gloats. "He always comes back to me."

"Sheila, please," Logan says. "I am talking to my wife."

Now he remembers he has a wife.

"Isn't it about time you told her everything? How much longer do I have to wait?" Sheila reaches for Logan. "You promised."

"Shut up, Sheila," Logan glares at her. "Shut the hell up."

Sheila rolls her eyes at Logan and bends to pick up her panties with more dignity than I thought possible in this situation.

I ignore her and turn to Logan. "Let me get this straight. You've been having an affair with your secretary that dates back to before we were married. And you told me I was crazy for even thinking you were unfaithful. Is our whole marriage one big lie?"

I fold into myself and land on the sofa. Get it together, I tell myself. I will not give them the satisfaction of tears.

Logan kneels in front of me. "I'm so sorry, babe."

I look into the face of the man I've spent the last four years with and see a stranger.

"Is it?" I repeat. "Is everything between us a lie?"

Logan hangs his head. "You lied too."

"What? Now it's somehow my fault you cheated."

"You know what I'm talking about," Logan peeks up at me.

I am clueless and wonder where this is going. How did this happen? Why didn't I see it sooner? My ruminations are interrupted when Sheila speaks.

"You think you're better than me, Mrs. Rutherford. At least I'm having his baby." She emphasizes the word his.

It takes a moment for it to register. I look at Logan, and he shakes his head. "Damn it, Sheila."

"Now she's pregnant." I laugh, and it sounds like I'm strangling.

Logan nods, and Sheila smiles as if she won a prize.

"For someone that didn't want any kids, you sure are cavalier about making babies," I say.

"You're right. I didn't want any children," Logan shoots Sheila a look, and she shrinks back against the wall. "If she's even pregnant, that baby would be my first."

I shake my head. "What are you talking about? I guess Nicholas doesn't count now."

"Let's talk about Nicholas since we are being honest with each other. You want the truth. You tell the truth. Who is Nicholas's father because it sure as hell isn't me?"

A cold sweat runs down my back, and my heart pounds so fast I can barely breathe. I grip the arm of the chair. I want to stand, but my legs feel like jelly.

Logan looms over me. "I admit I wasn't happy when you told me you were pregnant. We had just gotten married and I didn't want the burden of a child. For nine months, I tried to wrap my head around the fact that I would be a father. It was so hard growing up with Logan, Sr. No matter how hard I tried, I could not please that man. What if I did that to my own child?"

I can't speak, but Sheila does. "I think you'll be a great father."

"If you don't keep your bitch quiet," I growl. "I'm not having this conversation with her here."

Logan continues as if we haven't spoken. "And then he was born, and he was perfect. Mother had a grandchild, and I had a son. Remember how I insisted he have his own name?"

I nod. Sheila sits behind the desk. She wants to witness my further humiliation. I may have to hurt her.

"And then he got sick. Sickle cell. A genetic disease. We both got tested."

"And we both tested positive," I say. A statement of hope more than fact.

"No, you tested positive. I told you I did."

"Why would you do that?"

Logan shakes his head. "Because even though it killed me to learn from the paternity test that my wife had someone else's baby, I couldn't deny one fact."

"What was that?"

"I love you." Logan kneels in front of me again. "I still love you, Adrienne."

Sheila jumps to attention. "What about me?"

"Yeah, Logan," I say. "I caught you with your pants down. Literally."

"I forgave you. We can get past this."

Now I know the man has lost his mind. I stand.

"You never forgave me. You made me pay for that transgression every day." I didn't know what I was paying for.

"How? I gave you everything."

"Everything except the truth. Every time you badgered me about having a baby and made me feel guilty about not wanting to. Every time you ignored Nicholas. Hell, every time you slept with Sheila, you made me pay."

The great debater is rendered mute. His closing argument is unsustainable. For a moment, no one speaks. I feel a barrage of emotions. They run the course from anger, remorse, confusion and pain. Sheila maintains her stance by the desk with her arms crossed. She alternates shooting daggers with her eyes at Logan and me.

"You know what," I say. "I can't deal with this." I turn to leave.

"Babe, wait," Logan says. "Tell me what to do. What do you need me to do?"

Sheila pipes in. "I need you to be a father to our baby."

We both turn to glare at her. Her eyes widen, and she takes a step back.

"Baby?" Marilyn shrieks. "Logan, what is going on here?"

Marilyn stands in the doorway. The look of horror on her face tells us that she heard Sheila's declaration.

"Mother," Logan groans.

"Answer me. Why is she talking about a baby?"

Logan stands there mute, so I fill Marilyn in on the recent revelations. I don't leave out a sordid detail. I even tell the part about walking in on them sexing. It feels good to share the pain.

Marilyn's face twist like there is a rancid odor in the air. "Congratulations, son. You finally outdid your father."

The weight of her words strikes Logan with such force that he crumbles onto the sofa. Marilyn stands over him and berates him like the little boy he used to be.

"I told you to get rid of this floozie when you got married. It was time for you to stop chasing this girl like she was a piece of forbidden fruit. But you wanted to keep your mistress close. Your father did it, so you figured you could do it too."

Logan looks up at Marilyn. His eyes are wet with tears. "Dad cheated on you?"

"I was the one that helped him build that firm. I was right there answering phones, filing paperwork, helping him create a name." Marilyn continues unaware that Logan is clueless.

"I worked the whole time I was pregnant with you. So, when your father wanted me to stay home and raise our family, I agreed. Then he hired that woman, and she's been there ever since."

"Beatrice?" I don't realize I've voiced my thought until Marilyn faces me, hands on her hips.

"I knew about it from the beginning. A wife always knows."

I nod in agreement. I did know. I let Logan convince me I was imagining things. Marilyn turns back to Logan.

"How could you do this to your wife? How could you bring this shame to the family? I raised you better than this."

"Momma, I'm sorry," Logan chokes out.

"And if you think I'm accepting some half white baby as my grand-child, you are mistaken." Marilyn shakes her finger at Sheila and walks out.

Sheila's face flushes, and her mouth drops open. "Are you going to let your mother talk to me like that?"

Logan sits with his head in his hands. He doesn't respond. Sheila turns to me. "Can you believe what his mother said to me?"

I am not in the mood to tell her that she will never win in a contest between Logan and his mother.

"I believe you need to get out of my house," I say.

Sheila takes in my threatening stance, hands in fist, legs spread, and moves toward the door. She stops and makes one final plea to Logan. He lifts his head to stare at her with red-rimmed eyes.

"Get out, Sheila. You got what you wanted. Everybody knows now."

"But what about us?" she asks.

He shakes his head. "Leave."

"You need to go with her, Logan," I say.

The man has the nerve to look surprised.

"No," he stands. "We need to talk."

I shoot him a look that would have stopped a sane man from saying anything further. But Logan continues.

"I can't believe what Mother said about Dad?"

"Are you calling your mother a liar?"

"No, of course not. I can't…I mean…how could he do something like that? How could he hurt her like that?"

"Probably the same way you did it."

Logan does have enough sense to look ashamed. He clears his throat. "Babe, we can get past this. I need you."

"Get out," I say.

"I love you."

"Get out," I repeat.

"You still love me, right? Tell me you love me."

I look at this man and think about our time together. I think about the guilt that dogged our union from day one. I think of the way I let him manipulate my life. The way he treated Nicholas.

"Get out," I scream. "Get. The. Fuck. Out."

Logan grimaces. "Okay. Okay. I'll call you later, okay?"

I turn and grab a stapler, the first thing I find and aim for Logan's head. He ducks. I reach for something else.

Logan pushes past Sheila and runs from the room. A paperweight follows close behind. Sheila looks trapped.

"Do you have something else you want to say?" I ask her.

When she doesn't respond, I grab a picture frame and line up a shot. She yelps Logan's name and scurries from the room. The frame cracks against the wall and rains glass over the floor. I release my pent-up rage and ram sack Logan's office, the site of his ultimate betrayal. When I collapse in a heap, I am surrounded by torn paper, scattered files and a toppled bookcase. I take a moment to wipe my face and then I close the door on my destruction and go check on my son.

Nicholas is still asleep. Kim has changed his clothes and put him in bed. She is on her cell phone and mouths 'Rodney' to answer my unspoken question. I sit on the edge of Nicholas's bed and rub his leg. The tears begin anew.

Kim abruptly ends her call and sits beside me. "What happened?"

"It's over," I say and let my sister console me.

CHAPTER THIRTY FIVE

ADRIENNE

Numb. That's the word that describes me for the next few days. I've gone through the motions. Taking care of Nicholas requires that I maintain some semblance of my routine. I wake up every morning and take him to school. I sit at Kim's until he is done. Marilyn and I don't discuss Logan's absence, but I can tell she is distracted. Yesterday, she burned the chicken, and we ended up ordering a pizza. This is the fifth day since Logan has left, and we haven't heard from him. I assumed he was staying at Sheila's, but that woman had the nerve to call the house tonight and ask for him. I told her to kiss my ass before I hung up.

I know I have some hard decisions to make. I know my marriage is over, but I need to figure out if I need to look for a place to live or not. I did emerge from my stupor long enough to follow up on that teaching position. The money in our joint account is getting low.

And then there is Christopher. He has been calling every day leaving messages about needing to see me. I can't deal with him yet. I don't know what to say. Correction. I know what to say. I don't know how to say it. What if he rejects me and Nicholas? What if he is angry with me?

I snuggle further under the covers and hold Nicholas tight. He sighs in his sleep and burrows closer. Al Green laments of a broken heart and does little to soothe me to sleep tonight. The words from *Let's Stay Together* seem to mock my plight. When the disc gets to *Love is a*

Beautiful Thing, I am so full of competing emotions, I click off the cd and sob.

The smell of fermented potatoes brings me out of a fretful sleep. I lie on my back and let my eyes adjust to the darkness. A slight rustle draws my attention to the corner. The figure of a man bolts me upright.

"Logan," I stifle the scream and place a hand over my heart.

"I've been sitting here watching you," his words slur along the edges.

"Where have you been?" I ask. He hasn't been near a shower. Alcohol is not the lone smell permeating the room.

"Thinking about how to save this family," he says.

"Your mom is worried about you," I look around the room. If he makes any sudden moves, I can scoop up Nicholas and lunge for the door. I should be able to make it.

"I messed up," Logan continues. "But I've made some decisions that will help us get back on track."

I slide my hand toward the phone on the nightstand. How long would it take 911 to respond at 4 a.m.?

"So, this is how it's going to be," Logan sniffs and sits up straight. He is able to pull it off on his second attempt. "I'm done with the law firm, and I'm done with Sheila."

"What do you mean done?" I sit up and put my feet on the floor. "She is having your baby."

"I can't." Logan takes a deep breath. "You know you were right. I've been trying to impress a ghost, a man that didn't even deserve my respect. He cheated on my mother."

The pain radiates from Logan and threatens to suffocate the air. A part of me wants to comfort him, but I stay perched on the edge of the bed.

"I'm coming back home. We need to work on our marriage, and I need to be here with mother."

"What marriage? I think that was a done deal when you got your mistress pregnant."

Logan shakes his head. "We can get past that. I accepted Nicholas as my son. You can accept the baby too."

I fight to keep my voice low. "You didn't accept anything. You used that secret against me. Our marriage was built on lies. I think it is over and done."

Logan runs his hands over this head. "Built on lies, huh? Okay, all my truth is out there. Why don't you tell the truth?"

My stomach clenches. "What truth?"

"When did you have your affair? Who is Nicholas's father?"

"I didn't have an affair and what difference does that make now? You know it's not you." I toss the last statement out to turn the conversation in another direction.

"I want to know," Logan doesn't take the bait.

"You didn't want to know three years ago."

"I thought I could deal with it."

"No, you thought you could control me with it."

"Tell me who the father is."

I glance back at Nicholas. "It's not important now."

"Why won't you tell me? Do you even know?"

I shoot him a look. "Of course, I know."

"Just tell me. You know all my dirt. Let's hear yours."

I hesitate. I have been holding on to this secret so long, living with the fear that what I believed would be exposed. The words struggle to form.

"It was an ex-boyfriend," I whisper.

Logan looks confused and then his face shows remembrance. "The one you said left you? The one that hurt you so bad you never wanted to see him again?"

I nod. "That would be the one."

"Were you seeing him when we were dating?"

"No."

"Then how do you know he is the father?"

"I ran into him once. Before we got married."

"And what? You fell into bed for old times sake."

"No, it wasn't like that."

"Then what was it like," Logan's leg starts bouncing.

"Why is that important now?" I ask.

Logan stands and stumbles backward into the chair. "You know my shit. You know all about Sheila."

I look at Nicholas who turns over in his sleep. "Would you lower your voice?"

"Would you tell me the truth for once?" Logan runs his hands across the stubble on his face. He sighs. "Did you believe I was Nicholas's father or were you playing some sort of game?"

"I didn't know. I mean there was a chance you weren't the father. But when Nicholas got sick and we both tested positive…"

Logan winces and I continue. "I no longer had a reason to question. The bigger question is why you didn't tell me you knew."

He shrugs. "I didn't want to lose you."

I squint to read his eyes. "That's cute, but what's the real reason?"

"Thought I could get that one past you," Logan chuckles. "You could always read me, but I can read you too, babe. I know you don't want to tell me the man's name. Who is this ex-boyfriend?"

When I don't respond, Logan's leg starts bouncing again. "Who is it, Adrienne?"

"Christopher," I say and brace for the barrage of questions I know will come.

Logan brow furrows. "Christopher?"

I watch the truth register on his face.

"Michaels? You slept with Michaels? That's your ex-boyfriend?"

All I can manage is a nod.

"And you didn't tell me?"

I shake my head. I tried. It never seemed like a good time to tell my husband that his biggest client was the love of my life.

"Did you fuck him?"

My head snaps to attention. "What?"

"Did you fuck him?" Logan voice booms.

"That was a long time ago. Would you calm down?" I turn to smooth Nicholas's back.

"Calm down? You made me look like a fool and you want me to calm down."

I take a deep breath. "And how did I do that, Logan?" He does a good job of looking like a fool all by himself.

"Bet the two of you had a good time laughing at me behind my back. Is that how he agreed to let me represent him? You gave him a taste of the goods for his signature. So he could toss a little business my way."

Logan continues to rant, but I turn to comfort Nicholas who is now wide awake. "It's okay, baby," I tell Nicholas and try to make him lie back down.

"It's not okay," Logan shouts. "Tell me the truth. You let him fuck you, didn't you? That punk thinks he is better than me anyway. I bet it made him feel good to fuck you. He has everything, might as well take a piece of my wife."

"Stop talking crazy," I say. But, Logan is too far gone to reason with now. His eyes are wide and spit flies out of his mouth along with his vile words.

"Tell me, my wife, did he hit that spot?"

I ignore him and hope he'll take the hint. No such luck.

"Did he? Did he hit that spot and make you come? Naw, he can't put it on you like I can. Ain't that right, babe? I'm the only one that hit it like you like it."

"You couldn't hit it if your dick had a GPS system," I mumble. It is too early in the morning for this foolishness.

Logan is quiet and I take advantage of the peace to get Nicholas to close his eyes. I pull the cover over him and turn back to Logan in time to see his hands snake around my neck. The force of his charge pushes me back on the bed on top of Nicholas. I try to scream, but Logan tightens his grip.

"You bitch," he sneers blowing his foul breath full force in my face. "I'll teach you to cheat on me. You fucked him, didn't you? Didn't you?"

I struggle to get free. I feel Nicholas squirming underneath me. This man is trying to kill me and my child. My heart pounds loud in my ears, and I flail at Logan's arms. When that doesn't work, I try to reach his face, but he leans in closer. All I can do is pound on his back, but in my weakening state I'm not having much effect. I make one final push to sit up. I have to save Nicholas if nothing else. I'm able to maneuver enough that Nicholas rolls free.

"Momma," he screams.

That startles Logan enough that his grip slacks. I twist and bring my knee up to hit him in the groin. He groans and releases me. I reach for anything I can find. My hand grazes the cordless phone I should have used earlier. This time I don't hesitate and swing. I connect with his nose and Logan tumbles to the floor. I resist the urge to kick his ass and grab my son. Nicholas is trembling and crying. I cradle him and stand over Logan.

"Get the hell out!"

"You broke my nose," his voice is nasally. He holds one hand over his nose and the other between his legs.

"Get out before I call the police," I look for the phone. One piece is at Logan's feet with the other scattered across the room.

"It's over now," Logan says. "I came here tonight to try to work things out with your ungrateful ass."

"And when did that change into you trying to kill me?"

Logan wipes blood from his nose with the back of his hand. He shakes his head and looks up at me. "I'm sorry, okay. I lost it for a minute."

I go over to the door and point into the hallway.

He staggers to his feet. "I'll go. Is Nicholas alright?" He tries to reach for Nicholas, but my baby clings to me like Saran Wrap. I move away out of his reach.

"Nicholas will be fine once you are gone."

Logan limps out the door but turns for one last word. "Did you sleep with him?"

He stares at me, and his eyes plead for the truth. After years of marriage filled with guilt and longing and even love, I can at least offer the man the truth.

"Rest assured, babe," I tell him. "The only one who cheated in this marriage is you."

CHAPTER THIRTY SIX

ADRIENNE

It takes me two hours to get Nicholas calm enough to drift back to sleep. There would be no peace for me. To be certain Logan left, I follow him out and watch his car pull off. But, I don't feel safe. By the time the sun comes up, I am already dressed and formulating a plan. It is time to leave. Logan may be wounded and confused, but I know my husband. He will be back claiming we can work it out. Or trying to get back at me for Christopher.

Either way, I am not going to hang around to find out. I call Kim and fill her in on current events. After she curses Logan out and swears to "smack him" the next time she sees him, she tells me she is on the way over with a couple of guy friends for muscle and protection.

I let Nicholas sleep while I make phone calls. I don't have much, but I am taking all of Nicholas's furniture. Logan and Marilyn can have this house. It is no longer home.

Kim arrives while I am helping Nicholas get dressed.

"How's my favorite nephew?" she asks walking into the room.

"Hey, Auntie," he says with sad eyes and sticks an arm in his shirt.

Kim looks at me and I shake my head. Nicholas has been especially quiet since he woke up. She sits beside him on the bed.

"Where's my hug?"

Nicholas leans into her and wraps his arms around her. "Daddy is bad," he whispers.

My heart breaks. So much for my hope that he wouldn't remember last night.

"It's okay now, baby," Kim rocks him. "Do you want to come to Auntie's house?"

Nicholas nods. I turn to fold up his pajamas and compose my happy face.

"How about some waffles first?" Nicholas hasn't eaten, and I don't want him to get sick. He doesn't answer but stands. Kim takes his hand.

"You may want to talk to Marilyn," she says. "She was surprised to see me and two dudes at the door."

Shit. I don't have the energy to deal with Logan's mother. I follow Kim and Nicholas down the stairs.

"Where are these guys you got?" I ask.

"Marilyn insisted on getting them some coffee."

"How were you able to get somebody at a moment's notice anyway?"

We walk into the kitchen, and the answer to that question is sitting at the table eating a bowl of grits and sausage. It's Rodney the newspaper reporter. Kim avoids my look and smiles. Rodney can't take his eyes off Kim. The man is clearly smitten.

"How are you, Mrs. Rutherford?" he says.

"Please, call me Adrienne. I appreciate your help. I hope Kim didn't take you away from your plans for the day."

"No, we were planning to hang around the house," he says. The look he gives Kim tells me everything I need to know. Baby sister hooked another one. I pinch her and she moves away.

"Adrienne, this is Rodney's friend, Gary." Gary looks up from his plate long enough to nod a greeting. His bulky frame is barely contained in the chair, and he is stuffing sausages into his mouth as if he hasn't eaten in days.

"Excuse my friend," Rodney says. "Boy acts like he doesn't have any home training."

Marilyn laughs and spoons more grits into his bowl. "Let the man eat."

I help Nicholas into his booster seat and pour him a cup of milk. I microwave his waffles and sip a cup of coffee while everyone eats. Marilyn buzzes around the kitchen and seems happy to have people to cook for. She has to have figured out that I'm leaving.

Gary wipes a hand across his mouth and pushes back from the table. "Alright, man. Are we going to do this or what?"

Rodney looks at Kim who then looks at me.

"Uh, yeah. How about you guys start in Nicholas's room."

I wait for questions from Marilyn, but she continues washing dishes at the sink. I ask Kim to take Nicholas and clean him up and show the guys where to go. When everyone leaves, Marilyn says, "You're leaving."

"I think it's best for Nicholas and me to move out."

She doesn't say anything, so I begin to gather dishes from the table. I help her clean the kitchen. She washes and I dry, both of us lost in our own thoughts. I wipe down the table and fold the towel over the sink. I am about to walk out when Marilyn stops me.

"I envy your strength." Marilyn sits at the table with a mug in her hand. "That's what I liked the most about you. Your courage. I knew you were brave enough to deal with Logan."

"I don't feel very brave," I say. My stomach is churning, and I am second-guessing myself right this minute.

"But you are. You are the type of woman that challenges Logan. I love my son, but I know he is spoiled. I guess I tried to be the soft place he could go when his father's demands became overbearing. I probably did him a disservice."

"You did what any mother would do," I say. "The best you could."

Marilyn smiles an acknowledgement of the gift my words offer. "I thought about leaving Logan, Sr. all the time but made a lot of excuses to stay."

I join her at the table. "I thought of a few reasons to stay myself."

"Just lacked the courage is all." Marilyn sits up straight. "I want you to know that I understand. I do want you to let me see my grandbaby."

"Of course," I say. "But there's something you need to know." If I am going to deal in the truth now, I have to tell it all. I take a deep breath.

Marilyn shakes her head. "I already know what you are going to say."

My brow wrinkles. "You know what?"

"Nicholas' paternity. Logan told me years ago."

I hop out of the chair. "You knew? Did everyone know except me? Why didn't you say anything?"

"What was there to say? I thought I would spare you the embarrassment. Besides, I fell in love with that little boy, and Logan asked me not to say anything."

"Yeah, so he could control me," I mumble.

"I didn't tell you that to upset you." Marilyn walks over and takes my hands. "You did the best you could, right?"

I look for the mocking in her eyes, but all I see is understanding. Marilyn has gotten on my nerves over the years, but she is not the enemy. It's a shame I never saw her as an ally until now. But as soon as Logan tells his mom about the latest revelation that Christopher is the father, I'm sure she will be back giving him her full support.

I give Marilyn a hug and go to start the process of building a new life.

CHAPTER THIRTY SEVEN

ADRIENNE

I have come full circle. Six hours or so later, I am lying beside Nicholas in what is now my room at Kim's. We were able to remove all traces of our presence from the house and put some things in storage. I thought I would feel some regret about leaving but all I feel is relief. I have a lot of other major decisions to make, but right now all I want to do is rest.

The buzzing of my cell phone snatches me back to consciousness. I fear it is Logan, but it is Christopher. The man is persistent. I think I have avoided him long enough.

"Ms. Adrienne," he says after a slight hesitation.

"How are you?"

"Been trying to catch up with you," he says. "Are you okay? How is Nicholas?"

Christopher's simple and earnest question about Nicholas makes me sit up and pull my knees to my chest. I am a terrible mother. I think of all the time I allowed Logan to ignore my son and disregard his needs.

"Nicholas is good," I manage to respond.

"And how is Momma doing? You don't sound good."

I take a deep breath. Momma is a mess, but I simply tell him that I am fine.

"I know you're fine. But how are you doing really?"

"Still running that corny line."

"That's how I get all the ladies."

"What ladies?" I tease him back. "You must mean Mya."

"Naw, my baby had to leave me. She's with her mother this week."

We chat a little while longer before Christopher gets to the reason for the call. The reason for all his calls since the party.

"You know we need to talk, right," he says. "You told me Nicholas wasn't mine, and I accepted it."

My stomach clenches. "But," I say.

"But when you told me he was sick with sickle cell, I couldn't help but wonder."

"Why?"

"Cause I have the trait too."

And there you have it. Tears run down my face. They cleanse away the guilt. Christopher calls my name twice before I can speak.

"Did you hear what I said?" he asks.

"Yes. He is your son." And that piece of truth lifts the weight I didn't know was there, and I feel lighter.

"Wow," Christopher says. "I have a son."

I can't help but compare Christopher's response to the one Logan had. Christopher acts as if I have given him a gift.

"But are you sure? Because when I asked you before, you dismissed that as a possibility," Christopher says.

"Let's say some new information has come to light. If you want a test, we can do that," I say.

"We need to talk face to face," Christopher says. "Can you get away today?"

I can't do this right now. "How about I come by tomorrow? I'll answer all your questions then."

He doesn't like it but accepts it. We set a time to meet.

"Ms. Adrienne," Christopher says before we hang up.

"Yeah."

"Thank you."

I fall asleep with a smile on my face.

CHAPTER THIRTY EIGHT

ADRIENNE

The smile on Christopher's face is so big his dimples are slits. The man stands in his doorway and pulls me into a hug that I sink into. I breathe in his scent, clean and fresh, and the familiar feeling returns. I am safe.

"Ms. Adrienne," his breath caresses my ear.

"It's good to see you too," I say.

Christopher holds me at arm's length and looks down. "Where's Nicholas? I was hoping you would bring him."

"At school." I dropped him off this morning. It's important to keep some semblance of a routine since everything else in his life has been turned around.

"I figured we could talk without any distractions."

Christopher's smile wavers but he focuses on me, and his face takes on a different look. The man could always make me feel sexy. Even in a faded pair of jeans and a cotton button down shirt.

"You're right. Come on in."

I follow Christopher and the nutty scent of coffee into the kitchen.

"I made us some breakfast." Christopher has a platter of fresh cut fruit, a couple of pastries and a box of cereal. Scrambled eggs are warming on the stove. The counter is set with two place settings, one with a Sesame Street bowl and matching cup.

"Nice touch," I point to the centerpiece, a vase of fresh flowers.

"I aim to please," Christopher holds the chair for me.

I watch him move around the kitchen. He pours two cups of coffee and makes mine with vanilla creamer and sugar without being told.

"You remembered."

"I remember everything." Our hands touch when he presents the mug to me. I pretend it is the heat from the cup that causes tingles to crawl up my arm. He fixes our plates, and we eat and make small talk for a while.

"There is no easy way to transition into this, but Nicholas is my son, right?" Christopher lingers over the word son like he tastes something sweet.

I nod. "Yes, he is your son."

"What does that mean?" Christopher smiles. "I mean, I know what it means, but how does this play out?"

"I'm not sure," I begin.

"Because I want to be a part of his life. I want to get to know him, and he needs to know me. I know Logan is an issue…"

"Logan is not an issue," I sit down my fork.

Christopher leans back on the stool and waits for an explanation. I give him the condensed version. Tell him I walked in on Logan's affair with Sheila. The surprise pregnancy. And the reveal that Logan is not Nicholas's father.

"Logan knew all along?" Christopher asks.

"So it seems," I say.

"But why would he keep that a secret from you? What kind of man does that?"

"I don't know. I knew I shouldn't have married Logan," I confess. "I knew that from the beginning."

Christopher gives me a questioning look. I look him in the eyes and release the reality I have been denying for years.

"I thought the night before my wedding that I spent with you was about my need for closure and maybe some revenge. But the next morning, I was a mess. I knew Logan wasn't the man for me, but I made a promise to him and I felt that I had to go through with it. A part of me was hoping you would stop me though. Like in the movies when the guy rushes in and says, 'I object' and the bride runs back down the aisle."

"I should have," Christopher says.

I look away and fiddle with a piece of cantaloupe. "Anyway, I moved out this weekend. I plan to file for divorce as soon as I can contact a good attorney."

"I can give you the names of a few," Christopher says.

"Thanks. Logan will play rough." I rub my neck. "He thinks I want his money or the house, but all I want is my freedom." I ramble on about Logan and our dysfunctional marriage. Christopher listens for a while before he interrupts.

"What else do you want?"

"What do you mean?"

Christopher eases the mug from my fingers and takes my hands in his.

"I mean this," he kisses my hand. "I'm talking about us. Forget the past. Do you think you could want us?"

"I don't know," I say. "Maybe…eventually…after everything is resolved."

"Why should we wait for eventually when we have right now? This moment right here is the only thing that matters."

Christopher leans in closer. "I messed up when I left you. I messed up when I let you marry that man thinking you would be better off. I'm not making that mistake again."

I try to speak but he continues. "I'm not letting you walk out of here without having my moment of truth."

"What's that?" I whisper.

"You're the one, Ms. Adrienne. You have always been the one I love."

His lips meet mine and continue saying what his words convey. He kisses me with an urgency that takes my breath away. I sink into it and let Christopher lead the way. His hands caress my face and leave a trail of tingles down my neck and back. I mimic his movements and allow my hands to get reacquainted with the body I have been craving.

We move from the bar into the bedroom without breaking our embrace. When we break for air, I am panting. I look in Christopher's eyes and all I see is love and desire. I stand between his legs, and we begin to undress each other. My mind tells me all of this is too soon. It reminds me that I am a married woman, and I should tell Christopher this is wrong. But it doesn't feel wrong. It feels anything but wrong, and it has nothing to do with Christopher's lips kissing my navel and massaging my breasts, although that helps.

Being here with Christopher in this moment feels right. This is the man I was destined to be with. The father of my son.

"What the hell?" Christopher's question pulls me out of my trance, and I open my eyes. He is pointing to my neck. "What the hell is this?"

I close my shirt. "Nothing."

"It doesn't look like nothing. It looks like someone put their hands on you. Did Logan do that?"

"Yeah, but…"

"But what? I will kick his ass," Christopher is up and pacing.

I step in front of him and wrap my arms around his waist. "It's okay. I told him you were Nicholas's father and he snapped."

"That doesn't give him the right to touch you."

"No, it doesn't, but it's over and I'm fine. It doesn't matter because Logan is history."

Christopher takes a deep breath and hugs me close. I keep talking.

"It brought me back to you. This is where I am meant to be. It had to happen this way so we could be together. So I could see the truth."

I look into his eyes and say the thing I have felt for forever. "I love you, Christopher. You are the one that makes me feel safe. I know our timing isn't good. First, you were ending a marriage, and now I have a mess, but I want to be with you. Nothing else matters. I'm ready now."

The smile on Christopher's face is enough to fuel me for a lifetime. But when our lips meet, it feels as if time stops. The years apart are erased, and it is simply Christopher and I. Best friends and lovers.

Christopher steps back and licks his lips. His eyes travel up and down my body as he undresses me. When I reach for him, he shakes his head.

"Let me take my time," he says.

I watch as he slowly removes his clothing. My need for him grows from a dull ache to a smoldering fire of desire. Each reveal of his chocolate skin screams at me to touch, to taste.

Christopher takes my hand and guides me to lie across the bed. His hands followed by his mouth trace a path down my body until they hover over the part of me that is so moist I am afraid he may drown. But he dives in with a purpose, and I am moaning so loud I know the neighbors can hear but I don't care. He teases and tickles me with his tongue until I reach the peak, and my legs are quivering. He gives me a satisfied smirk. If I could form coherent words, I would tell him he is the best.

I need to feel him on top of me, inside me. I beckon him and he eagerly takes the cue. He covers me like a warm blanket, and I wrap my arms around his neck and my legs around his back. He slips inside and fills me completely. We find a slow rhythm and ride the crescendo of pleasure. As the heat intensifies, Christopher locks eyes with me.

"Talk to me, baby," he says. "Tell me how much you want me. Tell me you'll never leave me again."

I know he is reclaiming what has always belonged to him. I tell him that he is the man for me. The man I want. With each stroke, he promises to love me. He promises to never leave me. And with each thrust, I give those words back to him. We ride the wave until words are no longer possible. The pleasure is so intense and pure I forget to breathe.

I stare into Christopher's eyes, and I see the answer to the timeless question. How do you mend a broken heart?

By giving in to love when it stares you in the face.

CHAPTER THIRTY NINE

ADRIENNE

We spend the rest of the day in bed. We talk and make love as if we are the only people that matter. Making up for lost time. Christopher shows me in several ways how much he missed me. After one sensual session, Christopher gasps, "Girl, are you trying to kill me?"

"No way," I say and lick my dry lips. "I just got you back. You can't leave me now."

He pulls me close. "I'm not going anywhere."

I doze safely in his arms.

Later, Christopher kisses me awake. I stretch and purr, a sign of contentment.

"What time is it?" I ask.

"Almost 3."

"Wow. How long was I asleep?"

"Not long. You couldn't keep your hands off a brother," he teases.

I hit him with a pillow. "Making up for lost time."

"We have time," he says and hands me a bottle of water.

I gulp greedily. "I need to leave about 5. Kim is picking up Nicholas, but I want to get home the same time they do."

"Okay, I'll come with you."

"Why?" I try to search Christopher's face, but he is focused on the plate of fruit he set between us.

"I want to see Nicholas. I want to see my son."

"Whoa," I say. "You don't want to waste any time."

"I've already missed so much."

I pull the cover up to my neck. "And that's my fault."

"No," he says. "I'm not blaming anybody. I could care less about the circumstances. I've made enough mistakes of my own to not dwell on the past. I'm all about the new. This time with the woman I love and our son."

I relax my grip on the sheets and lean back. "Did I tell you that I love you?"

Christopher smiles, and I stroke his face.

"Don't try to distract me, woman."

I push the plate aside and pull him toward me. "I know you are anxious to get to know Nicholas, but I don't want him any more confused than he already is. Logan wasn't the most attentive father, but he is the one that Nicholas knows. He has been asking for his dad since we have been at Kim's."

Christopher settles beside me and I lean against his chest.

"Okay, I'll slow down," he says. "Tell me about my son."

"What do you want to know?"

"Everything."

I playfully swipe at his leg and start by telling him about Nicholas's favorite things. I describe his fascination with Spiderman, his love of peanut butter sandwiches and how he insists on wearing a baseball cap every time he leaves the house.

"How does he do in school?"

"He loves it. He started going a few months ago. But he is so smart."

"I know he is. Poor kid has a teacher for a mom." Christopher teases.

"It can be a blessing and a curse, I suppose," I say. "How much do you know about sickle cell?"

"When you told me Nicholas was sick, I did some online research. I know I have the trait but since Mya was negative, it wasn't something I thought about."

"It's all I think about."

Christopher turns my face toward his. "You don't have to carry that all alone anymore. Tell me everything I need to know to help you take care of Nicholas."

I tell him about Nicholas's hands and feet swelling at two months when his hands and feet were swollen, the endless nights with a screaming infant plagued by a high fever and not knowing what to do. The hospital emergency room visits and constant doctor offices. Watching this disease rob our son of a normal childhood. Watching a rambunctious child reduced to one that can't even manage a smile.

Christopher holds me close and strokes my hair. It gives me the strength to continue. "It's like being on guard all the time. As soon as I relax, the disease attacks my baby."

"It's not your fault," he whispers.

"I know."

Christopher kisses my face. "It's not your fault, baby."

We sit like that for a while. I soak up the security of his love. When I start to get sleepy, I lean forward to check the clock.

"I should get ready to go."

"Okay," Christopher says and rubs my arms.

"I need to take a shower."

"Okay." Now his hands move lower.

I roll away and stand up. "If you start that again, I'll never get out of here."

Christopher scrawls across the bed. "Playing hard to get. Okay, towels are in the bathroom."

I make a promise to get a soak in his tub, but a shower is quicker. Besides, his shower is huge. I adjust two of the four heads and step under the spray. The warm water washes over me and it feels good. I feel good. Being around Christopher is good for my soul. I feel free. Maybe this will all work out, I think. Maybe Christopher and I can work this out. Raise Nicholas and get him the procedure that could save his life.

I turn when the shower door opens.

"Thought I would join you," Christopher says.

"You can do my back," I toss him the washcloth.

"I can do more than that," he says. He backs me against the wall and shows me.

"Have you seen my shoes?" I call back to Christopher as I walk into the kitchen to get another bottle of water. I feel drained in a good way. I drink water and take a deep breath. I spot my purse on the counter and dig inside for my cell phone. I need to check in with Kim and see if she needs anything on my way home.

I have seven missed calls. My heart stops. Two calls are from Nicholas's school. The rest are from Kim. I don't take time to listen to voicemail.

"Kim," my voice shakes. "What's wrong?"

"I'm at the hospital with Nicholas. He's been admitted."

CHAPTER FORTY

ADRIENNE

Christopher speeds up to catch a stoplight before it changes from yellow to red. His face shows the concentration of getting us to the hospital. Getting to Nicholas. I glance over at him and think this is what love looks like. I fumble with my cell phone to keep my hands from shaking and repeat my mantra: Nicholas will be okay.

I don't realize I've said it out loud until Christopher takes my hand. "He'll be fine, baby."

I nod. The twinge of guilt that always lingers is replaced with trust. I don't have to do this alone.

"Did Kim say what was going on?" Christopher merges onto the highway with hazard lights flashing.

"The school called. Nicholas started complaining about stomach pain closely followed by vomiting. They tried to call me…"

"But you were unreachable," Christopher reaches for my hand. "It's not your fault, okay."

I ease my hand away. "Kim got there the same time as the ambulance."

Christopher sails down the exit ramp and is forced to stop at the light. He taps the steering wheel and his eyes dart from left to right.

"We're almost there," I say.

He nods. The light changes, and he goes through the intersection. Christopher pulls into the first parking space he sees, and we run through the emergency room doors. The front desk gives us Nicholas's room number.

Outside of the room, I grab Christopher's hand, take a deep breath and push open the door. No matter how many times he has been admitted, seeing my baby in that bed breaks my heart. Nicholas looks so small in a sea of white sheets. The drip of the IV is the only sound in the room. Kim stands when we enter and relief washes over her face.

"Thank you," I whisper when we hug. Nicholas looks peaceful, though Kim tells us he was screaming in pain on the way over.

"The doctor says it's an abdominal crisis," Kim says.

"What doctor? His doctor? Did they page Dr. Payne? Did they pull his emergency room chart?"

Kim's eyes widen. "Let me go get the doctor for you."

I look down at my son and stroke his face. A hundred thoughts run through my head and they all end with me in that bed instead of Nicholas. He doesn't deserve this. No child should have to go through this cycle of pain.

"He's going to be okay, right?"

I almost forgot that Christopher is here with me. Still holding my hand. I don't answer. Just pull him close. He looks at me with watery eyes and repeats the question. He has to be, I think. I'm not strong enough to handle anything else. Christopher reaches for Nicholas. Touches his hand. Touches his son. Not the ideal introduction.

"We're going to make him better, Adrienne," Christopher says. He takes a breath and looks at me. "Whatever it takes."

I lean against Christopher, taking comfort in his promise. We are going to make our son better. I don't know how long we stand like that, both of us touching Nicholas giving him our love and strength. Praying for his healing.

"Now isn't this a sight?" Logan stands in the doorway looking like he is ready for opening arguments in court. His suit is freshly pressed, shoes shined and hair recently groomed. The bandage on his nose is new. The sneer on his face isn't. "I see you didn't waste any time."

"Logan," I drop Christopher's hand. "What are you doing here?"

"The question is what is he doing here?" Logan crosses the room and stands on the opposite side of the bed.

Christopher takes my hand again. "My son is here."

"You sure about that, man? She had me believing this was my son too."

I cut my eyes at Logan. I wish I could break his nose again. "Why are you here?" I ask instead.

"The school called me when they couldn't reach you."

"As you can see, I'm here. No need for you to stay."

Logan doesn't say anything. He stands there glaring at Christopher. I decide to ignore him. Maybe he'll get bored and leave. I turn back to Nicholas and watch the IV pump fluids into my child. I know from past visits the IV will leave a bruise on his hand, and I know he'll have some kidney damage from this episode. I want him to be rid of this disease. Christopher squeezes my hand. It is good to have solid support. Whatever it takes, he said. I cling to that promise.

"Tell me something, Michaels. How long have you been fucking my wife?" Logan growls.

"What?" Christopher and I say in unison.

Logan gestures across the bed. "You two are all hugged up, disrespecting me like this. I have to ask, how long have you been at it? Did she give it up to you after the school tour?"

Christopher's hand clench. But Logan continues to spew his vile words.

"Tell me, man. I want to know. How was my wife? She's a good piece of ass, right? The best I ever had."

I step in front of Christopher to stop him from grabbing Logan. It would be up Logan's alley to try and trap Christopher into an assault charge.

"You have a lot of nerve standing there talking about disrespect. You were sleeping with Sheila for years, right? During our entire marriage if I remember correctly. Disrespect? Let's talk about you fucking her in our house and getting the woman pregnant." I point my finger in Logan's face.

"I told you the truth about me and Christopher. I was faithful to you. But this marriage is over."

Logan blinks. He holds up his hands. "I know I messed up. Okay, I fucked up big time. But we can work it out, babe. I love you."

I shake my head. "You don't love me, Logan. You hate to lose. It's obvious you didn't come here out of some concern for Nicholas. You haven't even looked at him or asked about his health. Please leave."

Logan stares at me, but I ignore him. I look toward the door and wonder what is taking Kim so long to find the doctor. A nurse scurries past and I go to stop her, but Logan's words give me pause.

"I know you are the client that's suing me."

Christopher takes his eyes off Nicholas and meets Logan's dare with one of his own. "Yeah. And?"

"You think I'm going to let you take my license and my wife? My family."

Christopher's laugh lacks mirth. "You are a terrible lawyer. You were charging me for hours you didn't work. And you are a bad husband. It's not my fault you couldn't hold onto your wife."

Logan's eyes flash. "Back off or I'll—"

"You'll what? And if you ever put your hands on Adrienne again, I will make you regret it."

Logan turns to me, his eyes a mixture of shame and regret. It passes.

"You need to stay out of my business," Logan tries to save face.

"Adrienne is my business," Christopher replies.

"What kind of man sleeps with another's man wife?"

"You tell me. You seem to know all about cheating on your wife."

Logan raises his voice. He threatens Christopher and promises to fight for his family and his reputation. Christopher looks at Nicholas and then me. I know he is trying to remain calm but is losing the battle. I debate whether to call security.

"Mommy." Nicholas is awake and reaches for me. His voice is hoarse. "Mommy," he repeats.

I perch on the side of his bed and pull him into a hug. "Mommy is here."

Logan and Christopher continue to exchange words. I hit Christopher's hand to get his attention. He sees Nicholas looking at him with wide eyes, and it calms him.

"Hey little man," he says. "How are you feeling?"

Nicholas's face scrunches, and he tries to sit up. "Mya," he says.

"Mya's not here, baby. Here, drink some water." I get Nicholas to take a sip. Christopher comes closer. We both soothe him. I manage to coax a smile before he turns and sees Logan.

"Daddy," Nicholas calls to Logan's retreating back.

Logan stops in the doorway. He turns and looks at Nicholas for the first time. He hangs his head in defeat, and then makes eye contact with me.

"Not anymore," he says and walks away.

"Daddy," Nicholas repeats. "I want Daddy."

"It's okay, baby," I say. That's the final act that confirms Logan is not the man for me. I wonder why I allowed that man to continue to disappoint my son. He couldn't even have the decency to make Nicholas feel better while he lay in a hospital bed.

Tears slide down Nicholas's face.

"Daddy…" I begin and stop. I don't know what to say.

"Daddy is right here," Christopher says.

Nicholas looks confused. "No, Daddy gone."

I climb all the way into the bed and rock him. I can't explain to a three-year-old that his real father is the man standing there looking pissed off at me. I have made a mess of Nicholas's life. How will he ever forgive me? How will I forgive myself?

"Are you going to say anything?" Christopher asks.

"About what?"

Christopher shoots me a look. "Are you going to tell our son that his father didn't abandon him? Tell him I am right here."

"Do you want to get into that now?"

"Now seems like a good time."

"I think we should wait until later. When he is better."

"Haven't I waited long enough?"

"I knew it. You do blame me. I thought you understood how this needs to work."

"No one blames you." Christopher rubs his hands down his face.

But that's not true. I blame me. My baby is sick and confused and the common thread in that is me.

"Leave." I don't realize I have spoken my thought until Christopher's eyes widen. I plow ahead. "You are confusing things, and I can't deal with that right now." Thankfully the medicine has Nicholas drifting back to sleep.

"Is that what you want?" Christopher asks.

I swallow hard. "Yes. Please go."

Christopher opens his mouth to speak, but then shakes his head. "No, is this some sort of test? To see if I will leave?"

"It's not a test. I want you to go."

"What makes you think I would leave you here?"

"You've done it before."

Christopher steps back. I know I am not playing fair, but I don't know how to stop.

"You can't keep playing that card with me. I thought we were past all of that. I thought today meant something to you. To us."

I am starting to lose my composure, and I need him out of here. "Go, Christopher. Get out. I can't think with you here."

Christopher throws up his hands and walks out. Good, I think. Let him leave now before I make the mistake of believing I can depend on him.

I collapse into the chair beside the bed, hang my head and fight back tears. Way to go. I ran off the man I love. But I can't dwell on that.

Nicholas has to have all my focus. I have to make sure he is well. I wasn't there when my baby needed me earlier, but I am here now.

"Dr. Payne is on the way," Kim returns with two cups of coffee.

"Thanks." I sip from the cup.

"I don't know how you deal with medical personnel. I had to run down a nurse, get into a near shouting match with her to get some answers, literally block some intern from getting on the elevator without answering my question and then cause a mini scene to get them to page Nicholas's doctor."

"They are busy," I mumble.

Kim continues her rant and looks around. "Where's Christopher?"

"He left."

"What do you mean, he left?"

When I don't respond, Kim kneels in front of me. "Please don't tell me he left you like this. Not when you need him."

Kim's face is similar to the look Nicholas had earlier. Confused.

I take her hand. "I made him leave."

"No, girl."

I fill her in on the scene with Logan and how we all got into it. I tell her how Logan walked out on Nicholas calling for his daddy. "Then Christopher starts telling Nicholas that his father is here which confused the child. I tried to tell him to wait for all that and now he blames me for this mess."

"Did he say that?"

"He didn't have to. I blame me so I know he does too. I figured I would end it now, before he had a chance to walk away later when it got hard."

"You do know this isn't healthy, right? I mean, this situation is delicate to say the least, but you deserve to be happy, sister. I know you love Christopher, and he is Nicholas's father. Don't you think he should have a chance to come through for you? He may surprise you."

"Maybe, but it's too late now."

Kim pulls me into a hug. "Everything will be okay."

I manage to get myself together before Dr. Payne rushes in. I stand to greet her.

"I am so sorry, Mrs. Rutherford. Nicholas has a standing order in his file that I am to be notified immediately if he is admitted. Seems as if the paramedics and emergency room staff overlooked it." She shakes her head.

"I'm glad you're here now. Tell me what is going on with my baby."

Dr. Payne takes a deep breath and flips through Nicholas's chart. "He has a severe infection, and we have started treatment. The school did a good job of reacting to Nicholas's sudden temperature. His hemoglobin levels are low, but that's to be expected. He is responding to the pain meds and the antibiotic therapy."

I look at my baby and wonder if this cycle will ever end. The hospitals, monitors, IVs and sterile white sheets are unbearable. Worrying about hemoglobin levels, daily doses of medicine and whether your child will ever have a normal month or even a day.

"Excuse me, sir. You can't be in here," Dr. Payne says.

I look up and there is Christopher. His face is a mask.

"It's okay," Kim says. "He's with us."

"Oh, I'm sorry, Mr. Rutherford. I haven't seen you in a while," Dr. Payne says.

"I'm Christopher Michaels," he extends his hand. "You're Nicholas' doctor, right? I have some questions about his care."

Dr. Payne looks at me. I walk over to Christopher. "This is Nicholas' father."

His eyes meet mine, and I send a silent apology. What I see reflected back is understanding and love. He takes my hand and lets me know he can't be pushed away. I make formal introductions.

"Christopher, Dr. Payne has been Nicholas's doctor since he was diagnosed."

And to her credit, Dr. Payne remains professional and shakes his hand when it is offered this time. "Mr. Michaels, is it?"

"Yes," I say. "Maybe you have a few minutes to discuss Nicholas's care with us."

Dr. Payne looks at her watch. "I have to leave for the office in about thirty minutes. Let's go sit in one of the counseling rooms."

Kim settles in the chair beside Nicholas, and we follow the doctor out. After some quick explaining about the soap opera that has become my life, Dr. Payne answers all of Christopher's questions. I sit and watch this man take full interest in Nicholas's care. I wonder again why I allowed Logan to treat Nicholas like an afterthought. I should have known from the beginning that his callous attitude was more than a man that didn't want a child. He didn't want a child that wasn't his.

"Adrienne and I would like to pursue the bone marrow transplant," Christopher says.

Dr. Payne smiles and looks at me for confirmation. "That's great. Why don't you call and schedule an appointment next week so we can get the process started? I can refer you to my colleague at the Atlanta Sickle Cell Center."

"Thank you," I say.

"It's a long process, but we'll walk through it together," Dr. Payne squeezes my hand. I squeeze hers back. She wants this for Nicholas as much as I do. Dr. Payne shakes Christopher's hand again and excuses herself. I go to follow but Christopher stops me.

"We need to talk for a minute," he says. The serious look on his face makes me return to my seat.

"Yeah?"

"Do you love me?" he asks.

"Yes." I have loved him forever.

"Do you know that I love you?"

I meet his intense stare. "Yes."

Christopher takes a breath. "Then that can never happen again."

I am quiet. I let the man have his say. He kneels in front of me.

"You can't shut me out like that. Don't try to make me leave you and Nicholas," Christopher continues. "I know our past. I can't change it. But I've been straight with you since I came back. I want you. I choose you. You have to decide. This is your moment of truth. Do you want this? I believe we can make it work. Do you?"

He waits for my answer. I look into the eyes that are like Nicholas, and I have never been surer of this feeling. Once I filter through all the mess that my life has become, dealing with Logan, worrying about Nicholas, all that remains is that I love this man. Everything in my life is crazy, but I need Christopher to keep me sane.

"I'm sorry," I tell him. His face falls, but I left his chin. "It won't happen again. I need you, Christopher. We need you."

He kisses me. "Tell me you love me."

"You know I love you, man. I've never stopped."

"Tell me you'll never leave me."

I take his face in my hands. "I'll never leave you or push you away."

"We're in this together, right?"

"Yes," I say. "Together."

He stands and takes my hand. We go to check on our son.

CHAPTER FORTY ONE

ADRIENNE

"In the matter of Logan Charles Rutherford, Jr., defendant versus Adrienne Rutherford, petitioner, I hereby grant the petition of divorce." The judge bangs the gavel and after a year of separation and a twenty-five-minute hearing, my marriage is over.

My lawyer turns to me. "That's it then. I hope you are happy with the outcome."

"I am, Roger. Even if you don't think so."

"I'm used to my clients following my advice." Roger O'Neal, Esquire, the best divorce attorney in the city stuffs a legal pad and copies of affidavits in his briefcase. For months, I had to negotiate with my own attorney as well as Logan. Roger latched on to the admitted adultery (the pregnant mistress made it hard to deny) and wanted to follow his scorched earth philosophy.

"We file on grounds of adultery, ask for alimony and have him agree to relinquish parental rights," he advised.

"I don't want this to get ugly," I said.

"It's a divorce, sweetheart. You have to get down and dirty."

And get dirty it did. Logan counter filed on adultery and tried to claim I had an affair and tricked him into believing that Nicholas was his son. My baby's medical records had to be presented as evidence, and we proved that Logan knew the truth when his secret paternity test became public. Then Logan wanted to fight over the house and how I refused to work and contribute to the household. After a while, I told Roger to remove any claims and let Logan have it. Roger tried to talk me out of it, but once I reminded him that he worked for me, he backed down. But, he didn't like it.

I place my hand on Roger's shoulder. "I appreciate your expertise and advice. But, this is best for me."

His rigid body relaxes. "I hate to think of the wasted opportunity. We had him dead to rights on adultery. You could have gotten alimony, the house…" The man starts to get worked up talking about the money we are leaving on the table. He has earned the nickname "Roger O'Dollar."

"All I wanted was my freedom and to legally clear up Nicholas's paternity."

Roger pushes his bulky frame from the chair. "Good luck to you then."

I take a deep breath and close my eyes. Send up thankful prayers that this part of my life is over. I reach for my purse beside my chair and a pair of black wing tip shoes comes into view. I look up and see Logan.

"Are you doing okay over here?" he asks.

"Sure," I stand and look around. We are alone in the courtroom. Kim must be waiting for me outside.

Logan clears his throat. "Umm, how have you been?"

"Doing okay. And you?" I've seen Logan a couple of times since that day in the hospital. He is still the good-looking man I married what seems like a decade ago, a little thinner perhaps.

"It's a little weird, isn't it?"

"What's weird?" I ask although being in a courtroom is a surreal experience.

"Talking to each other like strangers."

I agree. "Well, we haven't seen each other in months."

"And a lot has happened in between," he finishes my sentence. "I want you to know I'm sorry about…you know. Everything."

Now this is new. The Logan I knew wouldn't apologize for anything.

"Me too. I want you to know I didn't set out to deceive you."

"I know you didn't."

The conversation is pleasant enough but I can't resist asking, "Then why did you file papers claiming I did?"

Logan shrugs. "Trying to get back at you, I guess."

I smile an understanding of the game. No one wins in a divorce, but it doesn't stop both parties from trying.

"I stopped practicing law," Logan says.

This is surprising. "Wow."

"Yeah, when my license got suspended I figured it was time to close the firm. I had paid homage to my father long enough."

"That's good." It is more of a question than a statement.

Logan smiles. "It was time. But if you are in the market for a house…"

"Real estate?"

He pulls a card from his pocket in a practiced move and flashes it. "I'm a realtor now. Used my connections to get on track with one of the agencies here. I deal mostly with high-end executive homes. Sold a half million-dollar house last week."

"But of course." We share a laugh and I drop his card in my purse.

Logan looks as if he wants to say more, but his cell phone buzzes. He checks the number but doesn't answer.

"Sheila," he says. "I told her I would call after the hearing."

The easy banter evaporates at the mention of that woman. I have let go of the anger, but I don't want to hear about her. I put my purse on my shoulder and turn to leave.

"You know, my mother still talks about you. She loves to remind me what I gave away."

I turn around. Logan shifts from one leg to the other. "She doesn't like Sheila at all."

I don't tell Logan that Marilyn calls me from time to time. And, he is right. She can't stand that woman.

"But she loves that grandbaby," I say. Marilyn had a difficult time adjusting to the circumstances of the baby's birth, but she came around.

Logan's face lights up at the mention of his daughter. "She's six months now," he tells me. "Want to see a picture?"

He is reaching for his phone before I can stop him. Shows me a picture of a pecan tanned baby with sandy colored curls and plump thighs. "This is Carla."

"She's beautiful," I say. "Seems fatherhood agrees with you after all."

Logan stares at the picture and nods. He catches himself and a look of shame crosses his face. "How is Nicholas?"

Now it's my turn to smile. "He's adjusting well. We haven't had a crisis for two months now."

"That's good. Is he looking forward to being a big brother?"

I almost drop my purse. I look down at my stomach and cinch my blazer.

Logan smiles that boyish smirk I remember. "Didn't think I would notice, huh?"

"I didn't think anyone would notice. I'm four months."

"Do you know if it's a boy or girl?"

I shake my head. I know that these two fertilized embryos were tested and are sickle cell free and a genetic match for Nicholas's immune system. I know that the twins growing inside me will have their cord blood transplanted into Nicholas's system and replace his bad stem cells with healthy ones. I know that I already love them for the miracle they are and the miracle they will be for their brother.

"Didn't waste any time, huh?"

I take a step back. "I know you are not going to stand there and judge me when you got a woman pregnant while we were still married? How old is your daughter again?"

Logan holds up his hands. "Whoa, I don't want to fight. We've already done that. I'm sorry, okay?"

"You should be." Neither one of us followed a high moral code. No need to play your sin is worse than mine.

After a beat, Logan says, "Well, congratulations."

"Yeah, thanks."

Kim sticks her head in the door. She rolls her eyes at Logan. "Are you ready?"

I tell her I'm coming and she disappears back into the hallway.

"Take care, Logan." I smile and turn away.

"Can I ask you something?" He follows me toward the door.

"Are you happy? I mean, was I such a terrible husband?"

I stop and take his hand. "You know, in the beginning, I thought we could save each other. I guess we had to go through all of this to learn we could only save ourselves. But our time together wasn't all bad. It wasn't meant to last. So, yes, I'm happy. I hope you are happy too."

Logan caresses my hand, his eyes full of regret. "I wish I had done things differently, you know."

Before he can continue, his phone buzzes again. He takes a breath. "Sheila," he says.

I lean forward and kiss his cheek. "Be good to yourself."

Logan's smile fades when he answers the phone. "What is it, Sheila? Does Carla need anything?"

I take one last look at my ex-husband and go find my sister.

"And what did our "ex" have to say?" Kim sits on a bench and doesn't look up from her text.

"Nothing much. Did you know he stopped practicing law?"

Kim looks up. "He dealt with those daddy issues, huh? That's good. He wasn't a very good lawyer anyway."

"Be nice," I tell her. "It's over now."

"And it's about time."

"Want to grab some lunch before we head home?" We walk toward the exit.

"I'm meeting Rodney for lunch at this spot around the corner."

I give her a hip bump. "Someone is getting serious. I think he is the first one to last this long."

Kim smiles and sashays through the automatic doors. I follow behind her chanting, "Kim and Rodney sitting in a tree. First comes love, then comes marriage."

"You can't even say the thing right. You left out the K.I.S.S.I.N.G. part."

"I didn't leave it out. I skipped it because I know you are fast and already did the nasty."

Kim laughs and tries to hit me. I bounce out of her reach. "Stop playing and tell the truth. You love this one, don't you?"

"Yes, I do. And it scares the shit out of me."

I hook my arm through hers. "It's scary, but doesn't it feel good?"

She gives me a hug. "It sure does. I don't want to keep him waiting too long. Tell Christopher and the kids I said hello."

I watch my sister race down the sidewalk. She'll be married by this time next year. I stand a moment longer on the courthouse steps and let the sun warm my face. I rub my belly and tell the babies it's time to go home.

CHAPTER FORTY TWO

ADRIENNE

I pause outside Christopher's door. It takes me a moment to remember I have a key. This is now my home.

I open the door, and Christopher looks up from the couch. The smile he gives me warms me like the sun.

"Hey," I say and toss my keys on the table.

"How did it go?" He moves his laptop aside and makes room for me. I sit and lean in for my kiss.

"It seems like it should take longer than twenty-five minutes to end a marriage," I say.

"It does. You were negotiating for months."

"That's true. Do you think it was right not to file under adultery? This could have been finalized a whole lot quicker."

"Where is this coming from? Roger was whining again?"

I lean back against the sofa and nod. I forgot how tired you get when you're pregnant.

Christopher walks into the kitchen and returns with a glass of juice. I smile my thanks.

"You know I supported your decision 100%. Roger is an excellent attorney, but this is your life. Our life."

I already know this, but it is good to hear. I am still getting use to having a partner to discuss issues with instead of telling me what to do.

I appreciate him even more when he starts massaging my feet. We sit in silence for a minute.

"How is Logan these days?"

I open my eyes and shrug. "The same. He gave me his card. He's selling real estate now."

"Alright for him."

"We may need to call him. When the twins get here, we are going to need a bigger place."

Christopher shakes his head. "I don't think he wants to do business with the man that initiated the investigation into his law practice. I can't believe he was able to get a realtor license."

"Enough about that. That chapter is done, and I'm all about the future. Our future together."

Christopher runs his hand up my leg. "I'm all about that. You know what that means, right?"

"Yeah, you think I'm going to marry you."

"What? You having second thoughts? Think it's too soon?"

I sit up and take his face in my hands. "Boy, you got me knocked up. I want to be married before these babies get here."

"And you will," he promises. When he kisses me, I feel that promise from his heart to mine.

I want to climb on Christopher's lap and take this kiss further, but the silence gives me pause. It is too quiet in here.

"Where are the kids?" I ask.

Christopher struggles to pull back from our heat. "They are in Mya's room. They must not have heard you come in or they would be out here."

"I better go check on them."

"Yeah, but tonight we have to finish this," Christopher stands and helps me to my feet.

"If you don't fall asleep first," I tease.

"Raising two kids will wear you out," he says.

"You wait until we have all four."

"That's why I'm getting all the rest I can now."

I stop off at the bathroom and then walk into Mya's room. She has every doll and stuffed animal lined up in rows around the room. Right smack in the middle is Nicholas.

"Hey guys," I say. "What are you doing?"

"Playing school, Ms. A." Mya puts down the book she is reading. "It's story time."

"I see. And is Nicholas being a good student?"

"Hey, Mommy," he says.

Mya shoots him a look. "It's quiet time, class."

"Well, I hate to interrupt, but could I get one hug, Ms. Michaels?" I ask Mya.

She taps her foot giving it some thought. "I guess so. Nicholas, you may get up."

Nicholas springs up and hugs my legs. I kneel down for a kiss. Today is a good day.

Nicholas has adjusted well. The first month or so after we moved out, he asked for Logan every day. Now he has accepted our new family. He adores his sister and follows her around when she is here. Christopher won joint custody so she is with us for the whole summer and most holidays.

"Mya, come here," I say. "Where is my hug?"

She gives me a gap-toothed grin and hugs me tight. I release the kids and let them return to their game. I stand in the doorway watching them play until Christopher comes up behind me.

"You need anything?"

"I have everything I need right here," I rub the babies and watch our kids play.

Christopher wraps his arms around me and caresses my belly. "Everything is going to work out fine, Ms. Adrienne."

I don't know what the future may hold, but I know I will have these babies. I know Nicholas's transplant will make him sick before it makes him well. I know he will grow up with two parents who love him and siblings to share his life with, and I know there is no more need for sad Al Green songs.

I pull Christopher's arms tight around me and feel his strong heartbeat in sync with mine.

"And that's the truth."

ACKNOWLEDGMENTS

Dreams do come true. That's the phrase I keep repeating as I get to the stage in my writing journey where I can write acknowledgments. In a book that I wrote. The book you are holding in your hand. Or reading on the screen.

I appreciate you, dear reader, for taking a chance on a new writer. I hope you enjoyed the story and I look forward to hearing from you. Stay tuned for the next one.

One thing I've learned is that books are not written in solitude. Well, the initial birth of an idea is a solo task but once the characters are set free on the page, you need assistance to help it all make sense.

And on that note, let me get to the thank yous.

Thank you to my husband, Stanley. When I told him, I wanted to write a book, he bought me my first laptop. Thank you for loving me in all my weirdness.

Thank you to my parents and sisters for always encouraging me and being my biggest fans.

Thank you to my writing tribe which includes some of the most generous people. They include my editor, Rhonda McKnight. Her encouragement helped me push through the fear and put my work out there. My copy editor, Felicia Murrell, made sure the grammar was on point and no one's name changed halfway through the story. Any mistakes are my own for not listening.

A big thank you goes out to mentor extraordinaire Victoria Christopher Murray, and my Sister Scribes. You ladies made all my creative quirks feel normal.

And finally, to my daughters, Ashley and Megan. Mom finally did it. You have no excuses. In the words of our Saint Beyoncé, "*I dream it, I work hard, I grind 'til I own it.*" Whatever it is you want out of life, go get it.

ABOUT THE AUTHOR

Michelle D. Rayford is a National Best-selling author whose pen sharpens spine-tingling tales of betrayal, lies, consequences… and their fallout when the truth comes out. Fitting for her brand of literary inspiration–shining the light in the darkness of deceit.

Her debut novel, *Moment of Truth*, has been applauded for its real-life characters and contemporary issues. Michelle lives in a Southern city with her husband and two daughters and can be reached via her website at www.michelledrayford.com.

Sociatap - https://sociatap.com/mdrayford
FB Author Page - https://www.facebook.com/MichelleDRayford/
Newsletter Subscribe Link - http://bit.ly/SubscribeMDR
Instagram - https://www.instagram.com/mdrayford/
Twitter - https://twitter.com/M_Rayford

ALSO BY MICHELLE D. RAYFORD

NOT THAT NICE (Short Story)
50 DAYS OF PLEASURE (Days of Pleasure Series Book 5)

Anthology Contribution:
CONFESSIONS: Secrets & Lies Revealed

NOT THAT NICE

Kelsee didn't open her eyes, bracing for the reprimand and anger. Both were as familiar as breathing.

She knew how much Alex hated the light shining in his face. She couldn't believe she'd forgotten to close the blinds.

Everything had to be perfect. Always.

When she couldn't take the silence a moment longer, she chanced a peek and released a sigh of relief at the sight of the empty pillow beside her. Then she remembered. He wasn't there. The reason, for the moment, escaped her.

Kelsee snuggled deeper in the sheets and stretched out in the middle of the bed. She tried to relax and reclaim sleep, but her brain was already churning. She couldn't shake the feeling that she'd forgotten something.

The phone rang, and she checked the caller ID screen and groaned. She composed herself before answering, "Hello, Mariam."

Her sister-in-law skipped the usual greeting of 'As-salamu Alaykum' and asked, "Are you ready?"

Kelsee's mind froze. *Ready for what?*

"I can't believe I have to do this." Mariam's usually strong voice cracked.

Memories flooded in. Today was the funeral.

Two days ago, her husband left to play "golf" at the Chandler Park Course in the Five Points area in Atlanta. Kelsee made him a fruit smoothie with spinach and a special ingredient – a hint of mint. He took a sip and mumbled, "Don't want to be late". He poured the rest in a sports bottle and left without saying goodbye.

Kelsee went about her regular Saturday chores of cleaning the house, stripping the sheets, mopping, and vacuuming. She was washing their dishes, thinking about what he wanted for their next meal and how much effort it would take to prepare when the phone call came. The call that changed everything.

Her mask firmly in place, Kelsee lied, "I can't believe it either."

She closed her eyes, listening as Mariam sniffed and repeated the same rambling from yesterday. "Why would Allah take him from me so soon? My baby brother. Why?"

Kelsee didn't respond. No one in that family listened to her anyway. Instead, she padded to the bathroom and stared at her reflection in the mirror, wincing at the fresh bruise. A final rebuke from her loving husband.

"Are you listening?" Mariam asked.

Kelsee clenched her jaw against what she really wanted to say. "Of course."

"I said, I'm sending some brothers from the mosque to drive you to the funeral. I'll meet you there. I know things are happening quickly and I appreciate you for following the customs."

Yes, Kelsee knew the customs. Unlike her husband, she studied the faith and used it to her advantage. Custom dictated a quick burial without a viewing. She thought she would at least get to see the body. Mariam handled everything.

"We need to get there at ten," Mariam continued. "The last thing I need on a day like today is to be stuck in I-85 traffic."

Kelsee ended the call and mentally prepared herself to play the part of the grieving widow. Make-up would camouflage the bruise. Dark shades would hide any other remnants of what had become of their marriage.

Or maybe she'd display what he'd done. This was one secret he wouldn't take to the grave.